Albert Jenkins has dedicated his life to opposing the oppression and tyranny of the High Chancellor and her Moralists. He has desperately fought against the flood that has engulfed the world and washed over friends and family till he is left standing alone against the tide. Now with the High Chancellor's agents searching for him and age pressing down upon him, time seems to be running out for the old man. Yet in Albert's darkest hour, God has delivered a child of wonders to him. But can he hold on long enough to teach the boy what he needs to know or will the flood finally sweep him under?

Edited by Susan Tripp

Noah

Book One
Of the
Moralist Trilogy

Michael Howard

For my sister Brenda
Without her support this book would never have been written.

Birthday

The wind kicked up a dust devil out on the dirt road that ran in front of Albert Jenkins's yard, and he wondered if there was going to be any rain soon to settle the dust. He was sitting under the shade tree in an old rocker sipping on a glass of iced tea watching the swirling dust spin its way along the road till it blew itself out, the dust falling back to the road bed.

"Probably not for a while," he grumbled looking up at the clear sky through the leaves of the old oak tree. "Not been a lick of rain in more than a month now; why should I expect it to change this late in the summer." Shaking his head, he reached for his glass and took another drink of the cold tea before sitting back in the rocker. Resting the glass on his knee, the condensation on the bottom soaked into his pants, bringing a grimace to his face for a moment.

"Well, that song has got a good beat don't it dog," forgetting the wet pant leg as he looked down at the young pup lying beside him next to the tree. The little pup's pink tongue was hanging out the side of his mouth as he panted in the heat. "I think I like this new music they're playing these days" he added. Tapping his foot to the beat, the old man grinned at the way the black pup's little head cocked to one side. The little pup appeared to be listening to the music as well but not sure if he liked the tune.

"One good thing about a dog for company, you don't talk too much, but you sure say a lot," he said laughing as the little pup shook his head. Evidently, the little pup decided that he did not care for the song and turned his attention to a grass hopper a few feet away struggling up out of the thick grass.

The old man turned to check on the sprinkler on the other side of him and set the glass back on the table. He was particular about his yard and wanted the grass to maintain a healthy green color no matter what the weather did. If that meant pumping out ten thousand gallons of water a day to achieve, then so be it.

"Drought my ass," he said looking back at the little pup that was on his belly inching towards the grass hopper. "When I was a boy, we had a real drought. Three years in a row with temperatures in the triple digits from May till October and barely enough rain to amount to anything even in the winter months. Be damned if I let my grass or flowers either one die for a couple of months without a little rain." He stood up walking over to take hold of the green hose running to the sprinkler and dragged it to a new position. The little pup gave the old man a look of exasperation as he walked away, because his movement had sent the grass hopper flying into the air, ruining his hunt.

"What do you think, dog?" he asked the black pup as it ambled over to sit next to him, watching the sprinkler rocking back and forth spraying the dry dusty ground and flower beds. "Reckon my roses will survive this summer" he grinned and reached down a pale wrinkled hand to rub the pup's ear. The little pup forgave the old man his earlier transgression and accepted the attention as just retribution.

"You know, dog, today is my birthday," he straightened and looked at the old house place. His thoughts were on the years spent here both good and bad, but his eye could not avoid seeing things that needed to be done.

The roof was in serious need of new shingles, and the walls could use a fresh coat of paint, but there was no sign of rot or termite damage. The old man paid as close attention to his house as he did his yard. "I'm ninety seven today dog, and I feel every bit of it." He shook his head deciding the roof would have to wait till fall, after the heat died down a little. "Reckon we can make a trip into town tomorrow and get some paint though. What do you say dog, you want to take a ride?" The little pup was digging at the ear the old man had been rubbing but stopped to look up when he heard the word 'ride'.

"Yeah that's what I figured," the old man smiled. Walking back to his rocking chair, the old man began snapping his fingers to the rhythm of the song that was blaring from the speakers in the old house, grinning as the little pup hopped along watching his fingers. "Like that one don't yah, dog," the old man said dropping into the chair and picking up his glass to take another long drink of the tea. The glass was covered in even more condensation now. He used a rag lying on the table to wipe his hands dry and the glass dry before setting it back down.

"Reckon that's Susie?" he asked the little pup who was whining in anticipation as he bounced on his front paws staring down the road. "It's about time for her to show up ain't it," the old man said looking at the sun's position. Susie was a daily visitor, part of a program set up to monitor the elderly in the district.

"She's a good woman, dog," the old man said as the sound of a vehicle on the road could be clearly heard. "She reminds me of Tizzy; that woman was always looking for someone to take care of." The old man's voice was split between fondness and sadness. The little pup's whine changed pitch sounding more worried and concerned as he looked up at the old man. "You would have loved her, dog." The old man continued, lost in his own memories and not noticing the little pup. "She died three years ago come Sunday." The old man spoke more to himself starring off into space seeing the past until he felt the little pup's front paws on his leg and his little tongue licking the old man's hand.

"Hey," the old man said softly pulling his hand back and raising it to rub the little pup's ear once more. "What's the matter with you?" The old man asked grinning as the pup turned his little head into the rub and started digging the air with a hind leg. "Well, go on with you then," the old man laughed as the pup dropped down and started running across the yard towards the road. Then the little pup curved cutting across the yard... his little bottom low as his hind legs dug deep

6

propelling him forward... and raced back to sit beside his chair wagging his little tail and looking up at the old man, almost appearing to grin with amusement as he panted in the heat.

"Now you behave yourself, dog." The old man had a broad grin on his face, and his tone was full of humor as he shook a finger at the little pup. Looking up, the old man watched Susie driving past along the dirt road and slowly pulling into his drive.

Her car was one of the new all electric vehicles, though new was relative to the old man's thinking. *Probably only a handful of people on the planet that remember what cars really were*, the old man thought. Susie's car looked like someone had stretched a bubble of plastic then cut the bottom half off, stuck four tires under it, made the holes for windows and doors then called it a car. It was old though; how old was hard to say because once they had gone into production thirty years or so ago, there had been no changes made in the styles or colors. Susie's was blue, though the color was nearly hidden under scratches and blotches of various colors from paint thrown on it. It had four doors with the windows and the windshield criss crossed with cracks from blows. The front grill was gone, the hood tied down with a piece of rope, and the rear quarter panel looked like it had been smashed in leaving a gapping hole in the plastic body. Which was a new addition since the day before and the old man couldn't help but marvel at some people's stupidity. He would have called it vandalism, but the local authorities did not see it that way.

"You going deaf, Albert" she called over the music blaring from the house as she crossed the yard towards him.

"When I was running wild and rutting like a buck, we used to say if the music was to loud, you were too old" he said giving her a meaningful look and then a smile when she grinned.

"Brittany used to listen to this all the time." A flash of emotion crossed the woman's face. The old man couldn't identify it for sure, maybe irritation, anger, or hurt or maybe all three at once. "I would expect you to listen to something a

7

little more adult," Susie grinned as she continued; acting as though the flash had never happened. She sat down in the rocker on the other side of the table from him.

"This music has a special quality to it that I find appealing," Albert grinned back, but his eyes held a twinkle of mischief connected to his words and a look of anticipation that she would ask about them.

"A special quality?" Susie asked unaware that she was being baited.

"Do you hear the lead guitar," the old man asked holding his hands up and strumming in the air with the music until the woman nodded understanding. "He's holding back, he's a lot better than this," the old man nodded to his hands. "All of them are; you can tell in the chorus when the beat picks up. They want to take it even faster and harder, as we used to say when I was about your age, but they're holding it in to get past the sensors and on the radio." The old man smiled as he played his air guitar with the music.

"I still don't understand" Susie said though her eyes had a glint that said she did, but it was dangerous ground, and she was not sure she wanted to tread on it.

"They are pushing at their boundaries, girl," the old man said leading the way out onto the uncertain earth. "That is the thrill of being young; you can push a little now, then a little more and before long you're a long way from where you started. I would love to be a fly on the wall when those guys are alone and just playing together for the fun of it. The rifts they must play with no fear of being reprimanded." The old man's fingers seemed to fly through the air for a moment as he grinned with excitement.

"I don't think that would be proper, Albert," the glint in her eyes sharper as she refused to follow after him.

"Perhaps you are right, girl." The old man let the guitar float away. "Probably just an old man's fantasy," he smiled at her and reached for the pitcher of tea sitting on the table. Pouring her a glass and refilling his before sitting back down then sliding her glass across the table. His eyes seemed fixed on the tasks, but he watched her closely judging the affect of his words and assessing a new strategy.

"Thank you," the words were for more than the drink as relief filled her eyes at being away from the dangerous topics. "This heat is miserable; I don't see how you can stand it at your age." She took a deep drink of the cold tea. Unbuttoning the top three buttons on her jacket, she fanned the collar against her neck trying to dry the sweat that soaked her shirt. Both shirt and jacket were deep blue as were her slacks all cut in a style reminiscent of the military, and she wore them to much the same standard.

"Well, for one thing," his tone was a little sharp at her reference to his age but he smiled humorously as she blushed. "I stay in the shade as much as possible and for another I stay out of the air conditioning that no one seems to be able to live without these days," he said tapping his foot to the song that had just started playing on the radio in the house. "For another, I dress for the heat" he grinned as he plucked the gray long sleeve thin cotton shirt he was wearing with a t-shirt underneath and the kaki pants he had on.

"You know I have to wear these clothes." She shook her head at him, her eyes wary at his words as she continued fanning her collar.

"Oh, yes I know," he smiled seeing a hint of anger behind her wariness. "I meant for me." His smile deepened, and he took another drink of his own tea to hide it.

"Maybe, but I think you're just too old to sweat anymore," she said smiling to show that she meant no offense but there was a flash of flash of anger in her eyes as she spoke that the old man saw clearly.

"Girl, I'm too old for a lot of things, but sweating ain't one of them" he said with a grin for her anger and her humor.

"Well, what shall we do today then, Albert," she asked with a matching grin and steering the conversation away from uncomfortable topics once more. "Are you hungry? I can fix you something to eat, or does the house need cleaning?" She always asked even though she knew his answer before hand.

"Just cause I'm old don't mean I'm crippled girl; if you're hungry, there's food in the fridge, and I clean my own mess up." His eye's twinkled with amusement. "Who gave your old jalopy its latest body work?" He asked jerking a thumb towards her car sitting in the drive way.

"Jalopy, what's that?" she asked confused for a moment by the word till she saw his thumb. "Just because something is old doesn't mean it has to be thrown away or else we might have thrown you away a long time ago, old man." She smiled ignoring the question and took another drink of her tea.

"Olds got nothing to do with it, girl" the old man said letting his question go unanswered. "I'm talking about dependable. Things keep going the way they are and that clunker's going to leave you on the side of the road one of these days girl. Anywhere is a long walk in this heat." He took another drink of his tea and then pulled a metal box from the shelf under the table.

"You know I should report you for what you are doing" Susie said stiffening her voice serious as she watched him set the box on his lap and flip the lid back.

"Bah... you wouldn't do that girl. Besides if they want to stretch my old scrawny neck on Sunday, they're more than welcome to. I've been on this earth longer than I should have anyway," he said taking a hand rolled thin cigar from the box then a bottle of clear liquid before flipping the lid back into place.

"Don't talk like that, Albert, you'd live forever if you didn't hurt your body with those chemicals." Susie's concern was mixed with a generous helping of condemnation.

"Nobody lives forever girl and that is a blessing you will look forward to if you reach half my age." He stuck the cigar into his mouth and then placed the metal box back on its shelf before sitting back up. "One thing those Moralists didn't think about is that not everybody wants to live a long time girl with

10

out having a little fun along the way. Worst thing that ever happened to this country if you ask me banning everything that was worth living for" he took a lighter from his pocket and lit the end of the cigar breathing the smoke in deeply enjoying the feeling of it expanding in his lungs.

"I don't want my children using those things and ruining their lives," Susie said almost angrily as she watched him open the glass bottle and take a drink of the clear liquid.

"Ah... man that stuff is smooth," he grinned at her before recapping the bottle and placing it on the table beside him.

"Why do you do this every time I come out here, Albert?" she asked, taking a drink of her tea and watching him over the top of the glass.

He took a couple of puffs on the cigar, rolling it in his withered fingers before answering. "I had hopes for you, girl; you're smart and strong willed. You deserve a better life than you have, and a little happiness in this world goes a long way." He held the cigar up at the last but didn't take his eyes off it as he continued rolling it.

"And you think these **things**;" she waved a hand at the cigar in his hands, "will bring me happiness?"

"Things don't bring us happiness, girl; you know that better than anyone." She dropped her eyes at this, but he continued. "Taking the blame for your husbands actions was admirable, girl, foolish but admirable. Now you are Bonded as a Servant to the People. Nothing can change that for you, but I think you have made your peace with it." He looked at her now to see the affects of his words and was pleased that she was staring him straight in the eye with the hint of anger now raging in them.

"You don't know anything about it, Albert," she said through clenched teeth.

"I know more than you think, girl." He took another drag off the cigar and reached down with his other hand to stroke the little pup still sitting beside his chair. The black pup had

11

started whining softly at the distress in Susie's voice. "I know your husband now sits on the Moralist Council in town and is soon to marry the Head Councilman's daughter..."

"So you know what everyone else in this district knows; that is not such a wonder," she cut him off, her voice carrying a touch of bitterness along with the anger.

"I also know that your daughter Brittany has called you for Punishment on Sunday the last three weeks. I know your son Edward has been accepted and will be leaving next week for Emerald City to join the Priesthood of the High Chancellor. I know you have not seen your children since you were Bonded two years ago, and they haven't wanted to see you at all since then. I do not say these things to be cruel, girl, but to make you understand that I know more about things than you think." He took another puff off the cigar and reached for the bottle.

"How do you know these things, Albert?" Her anger was slipping away as she stared at him. She had only heard about Edward the evening before. She did not know about Brittany but the old man's words had a ring of truth about them she could not deny.

"I know many things, girl. I even know the High Chancellor herself, the woman who started the Moralist Movement in the old days." He gave the little pup a final pat before using that hand to remove the cap on the bottle. "She was one of the biggest drinkers and drugges I ever ran with in my younger days, but she settled down like the rest of us." He took a sip of the clear liquid and squeezed his eyes shut for a moment. "Man, that's good stuff." He gave her a grin before continuing. "Married a wealthy New Yorker and joined the **proper** social groups. Then her husband became a politician. People who governed the nation back then," he explained as she looked confused at the unknown word. *Keep forgetting how much has changed since those days* the old man thought to him self. "Anyway, her first son was eighteen by then the legal age of adult hood back then. Well, he fell in with the same kind of crowd she run with at that age and got into some trouble.

12

Now this threatened her elevated status as a Congressman's wife. The scandal would be the talk of the social circle for months, and she would be too embarrassed to face those people knowing they were talking about her behind her back. So you know what she did?" He replaced the bottle on the table and looked across it at her. Too enthralled by the story to speak, she shook her head and leaned forward as he continued.

"She called the police; they were like the Magistrates now days. She had him arrested and thrown in jail, her own son." He shook his head still in disbelief that a woman could do such a thing to her own son. "Then she forced the boy to name each and every one of the wild bunch he had been running with. Using her considerable influence, she had all of them thrown into jail as well. Many of them were the sons or daughters of her social circle which put any question of her being embarrassed to rest. Now, since most of those parents were some of the more powerful people in the government and the populace was fed up with greed and double standards in Washington... Emerald City now... that, girl, is how the Moralist Movement began and the High Chancellor got her start. It was like a fever sweeping across the nation. Husband turned on wife, father and mother against son and daughter. The prisons and court systems were swamped under the onslaught. The poor boy that it all started with was still in prison, when his mother proposed that crimes should be considered as severe as sins. He was one of the first to hang for his Sins with his mother watching in satisfaction."

"You know the High Councilor," Susie said when he finished his story. Her voice was filled with awe as she looked at the old man with wide eyed wonder, totally missing the point of the story.

"I did but the important part is what she was and what she became, girl." He tapped the ashes from the cigar on the ground and looked across the table at her. "She was an unhappy drunken whore, and she became a hypocritical tyrant imposing her will on the whole country, girl."

"That's blasphemy, Albert." She said the words by reflex and was doubly shocked. First at knowing the words held no meaning for her and second to hear him talk that way about the High Councilor. Even after hearing the story, she still felt constrained to hold the High Chancellor above all else.

"The woman isn't God, girl, not by a **long** shot, but the point I'm trying to get to is that I can help you, girl, if you want it." He took another drag from the cigar looking at her through the smoke.

"Help me how, by corrupting me with your contraband," she asked sitting back with a laugh.

"I can remove those marks from your forehead for one," he said knowing what he offered was a death sentence for him if she reported it. The Mark of the Servant, as it was called always made him thing of three sixes. One at the bottom and two on top inverted with all three open arcs connecting at the same point and forming a triangle.

"And then what?" she finally said after a few minutes of silence had passed and he was beginning to wonder if he had gone too far and she indeed meant to report him. "Spend the rest of my days running or living in the wilderness like an animal. No thanks, old man, I am content with my life and besides I can't leave my children."

"You have already lost your children, Susie," he said softly and as compassionately as he could. "Wilderness life is not as bad as you might assume either. Many people have turned their backs on the Moralist and are forging a new life for themselves. I can help you get to one of their communities and they could use someone with your skills." He raised the cigar and took another puff letting her mull the idea over.

"I would think someone of your age would be past their rebellious years." Her eyes did not hold the off- handed amusement that was in her voice.

"Tizzy always said I'd argue with a sign post if I painted it myself. I guess this is just about the same thing only I wouldn't call it rebellion, more like just trying to make a little right in a world full of wrong." He rose and walked over to drag the sprinkler to a new place, and the pup followed along dropping his snout to lap up some of the water that had formed a small pool in a depression.

"You know there is a drought on and the Council has forbid any unnecessary use of water," she said behind him. He gave her another of his grins as he walked back to the rocking chair.

"I guess I didn't get that particular memo, girl. Besides, my yard is very necessary to me." He took a drink of his tea and puffed on the cigar smiling at her.

"How you get away with the things you do, I'll never understand." She shook her head in disbelief.

"We're at the back end of civilization, and I'm an old man; besides, this water comes from my well, not the Water Commission" he said with a grin as he flicked the ashes from his cigar.

"You've got an illegal well, too? It's a wonder you aren't Bonded as a Servant as well." She reached down to pet the little pup that had stopped in front of her to scratch his ear at her feet. "Your master is going to get himself executed before he has a chance to die of old age, and then who is going to take care of you." The little black pup looked up at her arching his back as she scratched it, his dark eyes reflecting her image back at her.

"We all die sometime; what matters, is how we live and how we face that death when it comes, girl." He laid the butt of the cigar on the table to let it go out and picked up the bottle once more.

15

"The words of the Moralist?" she asked cocking an eyebrow at him.

"Words that have been around a lot longer and without their narrow view of how we should live," he replied with a grin before taking another sip of the clear liquid.

"What is that stuff?" she asked as he squeezed his eyes shut tightly after swallowing.

"Moon Shine," he said enjoying the warm sensation that was slowly spreading out from his middle. "Corn liquor," he explained at her blank expression.

"Where on earth did you get that?" she asked incredulously.

"I'll have you know that once upon a time I was renowned for my Sipping Whiskey as well as a few other illegal products. Tizzy always tried to get me to give up my activities but she knew deep down how much I enjoyed them and that I would never stop. Part of it was tweaking those fools who were always trying to catch me in the act which is probably why I am trying to help you, girl. Same business just a different product; you might say it's just my nature."

"What makes you even think I want your help in the first place, Albert." She asked it with a voice so soft he could barely hear but with an under lying plea in it that cried for her to be saved. He did not think she even realized it was there.

"Help offered does no harm if it is rejected but no help offered where it is needed is a sin that blackens the soul. I plan on dying free of that particular sin if no other."

"What if I just decide to report you after all?" she asked looking at him intently.

"Then it would most likely mean that come Sunday I'll be strung up and hanged," he answered grinning with not a bit of fear in him.

"You're one crazy old man you know that," she shook her head in wonder.

"Maybe… they say people start getting senile at my age" his grin broadened. "Tell you what why don't you go inside the house there and bring us some of the cake I made. It's my birthday today you know."

"Well, happy birthday, Albert." She rose and stepped over to him then leaned down and gave him a hug. "Since it's your birthday, I won't report you," she said in his ear. "But I will get the cake." She grinned as she straightened back up and started for the house.

"You know, dog, if I was twenty years younger, I'd ask that girl to a dance or what ever they have these days." He looked down at the pup who was back to digging at his ear with a hind leg again. "Boy, you got fleas or something?" the old man asked as he reached down and petted the little black pup. "I think we're getting to her, dog," the old man said, glancing at the woman as she walked to the house, with a look of satisfaction in his eyes.

"Strawberry cake with white frosting" Susie said a few minutes later when she returned with two plates. "It was always my favorite." She handed one of the plates to the old man before taking her seat.

"Mine too for as long as I can remember" he said lifting his fork and cutting a chunk of the cake off then stuffed it in his mouth. "Tizzy always made me one for my birthday and other special occasions. Now if I want one, I have to make it myself, but I'm not a bad cook if I do say so myself," he grinned across the table at the girl as she stuffed a piece in her mouth.

"Excellent," she said around the cake in her mouth, and then they both continued eating without talking.

"You don't get much cake in the Compound do you," he said setting his empty plate on the table then refilled his glass from the pitcher. "They don't give you much of anything from what I hear." He looked over at her car then back at her with a suggestive look that said his words meant more than the obvious before taking a drink.

"Still trying to get me to run away and live in the woods like Robin Hood and his Merry Men." She smiled remembering the day the old man had told her that story and set her empty plate on top of his, then laid the two forks on top of the stack.

"Just making an observation, girl; you know I will help you get out and you can make up your own mind about whether or not to take it." He picked up the cigar and pulled his lighter from his pocket. "My door is always open to you day or night." He put the cigar in his mouth and lit the end puffing it back to life. "When you decide you've had enough of living like you're property, you'll knock on it." He smiled at her around the cigar.

"You sound like you already know what I'll do," she said pouring herself another glass of tea.

"Most everyone I have made the offer to eventually decide they would rather take a chance than live like a caged animal," he said lifting his glass to her before taking another drink.

"We're not caged... you've helped others?" she asked with eyes going wide with surprise as his words registered.

"Girl, as long as you wear those marks, you are caged, no matter where you go, and, yes I've helped quite a few people escape the High Chancellor and her Moralist." He got up still puffing on the cigar and moved the sprinkler once more to another section of dry yard.

"How many have you helped?" she asked hesitantly as if afraid to know the answer.

"Exactly I'm not sure but some where around seven or eight hundred." His tone was bland as if the numbers were not a major concern for him.

"How... where did..." she stuttered to silence just sitting and looking at him.

"Not till you decide that you want to start a new life, girl. That way you can't tell what you don't know. Now isn't it about time for you to be heading back to town?" he motioned to where the sun was sitting on the horizon to the west.

"Yes, it is." She rose and then paused to look at him once more. "I will… consider your offer, Albert, and I will keep your secrets as well."

"Don't take to long considering, girl, I'm an old man, and I might die in my sleep tonight." He flashed a grin.

"You've got years left in you, old man," she laughed as she started across the yard to the bubble car where she gave him a final wave before getting in and hitting the power button. He gave her a wave as she drove past, heading back down the road in the direction she had come, the whine of the electric motors fading into the distance.

"Dog, that there is a fine woman, and she deserves better than she's got." He flicked the ash from the cigar as he reached down to pet the black pup who was still staring down the road. "Now that song has a nice tune to it don't it, dog." He started tapping his foot to the music and reached for the bottle once more. "Good company, fine sipping whiskey, and a nice smoke what more could an old man ask for," he said to the little pup after taking a sip of the clear liquid. The black pup didn't answer; he was digging at his ear again with his hind foot. "We'll get something for them fleas when we go to town tomorrow, dog."

The sun had just slipped completely below the horizon before he spoke again; only this time it was not to the little pup. "Boy, if you can't even sneak up on an old man with out making enough noise to wake the dead, you might want to consider a new profession."

"I didn't want to give you a heart attack from surprise, old man," a male voice answered him from behind.

"Well, come have some tea, boy, and tell me how you been" he said without turning and then filled Susie's glass with fresh tea for the other man.

"How about a shot of that Shine and one of them cigars as well" the man said as he dropped exhaustedly into the other rocker.

19

"Help yourself, boy," he waved at the bottle sitting on the table and tossed his spent cigar beside the empty pitcher at the same time. "How were things up north?" He looked the man up and down as he took a sip of the Shine. He looked tired and worn from his travels, his clothes had holes in them and his face was covered in grime. He looked ten years older than the last time the old man had seen him only about two months earlier.

"Rough." The man might have been speaking of the alcohol from the pinched look on his face, but the old man knew he was talking about his trip. "The High Chancellor is cracking down hard now. I got about two hundred people following along behind me, and it was all I could do to avoid the Magistrates that are looking for us. There's more than a thousand stretched out from here to the northern border who were begging me to take them along, but I was afraid to try moving them all at once."

"Times are definitely getting harder for people that don't conform to the Moralists, and it's only going to get worse. That's the thing about tyrants, Michael, they're only option is to respond with force and inevitably that is their undoing. I'm afraid the High Councilor has too much power for any to strike against her right now." The old man took the cigar that Michael offered him and lighted it and then passed the lighter across the table.

"There were men talking about fighting back. Some in just about all the groups I talked to," Michael said after lighting his cigar.

"I'm too old to start a war, especially one that can't be won. She may have abolished the armies around the world, but she controls the weapons now and has more than enough fools willing to die in her name to kill us all in a matter of weeks. Open warfare is not the answer; we'll just have to keep doing what we have been doing." He took a drag on the cigar thinking through the problem and not liking any of the solutions he was coming up with.

"There is something else." Michael finally said with a voice that suggested he would rather not tell this part. "The High Council has put a reward out for your capture. A big one, even though out there," he swept his hand to the horizon, "you are only a myth to most people. They've started calling you Noah now and say you are saving the people from the flood of the Moralists. There's a description of you as well that is pretty accurate, and the information is wide spread from what I can tell."

"Really... well, as long as they don't call me Albert, I guess it doesn't matter; sometimes people need something to believe in to get them through one more day." He took a drag from the cigar then picked up the bottle from the table and took a sip. "How much is the reward."

"A million and forgiveness from the High Chancellor herself for any past Sins" Michael's tone said what he thought of the offer. He nodded at the old man's whistle of disbelief.

"You hear that, dog; I never thought I would be worth so much." He reached down and rubbed the pup's back. "Wonder if I could turn myself in and collect the reward then demand the old hag forgive me. We could go live on a beach somewhere it was warm, eh dog" the little pup looked up at him for a moment then laid his head back down on his paws.

"I don't think I would risk that if I were you, Albert. The Magistrates seem pretty intent on finding you and making sure you are dead by the end of the summer." He took a long pull on his cigar, the end glowing brightly in the darkness now surrounding them. "You **could** find you a little place by the beach though. You have done more than enough for the people already, Albert, and at your age you deserve it." He spoke quietly in between blowing smoke rings that were just light enough to see floating up into the dark air.

"Have you heard this song yet, boy" he gestured towards the house, his foot tapping rhythm in the grass, the motion barely visible in the darkness. "Even in the darkest days people still find ways to lift the spirit. I can not turn my back to

21

them no matter how old and tired I am. Do me a favor, boy, and go drag that sprinkler to the other side of the yard for me." He motioned towards the sprayer behind them with his cigar then reached for his glass of tea, and took a drink as Michael stood up.

"You do realize that I'm pushing forty don't you... old man," he said looking down at Albert in his rocker.

"Still just makes you a boy when compared to me. I turned ninety seven today, boy." He emphasized the word this time, "and there ain't many left in the world now that can claim that age or even close to it. Now run along and move my sprinkler before it drowns my roses. Then go bring your people in and we'll see to getting them fed and bedded down for the night."

"Well, happy birthday, Albert" Michael said with a grin in the darkness before turning to walk towards the sprinkler.

"Has been so far, huh, dog," the old man said as he reached down and rubbed the pup between the ears.

He replaced the bottle in the metal box and tucked it under his arm as he stood up. "Come on, dog; let's get ourselves something to eat." He picked up the pitcher in the hand of the arm holding the box. Dumping out the tea still in the glasses and placing them on the plates, he picked them up resting them on his hip. "We got a long night ahead of us, dog, and I already feel worn out." The pup cocked his head looking up at the old man then followed him into the house. He was hungry, and he knew the old man was going to feed him something special tonight.

Town

The sun was already up when the pup's whining, and scratching at the door woke the old man out of a peaceful sleep. He had been dreaming of Tizzy, when they had been young. *I haven't dreamed about her this much in all the time she's been gone*, the old man thought. At the pup's insistent scratching, he threw the sheet off of his thin boney frame, padded across the room on bare feet, and opened the bedroom door. The little pup scampered ahead of him to the backdoor, resuming his scratching, and whining. Opening it the old man followed the little black pup into the back yard, and watched as he ran around sniffing the ground until finding just the right spot to do his business.

"Better?" he asked the little pup when he ran back across the yard. For answer the pup dropped to his haunches, and started digging at his ear with a hind paw. Then bit at the paw before looking up at the old man.

"Come on, dog, I got business of my own, and I don't care to do it out here in front of the whole world." He held the door open for the little pup then followed him inside.

Pausing in the kitchen long enough to turn the coffee maker on he made his way back to his bedroom with the little pup following him. "You know, dog, you interrupted a really nice dream I was having. I usually don't have many of those kinds anymore." His tone said he was surprised by the recent change in that area. His needs hit him suddenly as it often did, and he crossed the bedroom as quick as his old legs would carry him; barely reaching the bathroom in time. "Maybe ought to have done my business outside after all," he said to the little pup as it curled up on the green rug beside the tub.

Finishing he turned to the sink, and started the hot water running. Reaching up to the shelf beside the mirror, he took a washcloth, and held it under the hot water then washed

23

his face and neck. "Well, I feel more awake now, but you look like you've only had a few hours of sleep." He said to the old man in the mirror in front of him. The pup on the floor looked up at the sound of his voice, but after a bit put his head back down. He was tired too, last night had been exciting with all the people, and the smells they carried with them. But the excitement was gone, and exhaustion was dragging at both of them right now.

Taking the glass from the counter top the old man dumped the contents into the sink, then rinsed the glass out, and replaced it. Digging his teeth out of the sink, he rinsed them as well, and then popped them into his mouth, settling them into position with his tongue, and smiled at the old man in the mirror. "Nothing beats a good pair of store bought teeth, dog." He said a grin spreading across his face that showed the even white teeth clearly.

Turning off the water he wrung the washcloth out and spread it on the counter to dry. Then went back into the bedroom, and made the bed, *just like Tizzy used to do* he thought to himself. The thought stirred up memories, and the memories brought a sense of loss that tugged at his heart. The old man spread out his clothes for the day, a pair of kaki pants from the closet along with a kaki shirt, fresh socks, t-shirt, and under wear from the chest of drawers beside the door; just as Tizzy used to do for him. Taking up the light gray suit spread across the chair where he had left it the night before he rehung it in the closet. He always liked to be dressed formally when greeting the people Michael brought in for the first time.

While the old man was doing this the little pup came out of the bathroom, and sat in the doorway watching the old man. He could smell pain on the old man, and wanted to ease it but did not know how. Dropping to the floor the little pup laid his head on his paws, and his dark brown eyes followed the old man seeming fixed on the him. Like the needle of a compass is inevitably drawn to north.

24

Dressing the old man's thoughts were drawn to the dream he had had, it was more a memory of the first date he had taken Tizzy on. They had gone dancing because she had told him how much she enjoyed it. He had found out that night how much he enjoyed dancing with her. It had been a wonderful night, and neither of them had wanted it to end. "But it did end just like everything else" he whispered to the room. The words brought him a sense of peace, knowing that even he would leave this world one day.

"Dog, you hungry?" he called turning towards the bath room as he scrubbed the unshed tears from his eyes with a wrinkled pale hand. The old man's face broke into a grin as he saw the black pup rise from the doorway, and try racing across the bedroom. But after his second stride the little pup's back end slid out from under him on the hardwood flooring. His momentum sent him into a full spin before he regained his stride, and bolted across the bedroom, and out the door. Laughing the old man filled his pockets with the articles lying on top of the chest of drawers then stepped into his shoes, and followed after the little pup.

In the kitchen he found the pup nearly bouncing beside his food bowl and went to the cabinet taking down a coffee cup, and a can of puppy food. "You're gonna have to wait till I pour me some coffee" he said over his shoulder, and lifted the pot from the coffee maker, filling the cup. "You know, dog," the old man said over his shoulder replacing the pot then opening a drawer. "The last time I had a dog was when my boys…" he reached into the drawer pulling out a can opener with one hand, and at the same time lifting the full cup to his lips blowing across the top of it. "…David and Jacob were just boys. Tizzy said boys should have a dog to grow up with" he took a shallow sip to test the temperature as he clamped the can opener onto the top of the can. "I wound up taking care of that dog too" he grinned over his shoulder at the little pup as he set the mug down to cool a little more.

25

"Reckon you'll get your breakfast before I have my coffee" he said turning his head back around to open the can. Then dropped the opener back in the drawer and closed it with a swing of his hip. "How about chicken for breakfast, dog" he said carrying the open can over to the island in the center of the kitchen. Dropping to a knee by the little pup, and his food bowl, the old man emptied the can into it, and stroked the pup's back. "You sure are hungry this morning." He said to the little black pup, gently petting him as memories of the other dog worked up from the depths of time. "You remind me a lot of that dog too" the old man said grinning as the pup looked up from his food. "Tizzy brought him home from the pound. When I came in that evening, he was sitting on the porch looking miserable just like you." The little pup had been on the front porch last Sunday when the old man had come home from town.

"I think I'll just have coffee this morning." He told the pup, who seemed to nod in understanding before turning back to devouring the food, but watched the old man closely as he walked over to the counter.

Picking up his cup, the old man returned to blowing on the hot liquid as he crossed the kitchen, and then went through the dinning room into the front room. He paused long enough to turn the radio on, and set the volume to a comfortable level that he would be able to hear from the front porch. Nodding his head to the music he retrieved his metal box from the shelf beside the door, and then opened the front door wide to let the cool morning air blow into the house. "Ah… now that's nice" he said aloud as the cool air hit him in the face. The day was going to be hot and muggy so he enjoyed the relatively cooler air now,

Stepping outside he kicked a piece of brick in front of the screen door to prop it open for when the pup finished his breakfast, and would come out side to join him. Walking along the porch he took a seat in one of the wicker chairs that Tizzy had made him buy for her a **long** time ago. He had not particularly cared for them at the time, but had no intention of getting rid of them after all this time. They were another reminder of the woman that he loved deeply.

Sitting the box on the table, he tested the temperature of the coffee once again, and found it tolerable then took a deep drink of the dark bitter liquid. Smiling he set the mug down beside the box then flipped the lid open, and retrieved a wooden pipe, and another smaller metal container. The paint on it was so faded that a person could barely tell that it had once been red, and the lettering across the top of the front was nearly gone. Leaving only the letters "Prin" on one side and "ert" on the other still legible, and below them the image of a man's proud face was all that was left of the picture that had covered the front of the can, and it was nearly faded away as well. Opening the lid of the container the old man stuffed the sticky green contents into the bowl of his pipe then closed the lid, and replaced the small container back in the larger.

Closing the lid of the larger box, and flipping the little clasp that held it into place the old man stared at it for a moment. He had had one just like it once, a dozen lifetimes ago when he was a boy, and had carried his lunch to school. The lid was faded, but the image of a man dressed in blue, and red with one arm thrust out ahead of him, and a city below him as if her were flying could still be made out though his face was completely erased. *A hero sent to save humanity from itself, where are you now that we need you the most* the old man wandered as he pulled his lighter from his pocket. The sides of the box had had images on them as well but they were faded past recognition, and too much time had passed for his memory to recall what they had been.

Holding the flame of the lighter to the bowl of the pipe he took a deep draw, filling his lungs with the smoke. Exhaling he sent a pair of smoke rings through the air, and watched them break up as they struck the box. Picking up the cup he took another deeper drink of the cooler liquid then set it down, and took another draw from his pipe.

27

"Did you get full, dog," he asked the pup a few minutes later when it ambled out the doorway. The little pup paused to look at the old man then started towards the front steps. "Hey, mind your manners, dog, close the door behind you. I don't want any flies in the house. It's a pain chasing them out" he pointed to the brick holding the door with the pipe, and gave the pup a steady look. After a moment the little pup walked over to the brick, and set his mouth around the edge. Tugging with all his might on it till the screen door slide past, and closed. "Good dog" the old man said nodding at him in approval. "I knew you were a smart one."

"Now, go about your business" the old man said nodding towards the yard as he held the lighter to his pipe, and took another puff. The little pup made his way down the steps. The old man sat drinking his coffee, and puffing on his pipe as the little pup made a circuit around the yard pausing now and then to sniff the ground. He would raise his head, and look at the old man sitting on the porch each time as if telling him that something had passed here in the night. Then cocking his head to the side added that he was on top of it, and there was nothing to fear now. After completing his rounds the pup climbed the stairs, and bounced down the porch with its little tail wagging so hard his butt moved with it.

"Did you find them all, dog?" The old man said grinning as he laid his empty pipe on the table beside the box before reaching down to scratch the little pup behind one of his ears. "You know I think I will have some breakfast myself this morning dog" he said rising, and picking up his cup before leading the little animal back into the house.

In a few minutes he had sausage frying in a skillet, and batter made for pancakes the whole time talking to the little pup like he used to do when making breakfast for his wife. It never occurred to the old man that had anyone seen him they might have considered that he was crazy. He knew the little pup wasn't his wife but he served a second best for voicing his thoughts to while making breakfast. *Better than talking to my self like I have been* the old man thought. Occasionally the little pup gave a low bark or growl in response to the old man's words, but more to the tone, and most times the old man agreed with the little pup completely.

"Well, I feel ten time better now" the old man said after taking the last bite of his pancakes, and reached for the coffee cup which he noticed was nearly empty. "How about you, dog, you getting full?" He asked the pup who was still chewing on his pancake, and paused for a moment to look up at the old man as he filled his cup once more.

"Now, I need a smoke to top off a good meal." The old man said heading back outside to take one of the cigars from the box then carried it back inside, and replaced it on the shelf. "Let me clean this mess up, dog, and then we'll go to town" the old man said after lighting his cigar.

"You about ready to go for a ride, dog" the old man asked later after having washed the dishes, and put them away. The little pup answered by rising to his feet, and wagging his tail. "That's what I thought, you're always ready to go for a ride, aren't yah." The old man grinned as he walked past the little pup who fell in beside him tail and bottom both wagging as he followed along.

"Step along, dog," the old man said holding the screen door open for the little pup to go scampering through. "I know where the truck is, dog" the old man told him as the pup waited at the top of the steps for him. "And I think I can still climb a couple of steps without you watching out for me" he told the little pup as he slowly went down the steps using the railing to help support himself. "Be my luck one of these knees goes out just cause you're watching me, dog, then who's going to feed you pancakes for breakfast" the black pup continued watching him make his way down the steps just the same. Then lead the way across the yard to where the bubble truck was parked beside the house. The old man had gotten the thing because gas usage by Citizens had been outlawed, and it was his only option. He hated the thing, but he did what he had to do, sometimes.

"I'm coming, dog" the old man said shuffling around the house, and hearing the pup whining to get into the vehicle. He reached for the handle, and opened the door then bent down to pick the pup up, and set him on the seat before climbing in behind him. As soon as the old man was behind the wheel, the pup crawled into his lap, and put his front paws on the door then pushed his snout against the glass and whined.

"Well, give me a minute, dog, I ain't even got settled in yet" the old man said trying to get comfortable while the pup struggled to get his head past the window. "There you go" the old man said with a smile as he pushed the big power button on the dash then hit the window button and the glass slid from view. If he was going to have a plastic bubble for a truck, he had made sure to get one with all the bells and whistles. Putting his arm on the door, the little pup took position with his back paws on the old man's leg, and his front ones resting on the old man's arm. His little head stuck out the window where he could catch all the scents along the way.

"Hang on, dog, here we go" the old man said grinning as he dropped the gearshift into drive, stomped the accelerator, and the bubble truck jumped forward heading down the drive. "This song has a good bass beat don't it, dog?" he leaned forward to turn the radio up a little more, and started tapping his left foot to the beat. "Let's go to town, dog" the old man grinned broadly as he pulled out of the drive, and onto the dirt road heading for town.

Almost an hour later, and more than a dozen turns the old man drove into town from the east, coming in on the opposite side from where he lived. "This will have'em wondering, and coming round to ask questions dog, you watch and see" the old man said with a grin as he looked up at a camera mounted on a power pole. "All that old world technology we had to keep an eye on our supposed enemies. Well the Moralists are now using it to monitor the people in their brave new world. Only a fool says something disparaging about them on the phone, dog, they'll have him switched in public if he's lucky. If not Bonded as a Servant of the People, all his property confiscated, and even his family refusing to admit they ever knew him. Their brave new world is not all that pleasant for us free thinkers to live in, dog." The old man's smile at the pup was grim as he turned onto Main Street.

"We're here, dog" he said a few minutes later as he pulled the truck into the parking lot of the hardware store. The sign above it claming it was Durum's Hardware. "Used to belong to Phil Maxwell, dog, but he's a Servant now. He was a free thinker like us only he was a little to free with expressing what he was thinking. Pity too he knew what he was doing, Adam Durum on the other hand doesn't know a pipe wrench from a monkey wrench, dog." The old man chuckled at the joke then laughed loudly when the pup looked up at him with his mouth open, and his tongue hanging out as if he was grinning at the joke as well.

"Alright, dog, you wait here, I don't want your mouth getting us lashed in front of the whole town, and I'm too damn old to be serving anyone else." He set the parking brake, and rolled the other window down before poking the power button with a stiff finger. The low whine of the electric motors shut down. Then picked the little black pup up gently, and set him in the seat beside him. "Now, you stay here" he admonished as he opened the door, and got out closing it behind him. "I said stay there" he repeated when the pup's whine brought him to a halt, and turned his head to look over his shoulder giving the pup a sharp look. Which the pup accepted, and laid his head down on his front paws resting on the door. The pup watched the old man till he disappeared around the corner of the building, and continued watching the same spot anxious to see him reappear.

The old man shuffled along the side walk noticing that he had the street to himself, nobody traveled much these days with the Magistrates watching every move people made. He

31

shook his head at the foolishness of people. First they demand that safety required the suspension of certain civil liberties then were shocked when they were deemed a threat to society, and had no way of defending themselves. Now, safety only came with the appearance of fully supporting the High Chancellor, and avoiding those who held the reins of power. These thoughts were whipped away as he reached the door and swung it open to step inside. The blast of cold air coming out nearly knocked his frail looking old body back, *seems Adam's got his AC cranking full blast already* he thought to himself. Forcing his way past the escaping air the old man made his way inside and closed the door behind him.

"Hi yah, Albert" Adam Durum called from the counter on the old man's right. Adam Durum was a middle aged man with dark brown hair that had wings of grey starting to appear at his temples. His eyes were deep brown with a ring of black flakes circling the iris, and he was over weight by about thirty pounds the old man thought. Well beyond the limits of the Moralists standards, but that was one of the benefits of the man's position in the community. "Come in and cool yourself, it's already hotter than a griddle out there" the man said pleasantly.

How would you know what it's like out there the old man thought but out loud he said. "You definitely got it cool enough in here, Adam." Adam was a member of the Moralist Council and a devote believer in the divinity of the High Chancellor. Not a man he wanted to insult just because he could. *Didn't get this old being a fool, and there ain't no point starting now* he thought.

"What can I do for you, Albert?" Adam asked coming around the counter towards the old man.

"I need some paint, brushes, scrapers, and rollers. My old house is in serious need of a fresh coat of paint nearly as bad as me." The old man smiled, and Adam returned it missing the fact that the old man's eyes showed no sign of humor in them.

"We can handle that with no problem" Adam said nodding, his eyes taking on a harsh cast as he looked past the old man. "Servant Marcy, help Citizen Albert" he called loudly into the room, his eyes softening once again as they shifted back to the old man. "I'll fetch Servant Larry from the back to mix your paint for you, Albert, be back in a jiffy." His eyes took up the harsh cast once more as he turned, and walked along the counter disappearing behind the shelves that filled the large room.

"Citizen Jenkins, how may I serve?" Marcy said from the other side of the store, bringing the old man's head around to look at her. The woman was as thin as a fence post with long dark brown hair, and the most striking green eyes that were her only attractive feature. She was in her mid forties the old man thought, and she had the same marks on her forehead as Susie. Seeing the marks always made the old man think of the passage in Revelations about the Mark of the Beast. This made him glance down at his own hand, where a barcode had been set under the skin like a tattoo. *Are we all serving Satan...?* The thought left the old man cold inside. The old religions were gone their books burned replaced with the Moralist Bible, the High Chancellor taking the place of God. The old man often wondered if that had been Satan's plan from the start, but today his mind shied away from the subject, and focused on the thin woman.

"Hello, Marcy, how are you today" the old man smiled warmly and this time his eyes reflected the same emotions.

"I am well Citizen" her eyes shifted to the back of the store with fear filling them for a moment. "How are you, Citizen Jenkins?" her tone was neutral but when her eyes tuned back to him the fear vanished behind a warm light of genuine concern for the old man.

"Can't complain" his smile deepened to a grin at the smile that appeared on the woman's face for a moment then resumed its regular neutral expression. Servants were held to a

33

strict code of conduct, and any transgression was punished severely.

"What can I get for you, Citizen?" She asked stepping past him to pull a cart out of the short line beside the door.

"A half dozen paint brushes, scrapers, and rollers Marcy. And a dozen thick pads for the rollers please" he added giving the woman a smile as she wheeled the cart down one of the aisles, and disappeared from his view.

The old man shuffled along behind her, but turned up a different aisle inspecting the products hanging from hooks in their packaging or lying on the shelving. "Marcy could you add a couple of shovels, picks, and a pair of post hole diggers. Might as well get a couple of hammers and ten pounds of sixteen penny nails as well" the old man called across the aisles. He was thinking of all the people that Michael had brought with him the night before. Tools were an essential and scarce commodity in the wilderness, and whatever he could get without raising suspicion would aid them greatly.

"As you wish, Citizen Jenkins, anything else?" Her tone was neutral even lacking any sign of the question in her words. She had learned quickly, and survived a long time. Where many perished in only weeks after being Bonded as Servants she had lived for fifteen years under the harsh conditions so far. If he ordered it she would load up the entire store, or pound her head against a wall. The Servants served the Citizens. They had no other purpose in life after being Bonded.

"Yeah a couple of hand saws, axes, and sling blades as well please" he said bringing his thoughts back to her question. He shuffled on down the aisle looking at the items on display thinking of all the things the people would need, but thought he had better stop there, or questions might start being asked. He had answers if they were, but preferred not to raise suspicions at all if he could avoid it.

"As you wish, Citizen Jenkins" Marcy said her voice loud in the large room which was probably why she was careful about her words knowing that Adam could hear what she said

34

even in the back. The woman appeared down the aisle with the paint supplies already loaded in the cart. She smiled briefly at him as she passed heading to the other side of the room to gather the rest of the items he had requested.

"Servant Larry will mix your paint for you, Albert" Adam said appearing at the far end of the aisle with a young man in his early twenties following him. "I got some five gallon buckets that are on special if you would like to look at them" the man offered.

"Nope, Tizzy only likes the best" the old man said smiling inside at the other man's sudden widening of his eyes; sometimes being old had its advantages. "She'd roll over in her grave if I didn't do things right to the old house place" he added just so the man wouldn't think he was too far gone.

"Well, I understand completely" the man's eyes said that he thought the old man was going senile but if it increased his profit that was just fine. *Greed was still alive and well in the Moralist* the old man thought. "Servant, show Citizen Albert what we have in stock, and give him whatever he wants" his tone was harsh, and commanding as he spoke to the younger man. "I'll be at the counter when you are ready, Albert" like a switch the man's tone was back to friendly and accommodating. He gave the old man a nod before leaving the Servant to lead the way to the paint area.

"How you doing, Larry?" the old man asked his voice low, noticing the tightness around the young man's blue eyes, and the thin line of his mouth covering his clenched teeth.

"I am well, Citizen Jenkins" the sandy brown haired young man said just as softly, giving the old man a quick smile, and a nod as he watched Adam walking away. "If you'll come this way, Citizen I'll get your paint for you" his voice louder as he turned holding out his arm towards the back of the store. Allowing the old man to lead the way as was proper for a Servant. "Do you know what color you want, Citizen Jenkins" the younger man asked keeping his pace slow to match the old man as he shuffled along the aisle.

35

"Forest Green, Larry, if you want to go ahead and mix it. I need twenty gallons please and five gallons of Dark Brown" the old man said turning to look at the Servant.

"Twenty gallons of Forest Green and five of Dark Brown, our best quality coming up Citizen Jenkins," the young man said bowing slightly at the waist before stepping past the old man, and walking away down the aisle.

The old man turned the other way shuffling along, up and down the aisles till he finally found what he was looking for. Browsing the boxes sitting on the shelf he chose one, and took it down carrying it with him as he shuffled back to the front of the store. Marcy was holding up a shovel while Adam was using a hand held wand to read the bar code on the handle when the old man shuffled over to them.

"Add this as well, Adam" he said laying the box he had picked up on the counter.

"Got you a dog with fleas, Albert," the man asked as he picked up the box, and ran the laser across the bar code.

"Nope, my fleas got a dog, that'll get rid of him won't it?" The old man said with a sly smile that produced a smile on Marcy's face that she quickly wiped off when Adam gave her a sharp look.

"That's a good one, Albert I'll have to remember it next time" his tone said he would be remembering more than the joke, and he did not have the barest hint of a smile on his face. "You realize this is the third set of shovels you've bought in the last month or so" he asked looking at his monitor with a concerned expression.

"Well, now that couldn't be I just broke my old shovel a day or two ago, and I bought it six or seven years back when I was making a bed for Tizzy's Azaleas." He put his best confused old man's face on as he spoke.

"Well, maybe I'm looking at this wrong then" Adam said shaking his head.

Yeah thankfully greed will do that to a man sometimes the old man thought to himself. "It happens with them computers,

36

never did trust'em, their going to take over the world one day." He waved a finger at the monitor as he spoke, and Marcy hid another smile as she held up one of the picks for Adam to scan.

"I don't really think that this one is going to do anything like that Albert." Adam waved his wand at the monitor, and inside Adam felt a momentary relief over diverting the conversation.

"Don't bet on it" the old man said laying a finger alongside his nose, and giving Adam a wink as he did so. Adam just looked at him for a moment confusion written on his face then scanned the pick Marcy was holding without saying another word.

The old man shuffled away from the counter, and stopped at a display that had bundles of leather work gloves, but after a brief inspection moved on. The stitching was already coming loose on most of them, and they wouldn't last a day of actual work. Most of the goods produced these days were of the same quality, and he wasn't going to waste time with them.

"Here's your paint, Citizen Jenkins" Larry said a little later as he pushed a buggy along the aisle with five, five gallon buckets sitting on it. "The best we had" he said in a lower voice as he reached the old man with a tone that said it was still not very good.

"Thank you, Larry, if you don't mind, load it in the back of my truck please" he gave the boy a nod of understanding, and shuffled along after him. Then made a little turn, and quickened his pace to reach the doorway before Marcy so he could open the door for her.

"Watch out for the dog, he's a ferocious beast" he said as he held the door for her to drive the cart through.

"Really, Citizen" her face matched the concern in her voice.

"Take an arm right off." He used his free hand to make a chopping motion across the arm holding the door as she went through looking back at him over her shoulder with fear growing in her eyes.

37

"Thank you, son" he said to Larry as the young man followed Marcy with his buggy. "I'm too old to be packing heavy stuff around anymore."

"I live to serve, Citizen Jenkins" the young man said as he passed.

"You should not be polite to them, Albert, they do not deserve it" Adam said sharply from the counter after the old man let the door swing shut. "They have lost their rights as people for punishment of their sins against the High Chancellor, and you would do well to remember that."

"Apologies, Councilman" the old man said as he shuffled across the room. "My mother beat manners into me so hard that I can still remember the feel of her belt even at my age."

"See that you correct your ways, or you may find yourself being whipped again even at your age." The man's words were a warning but his tone implied that he hoped the old man would not heed it. The weekly punishments held in the square were like a celebration that most Citizens looked forward to with anticipation.

"I will try to follow your example in the future, Councilman" the old man tried to scrap the sarcasm from his words before they escaped his mouth and he thought he managed it enough when the man said no more about it.

"Do you need anything else, Albert" he held up the wand as the old man reached the counter.

Just for people like you to not be in charge of things now he thought. "No that will be it Councilman" the old man held out his right hand for Adam to pass the wand over the bar code imprinted on the back of it.

"My goodness, Albert, you've got quite a large sum in your personal account, how do you manage that?" The man's question was more wonder than suspicion.

"Simple living, Councilman" the old man said as he took his receipt and shuffled towards the door where Larry was just now coming back in.

When the young man looked up at him, Albert gave him a wink and a smile before speaking. "Servant, if you can't perform your duties with out more speed than you have shown me today, then perhaps I should speak to the Magistrate before I leave town."

The young man's face turned pale and he dropped his head holding the door open for the old man who looked over his shoulder, and received an approving nod from Adam. "Sorry son" he said quietly enough that only the young man could hear as he walked past him and out into the heat. He shuffled along the building to the corner in time to see Marcy petting the little pup who was suffering the attention as he watched the corner where the old man had last been seen. When he saw the old man reappear his head come up off his paws, and the old man knew his tail was wagging even without seeing it.

"Careful girl he's liable to take your arm off any second now" the old man said with a grin as he shuffled towards the woman.

"I can see he's just a terrible monster ain't he" she laughed and then clamped a hand over her mouth, but he caught the surprise in her eyes that said she did not think she was capable of finding anything amusing any more. "I've got to go, Citizen Jenkins please excuse me" she said hurriedly her tone back to its normal neutrality and was already starting to leave before she finished speaking.

"Wait a moment, Marcy, I need some help here" he said nodding to the back of his truck. "I'm too old to be climbing in and out of the bed of a truck." He turned his head, and smiled knowing that there were two cameras watching them, but made sure that neither could see his face.

"My duty to serve, Citizen" she said crossing her arms against her flat chest and bowing in the formal form that all the Servants were required to use in public.

"Climb up in there, and open the truck box" the old man motioned to the back of the truck. "And hand me the rope in there, please" he added shuffling around to the tailgate. "Have you heard of Noah girl" he asked leaning over the tailgate and watching her. So he saw her freeze for just an instant as she was climbing into the bed one foot on the tire using it for a step and the other suspended in the air.

"No, Citizen, I do not know of whom you speak" she said stiffly continuing into the bed.

"You can drop all that propriety with me, girl, and I know you know who I'm talking about too." *Might as well use the rumors to my advantage* he thought. "I can get you to him girl" he said watching her shoulders tense as she opened the box. "You can start a new life girl" she turned, her face blank, the rope in her hands. "You're a good woman Marcy too good to be treated like this in my opinion." He took the rope she offered, her face tight but expressionless, and untied the knot that bound the loops together.

"Think about it" he took one end of the rope and ran it through the metal ring on the inside of the bed and tied a half hitch knot to secure it. "I can promise you a life where you don't have to worry about laughing in public getting you a whipping at the end of the week." He turned unrolling a couple more loops into a gesture that indicated the cameras watching them, and saw by the look in her eye that she understood.

"If there is anyone else that you know that might be willing to take a chance as well bring them with you" he ran the rope through the handles on the buckets. "I think Larry would take the chance, and I know how you two feel about each other" her gasp was proof that he had hit the mark in the dark on that one. "You two could have a real life together" he ran a loop of the rope through the metal ring on the other side of the bed, and pulled the rope tight pinning the buckets against the tailgate then tied another half hitch knot with the loop of rope.

"That should hold'em till I get home" he looked up at the woman standing in the bed of the truck her face bone white as she looked down at him. "Think about it girl my door is always open day or night to you two" he wrapped the other

40

end of the rope around the excess and tied another knot in it then dropped the bundle in the corner of the bed. "Now, climb down out of there, I've other business to attend to while I'm in town today, and I'll not haul you around with me" he grinned as he held a hand up to her.

She waved the hand away, and stepped over the buckets and tailgate placing her foot on the bumper then swung her other leg over and dropped to the pavement staggering a little. "When could we come to your home" Marcy whispered the words when the old man reached out a steadying hand to keep her from falling.

"Any time" he said just as quietly.

"Tonight then" she said before stepping away from him. "An honor to serve, Citizen" she said in a more normal volume before turning to walk back towards the store.

The old man smiled as he rested a hand on the tailgate and used it to help support himself as he shuffled back around the truck. He saw the little black pup's head sticking out the window looking at him. "I'll be there in a minute, dog, I ain't as young as I used to be you know." The little pup looked like he was grinning at he old man as he watched him shuffle along the bed.

He had reached the cab and had his hand on the door latch when the sound of another vehicle entering the parking lot brought his head around. The car was black and sleek, its motor sounded deep and powerful, and the seal of the Magistrates was boldly emblazoned on the driver's door. The old man turned and waited when the car stopped right behind his truck.

Magistrate Maxwell's black uniform stretched around his pot belly and accentuated the little man's bald head that was shinning in the sun. The old man had to stop himself from smiling at the man's nose that was much too large for his face giving him a comical looking face. There was nothing similar between the Magistrate and his brother Phil Maxwell the previous owner of the hardware store which might account for

41

part of the reason the man was now a Servant. Jealousy and envy were powerful motivators in some people and Phil had been a popular man in the community, a voice of reason in a world gone mostly insane. Magistrate Maxwell's dark eyes drew the old man's gaze because they held the fanatical light of one of the true believers and that made him a man to be cautious of if not out right feared.

"Citizen, a word with you please" the short man said in a tone that made it a definite command and not a request.

"Good day to you, Magistrate" the old man smiled as he dropped the man a bow before shuffling forward to meet him.

"What business did you have this morning that took you around the north side of town, and then brought you in from the east." The Magistrate's voice was filled with suspicion, and impatience at having to deal with the old man but his eyes were surveying the contents of the truck bed.

Always watching the old man thought. "Citizen Tom Duncan, over on the north side of town spoke to me last week about swapping our bulls since his wasn't performing his duties with the cows any longer. You know how bulls are. Then I felt like driving over by the river and seeing if the drought had dropped the water level to any noticeable degree, Magistrate." The old man put just a hint of question in his voice as if he was uncertain how he could have done anything wrong. This was always a wise tone to take with Magistrate Maxwell.

"Yet, you stopped at neither of these places, why is that" the Magistrate turned his full attention to the old man now, his eyes burning with his fervor seeking the truth that lay beneath the old man's words.

Dangerous ground here for some reason. "Magistrate, Citizen Duncan's bull was in the field when I passed and I saw no reason that the trade would not be good for both of us. For the river the highway goes along it for over a mile and it was plain the river has dropped several feet because of this drought." He almost had to bite his tongue to stop from asking whether he should call the Magistrates office before leaving his

42

house next time he went out. *You brought the attention on purpose, remember. You thought it would be fun to make them come out in the heat to question you remember* he said to himself wondering if it had really been such a good idea now.

"Did you notice anything odd in your travels, Citizen" the Magistrate was looking at him intently now.

"No Magistrate" the question itself was odd making the puzzlement in his voice honest.

"Be vigilant, Citizen, for the Sin of Sedition by those you know and trust" the Magistrate's voice held a warning that failure in doing so might result in equal punishment.

"Magistrate I will watch closely" the old man said his tone conveying an earnestness to do so.

"Go about your business then, Citizen" the man turned abruptly and walked briskly to his car leaving the old man wondering what was happening that he did not know about.

The old man shuffled back to the cab his mind racing with fearful thoughts and possible actions that he dreaded he might have to take. "Slide over, dog, we got one more stop to make before we go home" he pushed the little black pup gently off the door before opening it and climbing in. "I got you something for them fleas dog" he watched the pup digging at the back of his head with a hind paw before the little pup climbed into his customary place. "You ready to ride, dog," he asked as he slapped the power button, and the electric motors started to hum. The little pup looked up at him with his tongue hanging out the side of his mouth then stuck his head out the window.

The old man grinned at the little pup as he backed the truck up, and pulled back out onto Main Street. Turning left he continued on down the street till he reached Moralist Square. In the old days the area had been a school but that had been cleared away along with dozens of buildings to make the giant square. On the far side was the Magistrates Hall, the massive three story building faced in a black stone that seemed to suck the light out of the air around it. Three Deputy Magistrates were climbing the steps to the main entrance high above ground level, their uniforms blending into the dark stone.

On the right side of the square was the Hall of Councilors. The tall six story building was covered in glass with a tinted film that made it appear dark blue. The building was the center of power for the district all the decisions made there concerned the Citizens in the district. What crops the farmers were to grow, the production schedules for the half dozen factories in the town and the management of the local utilities, including water usage during the drought. The building sat on high foundations as well and had steps that stretched the width of the building, rising to the entrance.

On the opposite side from the Hall of Councilors was the Temple of the High Chancellor. The building large enough to hold more than five thousand people, faced with brilliant white marble and easily out shinning the other two buildings. A wide veranda stretched across the front with tall pillars of the white marble supporting a covering roof. Twin statues of the High Chancellor stood at ground level and tall enough that their heads nearly reached the roof of the veranda. Between them steps rose to the massive doors of the entrance where beyond the priests would be praying to the High Chancellor day and night.

Between the buildings the ground had been leveled and grass grew in between concrete walks that quartered the square and connected the three buildings. In the grass covered areas along the front of the Hall of Councilors wooden scaffolds had been erected on platforms so that all could see those who had Sinned so grievously that they warranted Hanging. The scaffolds were large enough that twenty people could be hung at once and in the beginning they had been filled several times on each Sunday but now they were used only occasionally for one or two people. Their main purpose was a reminder that death could be and would be the ultimate price for those who refused to live properly in the Moralist way.

In the area across the walkway wooden frames stood on raised platforms where men and women were tied and striped bare then lashed with the Tools of Punishment. Depending on the severity of their sins the punished could expect one or two of the implements or all. Most of those punished were Servants who had transgressed during the week or a Citizen who had Sinned and was being Bonded as a Servant.

In the center of the square a pavilion had been erected for the High Priest to lead the Citizens in prayer before they witnessed the Priests of the High Chancellor administer punishment to the Sinners. The pavilion was raised so that all in the square would be able to see the High Priest as well and hear his words. Every Sunday all the Citizens in the district were required to be in the square at sunrise to bear witness to punishment of the Sinners and then gather in the Temple for prayer and sermons that exalted the power of the High Chancellor until the sun set. The old man hated Sundays now but the only excuse the Magistrates accepted for absence was the person being on his death bed, and he better die well before sunrise, or else he would die alone because everyone else would be at the square.

The old man took the square in at a glance as he stopped at the intersection then turned right onto Moralist Avenue. The pup whined at the smells that came from the square, clearly unhappy about being near the place. "Yep, you're the lucky one not having to be here on Sunday, dog" the old man said absently as he quickly drove away from the square.

A few minutes later the old man pulled off Moralist Avenue into a parking lot of what had once been the big retail stores back before the Moralist had put an end to corporations. Now the Servants were housed in the huge vacant buildings that acted more like prisons these days. There were no fences or guards other than a couple of Deputy Magistrates who did a head count twice a day. Most of the Servants who ran were found within a day or so but most did not have the aide of the old man.

The old man drove through the parking lot half filled with nearly broken down old vehicles like the one Susie drove. He stopped in front of a small trailer that sat near the open entrance of the huge building. "You stay here dog" he said to the little pup as he set him in the seat and climbed out of the cab. He closed the door and started shuffling towards the stairs leading up to the door of the trailer when it opened. Out stepped a slim man with a long face and bright gray eyes that held a measure of intelligence but none of the fanaticism of the other Magistrates at any level. He was also the day guard at the Servants compound.

"Citizen Jenkins, a good day to you" Deputy Magistrate Mark Fines's voice had a distinct accent that held genuine joy at seeing the old man.

"Magistrate Fines, a good day to you sir" the old man responded with a smile for the younger man.

Deputy Magistrate Mark Fines was one of the few remaining Britons left in the world. In the early days of the Movement when the Moralists were spreading out across the world, England had refused to allow them access to their country. This had infuriated the High Councilor and she had sent a dire warning to the Prime Minister who after presenting the warning to the people of the United Kingdom had still refused the Moralist.

Within hours the High Councilor declared Great Briton a den of civil terrorists and Sinners. Her followers flooded the media with false accusations and evidence till the nation demanded immediate action. She sent the Navy to blockade the island nation and once it was in place, ordered bombing runs to begin. Thousands of incendiary bombs were dropped on the major cities and then the smaller towns and villages then finally on individual building till nothing man made stood. When this was done an army of more than three million of the most fanatical Moralists landed. They burned everything fields and forest from shore to shore, and behind them they salted the earth so that nothing would ever grow there again. The people

46

that survived the bombing were driven ahead of the High Councilor's army till their backs were against the sea in the northern part of the country. The killing took days and when it was done England was no more. Deputy Magistrate Mark Fines had already been a member of the Movement in America but the ruling body judged him untrustworthy and sent him here to serve.

"Come in and cool yourself, Citizen" the younger man said as he came down the steps and held out a steadying arm for the old man.

"Thank you kindly, Magistrate" the old man took the offered arm leaning his weight on it as the man lead him to the stairs, and helped him to climb them.

"The weather grows worse each day, Citizen, and you are too old to be out in the heat of the day. No offense intended Citizen." The man's heart felt concern was evident in his tone. "You should allow me to assign one of the Servants to you full time to ease your burdens, Citizen" the man made the offer each time the old man came here.

"I thank you for the offer, Magistrate, but my burdens are what remind me that I am still living" the old man gave him another smile as they entered the little trailer.

The small air conditioner was pumping cooling air into the room but thankfully it was only a little cooler than outside. The old man hated going from extremes, his old body did not deal with it as well anymore.

"Then how may I be of service, Citizen" the younger man asked waving to a chair sitting in front of the small desk. "Can I offer you some coffee, Citizen" the man took a pot from a coffee maker on a small table beside the door, and a cup from beside it offering both to the old man.

"I never turn down a good cup of coffee, thank you, Magistrate" the old man took the offered seat and the full cup when the man held it out to him. "I am in need of six Servants for two or perhaps three days at my home Magistrate" the old man said in answer to his first question then took a drink of the coffee.

"Six Servants" the man said as he poured himself a cup. "That is an unusual request from you Citizen. May I inquire why so many are required" he sat down in the chair behind the desk.

"Certainly Magistrate, I need my house painted and I do not believe I am up to the task myself" he smiled over his cup at the man before taking another drink.

"I see" the man answered taking a drink of his coffee as he thought. "Why do you require six Servants for this task" the man asked looking in his cup as he waited on the old man to answer.

"I do not wish the task to take overly long to accomplish and work spread across so many is done quicker and easier, Magistrate" the old man paused looking at the man across from him closer for a moment. "Is there a problem with my request Magistrate?"

"I received instructions earlier, Citizen, not to assign more than two Servants to a work detail for any Citizen outside of town" the younger man looked troubled by this. "I am sorry that I can not serve you better Citizen but I must follow the instructions I was given."

"Completely understandable Magistrate" the old man reassured him. "I suppose I will need the two Servants for at least four days though, if that is agreeable to you Magistrate."

"Certainly Citizen, I could even assign them to you permanently if you would allow it" the younger man offered once again.

The old man hesitated, considering the offer, but decided the risk was too great. "No thank you for the offer Magistrate, but honestly I am afraid that if I started relying on someone else to care for me that I would soon be in the grave, or worse a total invalid" the old man grinned at the younger man.

"I hope that I am half the man you are if I should be as lucky to live as long as you have Citizen" the man smiled appreciatively. "Is there any particular Servants you would like me to assign to you Citizen" the man sat up getting back to the business at hand.

"No Magistrate just as long as they are healthy enough to work in the heat, but if they know a little about painting it would be helpful." The old man took another drink as the man pulled a thick folder from a drawer in the desk, and opened it.

"Would you be opposed to using women Citizen" the man looked up from his papers. "Most of the men are assigned to Public Projects, and those that are not would be of little use to you I am afraid."

"I have known some women that could work most men into the ground Magistrate." The old man smiled at the memory of Tizzy still going strong in the evening when he was nearly exhausted, and nodded in acceptance.

"Then I will assign Servants Heather, and Angie to you, Citizen" the man said reaching into another drawer on the other side of the desk to take out a form. "When would you like me have them report to you, Citizen" he asked as he reached for a pen, and started filling out the form.

"Say around seven in the morning, Magistrate" the old man responded then took another drink of his coffee as he watched the man writing quickly. *I whish I could trust you enough to offer you a different life, boy. You deserve it maybe more than any of the others I've helped.*

"Sign and date here, Citizen" the man spun the form around, and slid it across the table pointing at the bottom, and laying the pen down.

The old man leaned forward in his chair, and set his cup on the desk then picked up the pen, and signed his name, Albert Jenkins along the line at the bottom then put the date July 2nd 47th YHC. *Year of the High Chancellor my foot, the year is 2067* but he kept the thought from showing on his face.

"Thank you for your service, and the coffee, Magistrate" the old man said rising after sliding the form back across the table.

49

"A pleasure to serve you Citizen" the man said rising, and coming around the desk. "Please allow me to help you Citizen" he said offering a supporting arm once again to the old man.

"Thank you, Magistrate" the old man took the arm, and allowed the younger man to help him out side and down the stairs to his truck.

"I see you have acquired a companion since the last time you were here Citizen" the man nodded to the little pup watching them approach.

"He was sitting on my porch last Sunday when I got home Magistrate" the old man said pushing the pup back from the door so he could get in.

"He seems like a smart animal Citizen" the man said when the pup took his position on the old man's leg, and allowed the younger man to scratch his ear. "I've always heard that dogs take on the characteristics of their masters. Did you name him Noah, Albert" the younger man spoke softly almost casually, but with a subtle undertone in the names that had a particular meaning.

The old man stiffened at the name, and knew that the other man noticed it. "No, I call him dog, Magistrate."

The younger man arched an eyebrow in question "I am not as blind as these other fools, Albert" the man continued scratching the pup's ear. "You should speak to the women, and do it quickly because they are coming for you... Albert" he emphasized the old man's name in such a way that it was clear he meant the other name.

"Why are you telling me this" the old man asked softly, starring at the younger man intently, searching for a clue in his face.

"Because I remember my country" the bitterness in his voice was clear.

"Would you like a chance at a new life son" the old man asked after looking into the younger man's eyes, and deciding that perhaps it was not such a risk to help the man after all.

"I can do more here for you now, Citizen" the man took a step back. "Good day to you, Citizen" he turned, and walked back towards the trailer.

"Well, dog, my scrawny old neck is on the chopping block now, the question is how long before the axe falls." He started the truck, and backed it up while the little pup looked out the window sniffing the air. "How about chicken for supper tonight, dog" the old man grinned as he drove out of the parking lot. The little black pup stuck his head out the window enjoying the feel of the air rushing over him, and all the smells it held.

Home

A half hour later the old man slowed the truck, and pulled into his drive way. "We're home, dog" he grinned down at the pup, and drove the truck up the drive past the house then backed it up to the barn doors. "Let's get unloaded, dog, I need a smoke bad" the old man said as he picked the little pup up, and opened the door then stepped out setting him down on the ground.

The old man walked behind the truck to the barn doors, and swung them both open, the frail old man routine unnecessary now that he was home. "Do your business, dog" the old man called to the little pup that was sniffing around the corner of the barn. He stopped to look at the old man at the sound of his voice then hiked a hind leg as the old man opened the tailgate of the truck.

"You know dog this has been one interesting day" the old man said dryly as he untied the rope holding the buckets of paint together. "It's got me worried some too" he chuckled as the little pup scampered over to him, and chased his tail for a moment before dropping his butt on the ground, and digging at the back of his ear. "Feel the same way" the old man said grasping the handles of two of the buckets, and dragging them off the tail gate then carried them both into the barn.

The old man returned for another pair lost in his thoughts, and this time the pup followed him into barn. Trotting along with his head held high sniffing the air that still held the scents of all the people who had passed through it the night before. One of them stood out above the rest, the little pup did not know why that was, but had an impression that it was important in some way. While the old man went back outside for the other bucket the black pup followed the scent to the far side of the barn where in the back corner the dirt floor sloped down to a concrete wall under the outside wall of the barn. In the center of the wall a metal door, and frame had been set into the blocks, and the little pup scampered down the ramp to sniff around the base of the door.

"Leave that be, dog" the old man said when he set the last bucket of paint down, and heard the pup scratching at the door. "We got other things to do today, dog" he told the little pup when he raced up the ramp and across the barn to where the old man was standing. "We got to unload this truck right now" the old man grinned as the pup went racing on by, and out into the yard.

Shaking his head in amusement the old man walked outside to gather up the shovels, and pikes, and carried them into the barn hanging one of each from wooden pegs in the wall. The others he set on the ground, and leaned their handles against the wall then went back out side for the rest of the tools carrying them inside, and laying them on the long work bench for now. After his last trip he closed the barn doors, and shut the tailgate then searched the yard for the pup. He was chasing a grass hopper near the back of the house. The old man stood leaning his elbows on the top of the tailgate as he coiled the rope back up, and watched the little pup stalking the grass hopper then leaping to try, and catch it when it hopped, and fluttered away.

Laughing when the pup missed his landing, and rolled over on his back the old man walked around the bed. Opening the truck box he tossed the rope inside, and closed it once again before heading towards the back door of the house.

"Come on, dog, you're still to slow to catch grasshoppers" the old man said to the little pup when he neared the back of the house. The little pup's head came around at the sound of the old man's voice, and he trotted over to lead the way through the door the old man was holding open for him.

"Now, ain't that a catchy tune dog" the old man said listening to the radio that he had not turned off before they had left the house. He walked over to the refrigerator, and got the jug of tea out, and poured some into the pitcher sitting it on the counter nodding his head to the rhythm of the music while the little pup sat by his food bowl watching him.

"You ain't hungry are you, dog" the old man asked without looking around as he replaced the jug then opened the freezer, and took out a pair of ice trays. He broke the ice loose, and dumped the cubes into the pitcher then refilled the trays with fresh water before replacing them in the freezer.

"Well, give me a minute dog" the old man said when the little black pup whined behind him prancing from one front paw to the other in anticipation. The old man opened a plastic container sitting on the counter, and filled the cup inside with the dry puppy food. "Just starving, ain't yah" he said dumping the food into the little pup's food bowl then picked up the water bowl, and emptied the old water into the sink, filling it with fresh. "Probably thirsty too huh, dog" he said when he set it back on the floor beside the eating little pup.

The old man tossed the cup back in the container, and put the lid back on then took two glasses from the cabinet. Picking up the pitcher with the other hand he carried them out of the kitchen, through the dinning room and into the living room where he set the pitcher on the table beside the door to open it, and took the metal box down from the shelf. Then tucking the box under his arm holding the glasses he picked up the pitcher and elbowed the screen door open kicking the brick into place to hold it for the little pup.

When he reached the whicker chairs, and table he set the pitcher down then laid the box beside it, and the glasses next to both of them. Then he picked up the pitcher to fill one of the glasses, and set it back down before plopping down into the chair. "Dog, it's been an exhausting morning" he called over his shoulder as he reached for the glass, and took a long drink.

Opening the box he pulled a cigar out, and lighted it sitting back and mulling over the events of the morning. "Definitely not the trip I had expected when I got up this morning, dog" the old man's voice was too low for the pup to have heard him. He took a puff on the cigar rolling it in his fingers as he blew smoke rings into the air. "They're coming after me, or they're coming after Noah. Do they think I'll lead them to him if they don't know it's me or do they know I'm him. Which is it I wonder" he spoke to the air, and reached for the glass of tea to take a drink.

"Mind your manners, dog" he said when the little pup came out on the porch. "You know I don't like flies in the house" he smiled when the pup pulled the brick out of the way, and the screen door swung closed. "Good job, dog" the old man gave him an approving nod of his head to go along with the words. "Have a seat" he said patting his leg then put the cigar in his mouth so he could reach down, and pick the little pup up, and set him in his lap. "Still having trouble jumping that high, huh" he said around the cigar.

"You'll grow into it, dog" the old man said reaching into his shirt pocket to take the box from the hardware store out. "Told you I would get something for them fleas, didn't I" the old man said when the pup sniffed the box. Opening the box he took the tube inside it out, and broke the end off then tossed it, and the box onto the table. "Now hold still dog" he said gripping the pups head in his hand, and holding him still. "This ain't gonna hurt you, but you ain't gonna like it either" he said as he squirted the contents of the tube along the pup's backbone.

"Told you that you wouldn't like it, but it'll get rid of them fleas" the old man said smiling when he released the little pup's head, and he jumped down, twisting around trying to get to the stuff on his back. "It'll quit burning in a minute, dog" the old man told the little black pup as it rolled over on its back squirming across the porch.

He slid the empty tube back in the box, and took the cigar out of his mouth with his other hand to take another drink of his tea. "Starting to feel better already ain't it dog" he said a few minutes later when the little pup quit squirming, and looked up at him uncertain if he liked the old man anymore after this kind of treatment.

"Fleas are already starting to abandon ship" the old man said with a smile pointing his cigar at tiny black specks that were appearing on the porch's boards around the pup. The little black pup stood up turning a circle sniffing the dying things that had been irritating him for so long then looked back up at the old man rethinking his earlier decision about leaving. The old man did take him for a ride today too so maybe he would stay with him a little longer.

"Not mad at me anymore are you, dog" the old man said taking a puff on his cigar as the little pup curled up beside his chair, and tucked his nose under his tail. "Yeah a nap sounds like a good idea dog" the old man took another puff on the cigar then reached into the box to pull the bottle out, and take the cap of to get a sip of the Shine. "We didn't get a lot of sleep last night did we" he took another sip before replacing the cap, and laying the bottle back into the box then closed the lid. "The problem is I got too much on my mind to sleep like you, dog" the old man said around the cigar then puffed on it for a few minutes.

The old man smoked his cigar through, and was half way done with another one before his nerves were finally starting to settle down. It was always like that when he went to town, which was another reason he hated Sundays now. When you're one of the few sane people in a world full of insane fools that could decide at any minute you deserved to die because you were not devout enough tended to wear on a person's mind. He had survived for years in this world, but feared that his time was finally running out.

"Well, dog, sitting here worrying ain't gonna do any good is it" the old man finally said when the second cigar was finished. Tossing the butt over the porch railing into the flower bed the old man got up, and poured the last of the tea from the pitcher into his glass then picked it, and the box up. "You gonna lay out here or you coming with me, dog" he asked the

56

little black pup who was looking up at him when he turned, and started along the porch. Thinking about it for a moment the little pup finally decided to rise, and stretch then scampered after the old man.

"Move along, dog" the old man said pausing to hold the screen door open for the little pup before going inside. He walked across the living room, and turned the radio down to a more comfortable level for being inside. "This way dog" the old man called to the little pup that had started for the dining room, and went through the other doorway into the study.

The room was sparsely furnished a desk on the left hand side of the door in front of two windows so he could look outside while he worked. The far wall was a floor to ceiling book case that was now bare of books except for his account binders. Only a few interesting objects that he had found over the years now sat on the shelves, a bleached white skull that could have been a wolf, or a dog he did not know which, a rock with a fossilized leaf of some plant, an old bottle made of thick dark green glass along with a dozen pictures of his family. The wall on the right had three large pictures hanging on it, the center one was of him and Tizzy with their two sons David and Jacob. The one on the left was of David, his wife, and their two daughters; the one on the right was of Jacob, his wife, and their son. The old man ignored the pictures as he always did when entering the room, memories of the dead brought no comfort to the living in this world now.

It had been many years ago now but the memory always resurfaced when the old man came into the room, the pain still fresh, and raw as if it had just happened. The Moralists had secured their power in every level of government from local to state to federal and the High Chancellor was newly elected to the Presidency, the first woman to do so. She was making changes to the Constitution that would insure that she held on to the power she now had. A peaceful rally was organized to protest these changes, and his sons had felt the need to show their support. They had traveled to Washington with their families to march along with nearly sixty thousand other Americans.

The High Chancellor was ruthless when it came to anyone opposing her, and when so many had taken a stand it drove her into a killing frenzy. She gave the order, and her most zealous followers obeyed without question. The protesters were surrounded; all avenues of escape blocked, and then the killing began. It did not stop till everyone man woman and child was dead. Even those who had simply gathered to watch the march were slaughtered. The streets were piled with dead bodies, and the gutters ran full with their blood. The images had been broadcast on all the TV channels, and the old man had watched the coverage closely, looking at all the faces on the screen for any sign of his family; he never saw anyone that looked like his sons or their wives or his grandchildren. Tizzy never left his side searching the screen with him in hopes of knowing for certain the fate of their family. It took three days, and nights to remove the dead, and the coverage never broke away. The bodies were taken to an incinerator, and burned to deny the families the chance to bury their dead; a warning to everyone about opposing the High Chancellor. It took months and a miracle for him, and Tizzy to finally come to terms with the death of their children.

It had happened so long ago that the old man could not remember the exact number of years, but the memory of his loss was as fresh as if it had happened only moments ago. Many times before he had considered taking down the pictures, but he knew that it would change nothing so they remained hanging on the wall, and he suffered the memories each time he entered the room.

The old man set the box and glass on the desk as the little pup stood at the door sniffing the air in the room. This was the first time the black pup had been in here, and he did not like the way the room made the old man smell of hurt. As the old man walked around the desk, and opened the windows though his hurt lessened, and the pup eased a little farther in sniffing for what had caused the old man's pain.

"Go ahead, and sniff around, dog" the old man waved a hand around the room. "Get used to it, we have to come in here sometimes too" the old man grinned when the little pup looked up at the sound of his voice, and cocked his head to the side then started around the room trying to smell out the source of the old man's pain.

"Well, let's see what we can find out" the old man said pulling the worn leather office chair back from the desk, and taking a seat in it. The desk was much older than the chair, its wooden top scarred, and cracked. On the right side of the desk was a set of drawers, one side of the middle drawer was off its guide, letting it drop on that side causing it to catch the lower drawer, and preventing it from closing all the way. But the old man paid no attention to the desk, his focus was on his computer system. He leaned over past the hanging drawer to the side of the desk, and reached down to push the power button on the black tower sitting on the floor then sat back up to power up the monitor sitting on the desk top in front of him.

"Seems like this old thing takes longer to load up each time I use it, dog" the old man said to the little pup. He had worked his way along the wall holding the pictures, and was sniffing around the corner of the book case. The old man smiled at the little pup then turned back to other side of the desk, and opened the top drawer to take an old washcloth out. Picking up the glass he took a long drink of his tea. Using the cloth he wiped the condensation from the glass, and off the desk top before folding it then laying the cloth on the desk. Taking another drink the old man set the glass down on the cloth.

Tuning back to the monitor he used the mouse to click on the little box in the middle of the screen, and then when an empty bar appeared with a flashing cursor he used the keyboard to input a sixteen digit pass code to unlock it. Tizzy had made the system as secure as possible with a fail safe that if the code was entered incorrectly even once then the hard drives in the tower would erase themselves. An incendiary device of his creation would then trip burning the tower to nothing in minutes. *Probably burn the whole house down with it as well* this thought came to him each time he used the computer. He had good cause for these precautions however considering what was on the hard drives.

"Put your hand in a bee's nest, and you might get some honey or you might get stung huh, dog" the old man said clicking on one of the icons on the main screen. "The question is which one this time" he sat back in the chair glancing to where the little pup was sniffing along the bookcase ignoring the old man's voice as he continued his search.

"Gonna take a while, ain't yah" the old man said to the monitor then reached for the glass of tea taking another drink. Sitting the glass back down he glanced at the clock on the wall between the windows then opened the lid on the box, and took out the pipe and faded little can with the man's face on the front.

"I imagine I got time for my own lunch dog" the old man said as he stuffed the bowl of the pipe full. Sitting back he pulled out his lighter, and puffed the pipe alight while he waited for the computer to connect to a server on the west coast. The server was located in Seattle, and was a part of the Moralist network which was why it took so long to connect. The program was designed to infiltrate the network without tripping any security protocols in the server, and without leaving tracks that could lead back to the old man. If this failed there were a dozen other servers around the country that it would try to connect to, but the one in Seattle was usually the most cooperative. Thanks to a friend long dead now, hanged for his Sins against the High Chancellor.

The old man had finished his pipe, and replaced it in the box, and was puffing on a cigar by the time a window finally opened on the screen with the heading Moralist Healthcare of Seattle. The old man immediately sat up using the mouse to hit the minimize button in the upper corner, and clicking on an icon that was the image of a pit bull's head with a spiked collar around it's neck. This program would run in the background, and if an administrator should happen to check to see who was using their system it would sever the connection immediately.

Then the old man clicked on another icon with the image of a bald eagle with its wings spread, and talons extended in front of it. A task pane opened on the screen, there were six slots with a bar blinking at the edge of the first one below them a list of numbers that designated servers, and satellites around the world. Scrolling down the list the old man clicked on six randomly, each one copying itself in a slot, and then hit the execute button at the bottom of the pane.

"This will take a while, dog" the old man said to the pup. He had given up on his search, and was lying between two of the legs of the chair. "Watch yourself dog I'm getting up" he eased the chair back from the desk, and the little black pup rose getting out of the way of the rollers. "You want some ham dog" the old man asked as he grabbed the empty glass, and headed for the door.

In the kitchen the old man set the glass, and pitcher he had retrieved from the front porch on the counter. Opening the refrigerator he took out several plastic containers that were so old the plastic could no longer been seen through, but the old man knew what each one contained. Sitting them on the counter he took a plate down from one of the cabinets then opened the loaf of bread sitting against the back of the counter. Taking out four slices he closed it back up, and tossed it back on the counter.

"You want a piece dog" he asked the little pup who was sitting with his tail wagging beside the old man's foot looking up at him expectantly. Opening the largest container the old man took out two thick slices of the smoked ham, and laid each on a slice of bread. Then he took out a third piece pulling off a small chunk, and dropped it to the black pup. He caught it in mid-air, and started chewing on it.

Smiling the old man laid the rest of it on the edge of the plate before replacing the lid on the container then opened the other three, and placed a tomato slice, a piece of lettuce, and a slice of cheese on each of his sandwiches. After returning the containers to the fridge he made another pitcher of tea then put a pot of water on the stove with tea bags in it to make another jug.

"Makes a pretty good lunch don't it, dog" the old man said around a mouthful of sandwich as he sat on a stool at one end of the island in the middle of the kitchen. He pulled another chunk of ham off the extra slice on his plate, and dropped it to the little pup that just barely missed it but quickly picked it up from the floor. "Let's check our progress dog" he said after washing the bite down with a drink of tea then pulled off another chunk of ham, and picked up his sandwich carrying it with him as he went back into the study.

"Not bad, dog, we've got the third connection and working on the fourth one" the old man said dropping the chunk of ham to the pup, and taking another bite of his sandwich.

"Now I like this song dog" the old man said after swallowing his bite. "The lyrics might be about the High Chancellor but they could be about any woman loved by a man as well." He grinned down at the dog that was chewing the ham, and not paying attention to the old man. "The music is slow too, a song to dance with your woman held close on a Saturday night, eh dog" the little pup paused in his chewing to look up at the old man as he started turning slow circles. The sandwich in one hand, and his other extended out to the side then the dog went back to chewing.

With the music playing and the lyrics echoing in his head the old man danced his way out into the living room where he and Tizzy had danced together in happier times before the Moralist had come.

Her golden hair so fine

62

She makes the light of my life shine

Tizzy had light brown hair that would shine so brightly in the sun that it almost looked golden. He thought of her when they had been young and how beautiful she had been in his eyes.

In a world full of darkness
Her touch leads me into the light

Tizzy's touch could set me on fire or sooth my pain. He thought of so many times in the past and could almost feel her in his arms as he danced around the room. He could almost hear the sound of her laughter in the music.

The High Chancellor makes my life…

Hell. The moment was gone and he ached to have it back but it was lost beyond recall just as she was gone from him.

"I don't know why I listen to this crap dog" the old man said wiping the tears from his cheek before taking another bite of the sandwich. He wasn't hungry any more, but he knew he still needed to eat to keep his strength up; the thought was arbitrary flashing through his mind.

"Let's check on the tea dog, and get you another piece of ham" the old man said ignoring the song on the radio, and striding back into the kitchen with the pup following. He was sniffing the air looking for what had caused the old man to smell hurt this time, and was confused because he could find nothing in the air. He caught the meat the old man dropped to him, but he chewed it more out of reflex than desire now as he watched the old man, and worried for the hurt he could smell coming off him in waves.

"Tea's done, dog" the old man grumbled unaware that he had done so, and turned the stove off then retrieved the jug

63

from the counter beside the fridge, and rinsed it out in the sink before filling it half full. Sitting it on the counter he took the roof off the little brown ceramic house that held sugar, and dumped two cups into the jug.

"Melanie... that was Jacob's wife dog, gave Tizzy this little house for Christmas" the old man held the roof shaped lid looking at the detail that showed the individual wooden shingles, and the chimney. The little black pup stared up at him as he stood looking at what he held in his hand the smell of hurt coming off him even stronger now.

"I'm an old fool dog" the old man said after a few minutes placing the roof back on the little house full of sugar. The pup wondered why the man wasn't on the floor whining. The little pup knew that if he hurt that much he would be snapping at whatever had caused it.

"A man can't live in the past, and he can't lie down, and die either dog" the old man's voice was harsh as he took the pan from the top of the stove, and gathered the tabs of the tea bags in his other hand. But the pup understood that the old man's tone wasn't meant for him, and tried sniffing the air again looking for the source of the old man's pain.

Shaking the tea bags free of any clinging water the old man dropped them into the trash can beside the stove then poured the contents of the pan into the jug, and tossed the pan into the sink angrily. "I shouldn't be like that dog" the old man said sighing, and the pup was amazed that the hurt smell was just gone.

"The past is done" the old man said picking up the jug, and finished filling it with water in the sink. "I have to do what I can now, and let the past go" he took a wooden spoon, and stirred the tea briskly for a couple of minutes then set the jug in the fridge.

"How about another piece of ham, dog" the old man said pulling a good sized chunk off the slice, and dropping it to the little pup. He caught it out of the air, and started chewing it, but was still worried about the old man. The hurt smell was there then it was gone then it was back, and his little mind could not understand it.

The old man filled his glass from the pitcher then set it in the fridge, and picked up his other sandwich, and what was left of the slice of ham. Then laid the plate in the sink, and picked up the glass in his other hand. "Let's go see what the computer's doing, dog" the old man said leading the way back to the study. He paused in the living room long enough to turn the radio off. "That's enough of that rubbish, don't you think, dog" the old man said with out looking at the little pup. Who was on the point of whining for the old man, the hurt he smelled on him was so strong.

"Well it's getting there, dog" the old man said when he reached his desk, and looked at the task pane before setting the glass back on the cloth. "We got the fifth connection, and it's working on the sixth" the old man said taking his seat before biting into the sandwich then laying it on the desk. He pulled a chunk off the slice, and held it out to the pup. "Better to be slow, and cautious when you're a mouse in the jungle, dog, remember that" the old man grinned as the pup delicately took the meat from his fingers. The hurt smell was strong on the old man again, and the little pup didn't want to hurt him anymore with his teeth.

The old man was nearly finished with his sandwich, and the pup was chewing on the last of his slice when the task pane disappeared from the screen, and a new window opened. The heading on the window was Hall of Magistrates, and the page depicted the Seal of Magistrates with a slot below with a flashing bar awaiting the pass code to enter the site.

"Here we go, dog" the old man said then took a bite of the sandwich before laying what was left on the desk, and lifted the second drawer so he could open the third. Reaching into it he took out a scanning wand, and laid it on the desk beside the sandwich then pulled a folder out of the drawer, and opened it. Inside were a dozen pages with barcodes covering them in columns, and each code had a name written underneath it.

Glancing at the clock once more the old man pulled a page from the middle, and scanned down the page till he found the one he wanted then picked up the wand. Holding the page up he pulled the trigger on the wand, and on the screen the little flashing bar sped across the slot leaving a row of asterisks behind it.

"We're in dog" the old man said with a grin as the window changed to Magistrate Pearce's home page. "This fellers second only to the High Magistrate herself, dog" the old man said picking up the sandwich, taking another bite as he scanned the screen.

"What do you say, dog, start with his email" the old man asked around the mouthful of sandwich then moved the mouse to click on the tab labeled mail, and typed Noah in the search box. "Nothing that way dog" the old man said absently to the little pup that was no longer in the room with him. The smell of hurt had left the old man, and after finishing the ham the little pup had trotted back into the kitchen to get some water.

"Let's try this, dog" the old man said still unaware that the little pup was not with him, and typed High Chancellor in the search box. "That's better" he mumbled when a list of emails appeared, and began scanning the list as he took another bite of the sandwich. Occasionally he would click on one, and open the email to read the content then close it, and continue scanning down the list. After half a dozen or so he returned to the main page, and clicked on drafts, and did a search for the High Chancellor. He opened, and read the first three still eating the sandwich mechanically not even aware that he was doing so.

"Oh this is bad, dog" the old man said popping the last of the sandwich in his mouth, and sitting back in his chair to look down at where the little pup should have been. "Where'd you go, dog" the old man looked around the room, but there was no sign of the little pup, and he was about to get up, and go search for him when the little pup trotted back through the doorway.

"There you are, dog, where you been" the old man asked as if the little pup could answer him. "We got some serious trouble heading our way, dog" the old man gestured to the screen. "The old witch is riding'em hard to find out who is helping Servants to escape her justice. The only thing they can produce is rumors of an old man which wouldn't be bad except that they've pinned it down to our district boy. Since I'm the oldest old man around here it won't take them long to find us" the old man was looking at the little pup as he spoke, but the words were more for himself as he put together what he had read.

"It going to get interesting around here before long, dog" the old man said reaching for his glass, and taking a drink of the tea as his mind continued churning. "I still don't see where they got Noah from though, dog, and that's worrying me some" the old man said lifting the lid on the box, and taking out another cigar, turning back to the screen he lit it, and considered his options.

"Let's give this a try, dog" the old man said after a couple of minutes, but the pup wasn't paying any attention. With a full belly the little pup had curled up at the old man's feet, and was sound asleep. The old man wasn't paying attention to the pup as he moved the mouse to click on the archives tab, and typed in Noah in the search box.

"Now that's more like it" the old man mumbled and took a drag off the cigar as he clicked on the first report, and read it. It was dated almost two years ago, and concerned the death of a Citizen, and the theft of a truck load of packaged food. The local Magistrate had located an abandoned camp of dissidents nearby with the name Noah carved into a tree. The location given on the report was about three hundred miles south of where the old man's home was.

"So that's where Noah got started, dog" the old man rolled the cigar between his fingers thinking then put it in his mouth taking a deep drag on it as he closed that report, and opened the next one. It was dated a little over a year ago, and involved the death of four Magistrates during a raid on a camp of dissidents where the name Noah had been found once again carved in a tree. The location given was about two hundred miles to the east of the old man's home.

"Where ever you go people die don't they, Noah" the old man's voice was sympathetic as he mumbled around the cigar in his mouth, and closed that report then opened the next one. It was dated late the year before, and described a raid by dissidents on several warehouses in a town about two hundred and fifty miles north east of the old man. Twelve Citizens were killed during the raid, and the warehouses were burned leaving no certainty on what the dissidents had looted. A survivor had testified that he heard the leader of the dissidents called Noah by the others, but could give no description of the man.

"And it just keeps getting worse don't it, boy" the old man took the cigar out of his mouth, and flicked the ashes into the waste basket on the left side of the desk then closed out that report, and opened up the last one. It was the shortest, and was dated only a couple weeks ago, and involved a local Magistrate finding an abandoned camp where the word Noah had been carved in a tree. The location given was about four hundred miles to the north of where the old man lived.

"Damn, dog" the old man was so startled that he nearly dropped the cigar, and his tone brought the little pup to his feet with hackles raised looking for a threat. "It's alright, dog" the old man reassured him. "But this definitely puts a new spin on the old bottle" the old man added closing out the report then on a hunch did another search for reports with his district as the key word.

Only one result was found, and when the old man opened it he raised the cigar to his lips, and took a long pull on it. The report was dated two days ago, and had satellite photos that showed a large group of dissidents traveling south. There was a detailed plan to intercept the group that involved sending a special operative to take charge of the local Magistrate's forces. A notation stated that there was a high probability that

Noah was linked to this group in some way. The thing that disturbed the old man the most about the report was the fact that in one of the photos he could clearly see his own house.

"You know, dog, finding a nice warm beach to live out the rest of my days is beginning to sound like a really good idea" the old man said after taking a couple of drags on the cigar while he stared at the screen. He leaned forward, and closed the report then the window itself. He waited until the pit bull appeared on the screen a couple minutes later, and barked twice reporting that all traces of the old man's activities had been erased. Then closed out the other window, and this time the dog appeared on the screen almost instantly, and the old man shut the computer down completely.

"Come on dog, I've had enough of this room for today" the old man said rising, and glancing at the clock as he walked around the desk, and shut the windows. Picking up his glass he took a drink then flicked the ashes from the cigar into the waste basket then pulled the bag out of it, leaving no evidence of his smoking behind except for a faint smell of smoke. Tucking the box from the desk under his arm he led the way out of the room and pulled the door closed behind the little pup as it trotted through.

Servant

"Susie'll be here in a bit, dog" the old man said as he entered the kitchen dropping the bag in the trash can as he passed it, and setting the box on the island. "So, you be on your best behavior when she gets here" the old man grinned looking down at the little pup, his tail wagging so fast his butt was swinging again.

The old man run some hot water in the sink, and washed the pan and plate setting them in the rack beside the sink to let them dry, then got the pitcher of tea out of the fridge, and refilled his glass. After taking a drink he walked over to the trash can, and decided that it was full enough to warrant emptying. "Come on, dog" he said around the cigar still in his mouth, and grabbed the can, and headed for the back door. The little pup trailed after the old man then went ahead of him when he held the back door open.

"Gonna try to catch him again, dog" the old man asked when the pup went sniffing around where he had last seen the grass hopper. Another one or perhaps the same one jumped out of the grass at the old man's feet, and the little pup saw it, and raced across the yard to try, and catch it. The old man laughed when the grass hopper jumped towards, and then past the little pup who tried to stop, turn, jump, and bite all at the same time which caused it to go tumbling, and rolling while the grass hopper got away.

"Got to do better than that, dog" the old man grinned around the cigar then turning continued across the yard past the old oak tree that provided shaded for the back yard. Reaching the burn barrel he dumped the contents of the trash can into it, and picked a piece of paper from the pile, and lighted it then stuck it into the rest. In seconds the whole mess was flaming, and the old man turned away relighting the cigar before replacing the lighter to his pocket.

"Yard's starting to look bad, dog, may have to water it tonight" the old man said looking at the drooping grass that was just starting to show yellow at the tips of the blades. Puffing on the cigar he walked around the yard checking on azaleas around the oak tree which were showing signs of the heat, and lack of rain. "You caught that grass hopper yet, dog" the old man called across the yard where the little pup was sniffing in the flower bed at the corner of the house. Pulling his head from the hedges that ran across the back of the house the old man saw that indeed the little pup had a grass hopper in his mouth he also noticed that the hedges were in need of a good watering.

"Well, good job, dog" the old man said sticking the cigar in his mouth to puff on it while he clapped in appreciation of the black pup's achievement. The little pup was proud of the old man's praise until he bit down, and the juice from the grass hopper hit his little tongue making him spit out the foul thing. "Don't taste too good do they, dog" the old man said with a grin after taking the cigar from his mouth.

"Come on, dog, let's wait on Susie out on the porch, I could use some fresh air" the old man said waving a hand at the smoke coming from the burn barrel as he started towards the back door. The little pup scampered across the lawn, and sat down in front of the door wagging his tail eagerly as he waited on the old man. He was happy that the hurt smell was now completely gone from the old man, and he knew that Susie always made the old man happy when she visited.

"Just a little impatient are we, dog" the old man asked tossing the spent cigar butt behind the hedge beside the door before opening it to let the little pup go in ahead of him. Inside he replaced the trash can beside the stove then went to the fridge to get the pitcher of tea. Pausing by the island he tucked the box under his arm, and picked up his glass, and followed after the pup that was already waiting at the front door. "She ain't gonna be here for another hour or so, dog" the old man called from the dinning room as he crossed it.

71

Using his foot the old man shoved the screen door open, and followed the little pup outside onto the porch smiling as the pup stopped at the top of the stairs looking down the road towards town. "I told you it'll be a little while before she gets here, dog" the old man said with a shake of his head as he crossed the porch, and set his glass on the table. Taking the box from under his arm he set the pitcher down on the table then set down in his chair sliding the box underneath it before sitting back in the chair relaxing a little.

"Dog, we got trouble coming" the old man said thinking about what he had learned from the computer. He wondered what it was going to take to get himself through it, or if he even wanted to get through it. He was so old and tired. Maybe it would be better just to give up the fight. "No, I reckon not" he mumbled. "Might not be able to do much at my age, but I couldn't stop doing even that little bit if my life depended on it, and right now it does, dog." The old man was thinking of his dead sons, and the hurt smell was back making the little pup anxious again but a sound from the other direction down the road caught his attention.

The old man was taking a drink of his tea when his ears caught the sound, and he set the glass down on his knee looking up the road that was visible for nearly a quarter mile in that direction. "Looks like trouble really is coming, dog" the old man said because driving down the road towards him was a line of black vehicles. The Magistrates car lead the procession followed by five assault force vans each of which would hold twenty men. "One hundred men and I ain't even got a pea shooter, dog" the old man said with a smile shaking his head as he watched his end coming closer.

"Looks like I waited to long on going to that beach too" the old man stood up, and set his glass down on the table. "Dog, come here" he commanded and the pup crossed the porch quickly at the tone in the old man's voice. "Get up in the chair and stay there, you hear me" the old man gave the little pup a boost up then a stern look when the pup was standing in the chair looking at the approaching vehicles. "Ain't no way either of us can fight that many so we bend if we can, and maybe live another day, or they'll break us for sure. If that's the case I'll see you on the other side, dog" the old man grinned, and rubbed the little pup's ear. Then the old man started shuffling along the porch as the Magistrate's car pulled into his drive, and two of the vans followed while the other three pulled to the side of the road along his yard.

As soon as the vans stopped the troops disembarked in a rush, a few securing the vehicles, the rest rushing the house. Most went to either side of the house but six of them came up the steps, and passed the old man streaming into the house. All of them were dressed in full combat gear that included automatic rifles. The old man made no move to stop, or question them simply stood out of the way, and watched with a curious expression on his face.

The man that got out of the Magistrate's car was not who the old man expected, he was a much younger man than Magistrate Maxwell, only in his early twenties if the old man judged correctly. He was tall, broad shouldered, and handsome with light sandy brown hair, and dressed in a black suit that looked tailor made for him. The old man noticed when he came around the front of the car that instead of regular shoes though the man was wearing the same type of boots as the troops.

So you're still a soldier like the rest, just dressed better the old man's thoughts changed when the man was half way across the yard however. *No not quiet like the rest are you.* On the man's forehead was the mark of someone who had been Bonded as a Servant to the People only where Susie's and the others were black this man's was golden.

"Citizen Albert Jenkins" the man stated more than asked as he climbed the steps to the porch.

"Yes..." the old man did not know the proper way to address the man and by the look he saw in the man's eye this was a normal occurrence and one to be taken advantage of.

73

"I am a Servant of the High Chancellor" the young man said as he reached the porch, and looked the old man up and down. "You will address me as you would any of the Servants" the man's tone created more questions in the old man's mind than his words answered.

Arching an eyebrow at the man curiously, and with just a hint of amusement in his eyes, the old man was reminded of what Adam Durum had told him earlier in the hardware store. "Well then Servant I would like an explanation as to why my afternoon tea has been invaded" the old man put as much loathing in the word Servant, and demand in his voice as he dared.

"There is Sedition and Sin in this district, Citizen" the young man said without any apparent negative reaction to the old man's tone. "The High Chancellor has assigned me the task of correcting this, Citizen" he turned his head back towards the drive way.

When the old man's eyes followed he saw that Magistrate Maxwell and his neighbor James Baker who lived up the road in the direction that the vehicles had come from were both standing beside the car with their hands cuffed behind their backs. *Interesting* the old man thought, but said nothing before turning to look at the younger man who was watching him intently gauging his reaction.

"Then perform your duty to the High Chancellor diligently Servant, or I will call you for punishment on Sunday myself" the old man kept the same tone, but inside he was sweating. The man was a Watcher and a good one evidently if he caught the Magistrate. He would watch people, and read their reactions letting them give their secrets away while politely conversing.

"Citizen, if you would please accompany me we will see how the inspection of your house has progressed" the man lifted a hand towards the screen door.

"Well, open it Servant" the old man said briskly, and hunched over he shuffled forward making a point of not looking at his chair, not even out of the corner of his eye as he passed the man.

Inside the living room looked like a whirl wind had been unleashed, the furniture was over turned, the cushions lying on the floor, the entertainment center sitting two foot off the wall, the TV and stereo sitting on the floor. It was a wonder that nothing was broken, but the men had evidently taken care during their search not to damage anything.

"Your animal shows uncommon discipline for one so young, Citizen" the man said behind him as he entered the room.

"I allow no disobedience in my house, Servant" the old man said still surveying the mess the living room had become. "I don't suppose your men are going to put everything back before you leave."

"If we find that you are free of Sin. Citizen, I will have a Servant dispatched to assist you in reordering your household" the, **if** was spoken no differently than the rest, but it was definitely significant.

One of the troopers appeared at the door leading into the study "Servant" the man called and beckoned with a hand.

"Shall we see what he has found, Citizen" the man asked holding out a hand indicating that the old man should lead the way while looking at him with penetrating eyes.

"He had better not have broken any of my pictures in there, Servant" the old man said shuffling across the room with the younger man following.

"His computer requires a security pass code" the trooper said stepping back from the door so the two men could enter the study.

"Explain this, Citizen" the man said walking past the old man to where the screen was waiting for the pass code.

"My late wife said I made a mess of her book work every time I used the thing so she set the system up to keep me out, and I have not had to heart to change it, Servant" the old man's voice was filled with real sadness.

75

"And what is the code, Citizen" the Servant asked unaffected by the old man's sadness.

"T...i... z... z... y, my late wife's name, Servant" the old man told him and the Servant entered code. The screen changed showing icons for the farm accounts and photos as well as a few applications.

"And these" another trooper standing on the other side of the desk indicated the folder with all the bar codes, and the wand lying on the desk.

"Can your men not read, Servant" the old man said with a hint of scorn in his tone. "Open up the icon that looks like a bull, Servant" when the man clicked on the icon and the screen changed the old man looked at the trooper. "Choose any one of the bar codes you like and scan it" the trooper flipped the folder open and pulled a page out of the stack then scanned one of the codes in the middle of the page.

"There is a box of cattle ear tags out in the barn, you will find one of them that matches that bar code" the old man said when the screen changed to a blank page. "Choose one that has a name under it" the old man shook his head, and the troopers face flushed red in embarrassment.

Scanning another selection the screen changed once again, showing a picture of a brown cow with a white face. Below the picture was a long list of information about the cow that included date of birth, weight, breeding dates, and offspring names. At the bottom of the list was a sale date and price.

"Check all of the codes including the ones in the barn, then do a system check on the hard drive" the Servant said to the trooper holding the wand then rose to look at the old man. "If you find nothing then remove the pass code option for the Citizen, and restore this room as you found it." The Servant was watching the old man with his dark brown eyes looking for any hint of distress in his face or eyes, but the old man simply looked back at him.

76

"Shall we continue then, Citizen" the man said offering to follow the old man out of the room with an extended hand.

The old man shuffled along out of the study across the living room and into the dinning room where a trooper was standing beside the door way into the kitchen. "The room is clear, Servant" the trooper said when the younger man appeared behind the old man.

Shuffling past him the old man shook his head when he entered the kitchen. All the cabinets had been opened, and their contents were set out on the counter, the island, and the floor. Through the doorway into his bedroom he could see that the bed had been tossed, and all his clothes taken out of the closet, and chest of drawers as well as Tizzy's, and the things from her bureau as well. Shaking his head at the mess he looked at the trooper who stood beside the doorway.

"Both rooms clear, Servant" the soldier said ignoring the look the old man gave him.

Turning the old man looked at the Servant who had not spoken since leaving the study. "I did say diligently, Servant, so is your inspection complete" the old man asked him.

"Should we not check the barn as well, Citizen, you did say diligently" the man asked slyly nodding to the back door.

"Hand me my cane, Servant" the old man nodded to a dark twisted length of wood leaning in the corner beside the doorway leading into the dinning room behind the younger man.

"Of course, Citizen" the man said turning to pick up the stick running his hands over it before handing it to the old man. *Probably looking for a hidden compartment or checking to see if I might have a sword in the shaft* the old man thought, but said nothing as he leaned his weight on the cane, and shuffled to the back door.

"What are you burning, Citizen" the man asked when they were outside, and nodded to the smoke still rising from the burn barrel. Two of the troopers were standing around it poking the smoldering contents with sticks they had found some where.

"Trash" the old man said simply, and continued shuffling towards the barn.

The barn had a dozen of the troopers around it; two were going over the old man's truck while the rest were standing perimeter guard. Out in the fields surrounding the house and barn the old man could see that the other troopers were spreading out in an arc their heads down intently searching the ground.

Reaching the truck the old man saw that the troopers had the hood up now, and glancing inside the open door he saw that every thing in the glove box had been emptied onto the seat. In the back one of the troopers was emptying out the truck box dropping its contents into the bed. The barn doors were open, and a trooper was standing just inside waiting to give his report. The old man shuffled past him, and turned waiting inside the cooler shade of the barn.

"Servant" the trooper glanced at the old man and there was a hint of sympathy in his eyes. "I believe you will wish to see this" the trooper nodded to the back corner of the barn.

"Shall we see what has the Lieutenant so concerned, Citizen" the Servant said to the old man, and nodded for the Lieutenant to lead the way.

The old man shuffled along behind the man with the Servant following him, and the old man could feel him watching. It made the hairs on the back of his neck stand up, and the old man was sure that the Servant noticed them, and saw them as a sign that they had found something.

"There is a large underground room here, Servant" the Lieutenant said when he reached the ramp leading down to the now open door set into the concrete block wall.

"Indeed" the Servant said going around the old man, and down the ramp to peer into the darkness past the door. "Your light Lieutenant" the man said without looking around holding his hand out for the requested item.

78

"Yes, Servant" the man pulled a short flashlight out of a pocket on his belt as he hurried down the ramp to place it in the extended hand.

The Servant turned it on, and entered the room disappearing from the old man's view. Waiting for a moment the old man shuffled over to a stool sitting beside the outside wall, and took a seat. The Lieutenant was dividing his attention between the old man, and what the Servant was doing in the room, but raised no objection to the old man sitting as long as he was still within sight. After several minutes the Servant reappeared, returned the Lieutenant his light, and strode up the ramp to the old man who stood up at his approach.

"What is the purpose for this room" the Servant was looking at the old man with a sharp penetrating gaze.

"Really" the old man's tone was weary and exasperated. "Are all your men from the city, Servant" the old man asked giving the impression that the question was foolish.

"Answer my question, Citizen" the Servant's voice suggested a hint of anger at the old man.

"The room has served several functions over the years, Servant" the old man said giving him a level look. "When I built it the primary functions were for a root cellar, and storm shelter, this region **is** prone to tornados."

"Root cellar, Citizen, I am not familiar with the term" the Servant said with an arched eyebrow.

"An underground room so that it maintains an even temperature where root vegetables are stored. Potatoes, carrots, turnips, beats and such" the old man added at the uncertain look in the Servants eyes at his explanation.

"What is its function now, Citizen" the Servant asked with a penetrating look at the old man.

"About the same as me, Servant" the old man said absorbing his look "Nothing."

"Still it is big enough to hold a large number of people now" the Servant's tone hinted at more to the question than was apparent.

"I told my late wife when she said I was making it too large, that if we ever got hit by a tornado we'd still have a dry place to sleep, and plenty of food to eat" the old man smiled at the memory of that day. "But if you wish Servant I have no objection to housing your men here in the barn" the old man said pretending to misunderstand the Servants meaning.

"I have no such wish, Citizen" the Servant said his tone hinting at anger again but his eyes calm, and appraising. "Have you seen any strangers in the last few days, Citizen, or had anything go missing, I noticed that you have purchased some new tools" the Servant watched the old man's reaction to the question.

"No strangers, Servant, and the tools are for a project I have planned for later on this month" the old man said nodding to the new implements on the wall at the last.

"I would like to know more about farm life, what sort of project" the Servant asked as if finding an evasion in the old man's story.

"With the drought the water level in my pond has dropped, and I plan to have some Servants deepen it" the old man said looking at the Servant with a questioning look as if to ask why he was interested in a few shovels.

"Citizen I..." the Servant cut off when one of the troopers trotted into the barn through the back doors.

"Servant, we have found the tracks of several groups of people about a half a mile to the west. They were heading towards the road, and Lieutenant Hopper is following them at this time" the trooper voice was excited as he gave his report.

"Very good Corporal remain for a moment" the Servant turned to the Lieutenant. "Recall the other squads, and dispatch one of them with the Corporal then load up, and prepare to move" the Servant was as excited as the Corporal, but hid it much better except the old man could see it clearly. "Have three Servants dispatched from town to help Citizen Jenkins restore his household" the Servant finished after glancing at the old man.

80

"Citizen Jenkins, my apologies for the intrusion" the Servant said to the old man as the Lieutenant began relaying orders on his radio and left the barn with the Corporal in tow. "I believe you are the first man with out Sin that I have met since arriving in this district" the Servant shook his head in disbelief as he started for the barn doors, the old man shuffling along beside him.

"Magistrate Maxwell has been stealing from the city treasury along with, I believe some of the Councilmen" the Servant's voice carried disbelief. "His fear when we first met was a stench that fouled my senses, and your neighbor Citizen Baker was as bad, he has been committing adultery with several of the Servants by threatening them with punishment on Sundays if they did not comply."

"That reminds me of the passage from the Moralist Bible 'Fear is an indication of a guilty conscious, and the Righteous does not know fear'" the old man said surprised, and wary at the sudden confidence the Servant was taking him into.

They left the barn, and were nearly across the yard with the troopers streaming past them when the Servant finally spoke again. "There is another passage as well, Citizen 'Sin is a stain on the soul, and the Wicked can not hide even in the darkest night from the Righteous'. Blessings be upon you, Citizen, I look forward to our next meeting" the Servant started to turn away from the old man's side.

"You have performed your duties with diligence, Servant, and I look forward to our next meeting as well" the old man said with true admiration in his voice.

"You honor me, Citizen" the younger man said giving the old man a slight bow of his head then turned following the last of the troopers along the side of the house.

The old man continued shuffling across the yard to the back door, into the kitchen, and by the time he reached the porch the last van was pulling out of his drive, and heading back down the road the way they had come. "Well, dog that was certainly not the most entertaining experience I have ever had, but I think I like that young man just the same" the old man grinned as he looked at the little pup still sitting in his chair.

"That man would have you strung up on Sunday if you said the wrong thing to him" a young male voice said from behind him.

Turning the old man saw a teenage boy standing inside the house looking at him through the screen door with a grin on his darkly tanned face. "Just who are you boy, and what are you doing in my house" the old man asked crisply.

"You bowed, and scrapped for them too much to use that tone with me old man" the boy said with the grin on his face deepening as he opened the screen door, and came out on the porch.

"Answer me boy before I take this stick to you" the old man said tapping his cane against the porch boards.

"You think you could whip me old man" the boys blue eyes shined with amusement as he walked past the old man, and picked up the little pup. Scratching the little pup's ear the boy walked around the table, and sat in the other chair with the black pup sitting on his lap. "Pull your box out old man, and have a cigar to calm your nerves those fools won't be back today to bother you" the boy grinned as he rubbed the black pup's belly making it's hind leg dig at the air rapidly.

The old man stood for a moment studying the boy, he was sixteen maybe seventeen the old man thought. His black hair was hanging down obscuring his face as he played with the pup that was nipping at the boy's hand as he tugged at the pup's muzzle. When he looked up at the old man his blue eyes looked ten years older as they studied the old man in return. *Been through a lot for having lived so short a time, ain't you boy* the old man thought. The boy was wearing a loose fitting pull over shirt of gray, a pair of pants made from what looked like tanned deer hide, and a pair of laced knee high boots with the handles of two knives sticking out of sheaths sewn on the outside of each one.

Walking over to his chair the old man sat down, and laid the cane beside his chair then reached under it pulling out the metal box with the long forgotten superhero on its lid, and set it on the table. Opening it he took out a cigar, and lighted it then reached for the pitcher of tea, and filled the extra glass sitting on the table. Setting the pitcher down he took up his glass, and took a long drink then set back to take a puff on the cigar.

"Now don't you feel better old man" the boy said with a grin as he reached for the other glass, and took a deep drink of the brown liquid. "Don't get much tea out in the wilds" the boy said with a smile of satisfaction, and set the glass down.

The old man continued puffing on the cigar, watching the boy, and waiting for him to decide to answer the questions the old man had asked in one way or another.

"Mad at me, ain't yah, old man" the boy said turning his attention back to the little black pup in his lap, and pulling at his muzzle once again. "Brenda says that making other people mad is second nature for me." The boy looked up at him, and grinned, but the old man just continued puffing on the cigar looking at the boy through the smoke.

"Alright, old man" the boy's grin slipped away. "What do you want to know first" the boy set the pup down on the porch, and turned to set an elbow on the table. Looking across it at the old man he picked up his glass, and took another drink of the tea.

"Start with why you think the Servant, and his troops won't be back today" the old man said quietly after taking the cigar from his mouth then flicked the ashes to the porch boards.

"My friends and I laid a few false trails that will lead them to the highway about three miles south of here. They'll figure that the people they're looking for got taken away by vehicles from there" the boy sounded sure of his assumptions. "Next" he asked with a grin.

"How do you know what they were looking for boy" the old man asked then took a drink of his tea.

"They're always looking for us, old man" the boy sounded like it should have been as plain as day.

"So you followed the others here, and then set trails to lead the soldiers away and now what" the old man asked placing the cigar back in his mouth, and puffing once again.

"No we were part of the last group to come here last night, and after we got some food, and sleep, Jen thought it would be a good idea to lay the trails. So we went back out early this morning" the boy reached down, and rubbed the little pup's ear who was trying to climb back into his lap.

"You went back out this morning" the old man was shocked to his toes.

"Yeah, it took us most of the day to lay the trails, it takes time for a dozen people to make it look like a hundred, or more have gone some where. You got a good plan making everyone come in on the road to hide their tracks, but you got them coming too close. Those soldiers would have figured it out sooner or later, and all they would have to do is open that door in the barn to find everyone. Which I'm surprised they didn't do while you were all in there" the boy seemed puzzled by this fact.

"You were watching us" the old man's shock climbed another notch.

"Yeah we were coming in from the east" he jerked a thumb over his shoulder towards the open fields on that side of the house. "When the soldiers showed up, so we went to ground watching, and waiting to see what happened.

"How did you get through the door" the old man asked rolling the cigar between his fingers and starring at it.

"How..." the boy cocked his head at the odd question. "It's a door I opened it" the boy shook his head grinning. "You ain't crazy, are yah, old man?"

"Maybe" the old man said looking up at him. "What's your name boy?"

84

"Noah, I don't know my last name so don't ask old man" the boy said a little bitterness in his voice.

"So you're the one…" the old man started.

"Someone's coming down the road" Noah said turning to the west then whistled shrilly and stood up. "We'll slip back through the door while we can, and I'll check on you later old man" the boy stood up setting the pup back on the floor then vaulted over the porch railing. When the view was clear the old man could see a dozen more teenagers in the open field running towards the back of the house. "See yah, old man" the boy said before disappearing around the corner.

"I'll be… I'll be…" the old man was shocked to the core, and sat for the next few minutes mumbling the words over and over. He wasn't even aware of the blue bubble car speeding down the road, and pulling into his drive way, or of the three women getting out of it, and racing across the lawn, leaping up the steps to the porch. Susie's words did not penetrate either, and only when she touched his shoulder did his focus return to the present.

"Albert, are you, ok" she asked him again her voice worried, and fear in her eyes as he looked up at her.

"Susie dear" the old man said a smile spreading across his face. "He opened the door" the smile turned into a grin, and he rose from the chair taking her by the hand, and danced around dragging the young woman with him across the porch.

"What have they done to him" one of the other women asked the third. Fear causing her voice to tremble.

"It looks like he's gone insane" she replied an equal amount of fear in her voice.

The old man stopped suddenly looking at the older woman who had spoken last. "I'll have you know that I am in full control of all my mental facilities Madame" the old man stood up straight, and held his head high looking at the two women in turn. "Just how did you get here so fast Susie" he asked with out turning his attention from the other women.

"We were at Citizen Martin's farm, down the road when Magistrate Fines called" the woman tapped the phone at her waist. "He ordered us all three to come here immediately, and as quickly as we could. He told us the Magistrates had been here" she added looking at the old man worriedly noticing the cigar in his hand, and glancing at the other two women hoping they had not.

"You two must be Heather and Angie" the old man said finally stopping his scrutiny of them, and grinning at the two women as Susie looked up at him with wide eyed surprise on her face. "The two Servants Magistrate Fines assigned to paint my house" he looked at them expectantly.

"I am Servant Heather, Citizen" the older woman with dark hair, and eyes said hesitantly still unsure of the soundness of the old mans mind.

"I am Servant Angie, Citizen" the younger shorter woman with light brown hair, and hazel eyes said with a bow to the old man.

"Enough of that Citizen nonsense, I've heard all of it I want for one day" the old man said with a frown. "Come on, let's have some tea in the kitchen we've got lots to discuss ladies" the old man put his cigar back in his mouth then smiling at Susie around it he gave her a wink. Walking back to the table he saw the little black pup sitting in front of it watching him with his tongue hanging out, and he winked at him as well. "He opened the door, dog, can you believe it" the old man said as he knelt down to retrieve his cane he rubbed the pup's head enthusiastically.

Tea

"Give me a hand Susie, I'm an old man remember" the old man said still grinning as he rose, and closed the lid on the metal box, and stuffed it under his arm. Then the old man picked up his glass as Susie came around him, and put her hand on his shoulder drawing his attention down to her worried face.

"Are you alright, Albert" her voice was soft but unyielding, and her grip was tight on his shoulder.

"Sweetie I can't remember the last time I was this happy" the old man said his grin dropping to a reassuring smile for the woman's concern. "Now grab the pitcher and glasses, and let's have some tea in the kitchen while we discuss your future" he turned to look at the other two women at the last including them in his statement.

"Come on, dog we'll find you something special too" the old man said over his shoulder as he started across the porch. The little pup looked at the three women for a second then scampered past them, to slow, and walk along at the old man's side.

"He isn't what I expected from everything I've heard about him" Heather said to Susie as she watched the old man walking away.

"Something has definitely happened to him today" Susie said picking up the pitcher, and half empty glasses from the table. "Maybe it has something to do with his visitor" she held up the glass for the other two women to see. "I doubt the Magistrates had tea with him" she added at their blank looks.

"Ah, crap on a cracker" the old man's voice was still filled with enthusiasm contrary to his words.

"What's the matter, Albert" Susie called looking to where the old man was holding the screen door open then started across the porch with the other two women following.

87

"I forgot about the mess, but we'll manage" the old man called back then disappeared through the door with the little pup leading the way.

"Mess" Susie questioned glancing over her shoulder at Heather then gasped when she reached the doorway, and saw the disarray through the screen.

"What were they looking for" Angie asked as she followed the other two women into the living room, and looked at the over turned furniture, and scattered cushions.

"Anything incriminating" Heather responded familiar with the scene as she began setting a chair back on its legs, and picking up the cushion to replace it.

"He's lucky they don't seem to have broken anything" Susie said lifting an end table up with a toe, balancing on her other foot, and then set the pitcher and glasses on it. "The Magistrate demolished my home when they arrested me" her tone was bitter as she knelt down to pick up a small lamp, and set it on the table as well.

"Help me with the couch Angie" Heather said from the far end of the overturned piece of furniture. The younger woman quickly stepped to the near end, and squatted down to help the older woman turn it back upright.

"But he's an old man" Angie said picking up one of the cushions, and brushing both sides before laying it on the couch.

"Age has no bearing in the Magistrates view point, Angie, you should know that best of all" Susie said picking up another couch cushion. "You and Larry were what, seventeen when the Magistrate arrested the two of you for Fornication. The Council didn't care then that you were so young, or that you two hadn't actually done anything either. The Council Bonded you just the same" Susie was picking up pictures from the floor, and setting them back on shelves, or hanging them from nails in the wall. She was trying to get them in the right place but she couldn't remember for sure where the old man had had them.

"The Magistrate arrests who he wants for what ever reason he cares to make up, and the Council follows his directions" Heather said her tone angry as she stood a small table back up in front of the window, and began picking up porcelain figurines of little girls and boys in different clothes and poses. Sitting them back on the table one at a time she continued speaking. "My husband Allan refused to testify against our neighbor William McIntyre, you remember him don't you Susie" she continued after the other woman nodded. "The Magistrate arrested us both, and then burned our house down to make a point; they hung Allan a week later. The worse though is that my children became Wards of the Council, I saw my daughter last month, and she had me Called for Punishment the next Sunday because I spoke to her before she gave me permission to speak"

"Councilman Sander's girl is your daughter" Susie asked in surprise starring at the woman across the room as the memory of seeing the older woman talking to the girl in town surfaced.

"Yes, I don't know what happened to my boy I haven't seen him since the night I was arrested" Heather set the last figurine on the table.

"He is most likely a soldier in the High Chancellor's Army, Heather" the old man said sadly from the doorway leading into the dinning room his expression sympathetic as he looked at the woman kneeling on the floor across the room. *He might have even been part of the Servants troops.* The old man thought of the ones he had seen earlier but could not connect any of the troopers with the face of the boy he remembered. "How would you ladies like to hear some real music" the old man smiled as he pulled a small silver rectangular object from his pants pocket, and shook it in air for them to see.

"What is that" Heather asked as she rose to her feet wiping tears from her cheeks.

"My dear this is a USB storage device probably one of the last ones remaining in the world not in the hands of the

Moralists" he grinned as he walked across the room to stand beside Angie who was still putting items back on the entertainment center. Kneeling down the old man put the rear cover of the stereo back into place then picked up the screws from the floor and tightened them as much as he could with his fingers. "That'll work for now" he said lifting the stereo, and setting it back into its hole.

"Would you plug the cord in please dear" the old man said to Angie as he fed it through the hole in the back panel of the entertainment center.

"Ok" she said puzzled at what the old man intended with his little device since she had never seen one before. "There you go" she called from behind the entertainment center which was still pulled out from the wall.

The old man pushed the power button and the radio started playing then he pressed the function button till the display read USB and lifted a small flap at the base of the radio and inserted the USB drive. "Now, we can listen to some real music" the old man said turning to where the three women were standing together looking at him. "Any of you know how to do the Hippy Hippy Shake" the old man asked raising his arms and waving them in the air as he swung his hips back and forth.

"He's gone over the edge" Heather said sadly shaking her head at the old man's antics.

"I'm beginning to agree..." Susie was interrupted by the sound of someone playing a fast rhythm on an electric guitar coming from the speakers of the stereo which was quickly joined by a heavy beating drum. Then a female voice joined in sounding wild and carefree as she sang lyrics that had been outlawed half a century ago.

The old man's gyrations changed as he danced over to Angie, and reached out a hand to take hers. Pulling her to him he began twirling her around to the rhythm of the music, and by the third twirl the young woman was enjoying the experience so much she began laughing. As their movement brought them

90

back to where the other two women were still standing, starring open mouthed at the pair, the old man passed Angie off, and reached a hand out to grab Heather's pulling her along with him. He danced her around the room, twirling her, and then pulling her back to him to drop her into a dip then back up to swing the two of them in a circle, and back to a twirl to start the whole thing over again till she too was laughing by the end of the first song.

As the song ended Heather twirled away from him to stand by Angie, and Susie stepped forward to take the old man's hand as the next song started up. He twirled her around, and started through the same steps just a little slower because this song was not quite as fast beat as the previous one had been. After the second series though the woman was laughing as hard as the other two had been, and when the next twirl came around he passed her off. Motioning for Angie to meet him he took her around the room three times before passing her off, and catching Heather who was running to meet him for her turn.

"Now we're living gals" he cried over the music, and laughed with Heather as they danced around the room. They all lost their worries, and cares caught up in the old man's excitement, and happiness as he danced the three of them around the room song after song. Even the little pup got involved, when he came to see what was going on, he began running around the two dancers leaping into the air every once in a while, and giving an occasional bark. *He opened the door* kept going through the old man's mind, and he would burst out with another round of joyful laughter as he danced around the room.

Finally after so many songs that none of them knew how long it had been, the old man had to throw up his hands, and shake his head to Heather as she came towards him to take her turn. "I could barely keep up with one woman in my prime ladies, and now I'm an old man who's starting to lose his wind" the old man said over the music.

"Thank you" Heather said when she reached him, and gave him a hug then stepped to his side making room for Angie.

"I've never done anything like that before" she had tears in her eyes as she reached out wrapping her arms tightly around the old man.

"That was wonderful" Susie said when Angie finally released him, and stepped aside. She stood on her tiptoes, and gave him a quick kiss on the cheek before hugging him.

"My goodness I haven't had this much feminine attention since before I was married" the old man smile at the three women with his eyes sparkling. "Now how about that tea ladies" he said grinning as he nodded towards the doorway to the dinning room. Before following them he hit the power button on the stereo, and pulled the USB drive from its slot, and dropped it back into his pocket.

"Did you have fun too dog" the old man asked the little pup who was looking up at him expectantly not realizing the dancing was over. "Let's get you something special like I promised" the old man said to him, and led the way after the women.

In the kitchen the old man found the three women replacing the dishes, and food back into the cabinets. Each had a glass of tea sitting on the counter near to hand, and it looked as if they had already been drinking liberally from the nearly empty glasses.

"Was that what life was like before the Moralists came" Angie asked when the old man entered the room. She was putting the stove back together, and looked up at him from her knees in front of it where she was sliding the racks back into the oven.

"Sometimes, and sometimes we had the same problems as we do today" the old man said. "Life is about ups and downs girl, one with out the other is a dreary life that is not worth living" he smiled at her as he picked up his own glass of tea from the island and raised it into the air. "To living life to the fullest" he shook his head at the puzzled look on her face, and glanced at the other two women who had the same looks on their faces. "It's called a toast; you raise your glasses" he demonstrated "and repeat the words of the toast, and then take a drink. They don't teach you kids nothing these days do they" the old man said shaking his head once again, but this time with a hint of a smile.

"To living life to the fullest" he called loudly, and raised his glass.

"To living life to the fullest" they all repeated sticking their glasses high in the air, and grinning at him before they all drank.

"Now you're learning kiddies" the old man nodded his head in approval. "How about you dog you want to live life to the max" the old man asked the little pup who was sitting beside his bowl waiting for something special.

"Let's see something special like I promised" the old man said to the little black pup who wagged his tail at the old man's words. "Something special" the old man circled the island squeezing past Heather who was clearing the counter beside the fridge at the end of the island. Opening the fridge door and dropping to one knee the old man inspected the crispers "At least they didn't empty the refrigerator out on the floor" the old man said.

Deciding that there was nothing in the crispers that could be considered special he raised his attention to the shelves. "You've already had ham today so that wouldn't be right" the old man continued his survey of the items. "I don't think you would like any vegetable would you dog" the old man dropped his head to grin at the little pup who was now sitting beside him looking into the fridge as well.

"How about a bath" Heather said above him as she put a stack of bowls on the top shelf of the middle cabinet.

At the word bath the pup looked up at her and almost growled then made his way around to the other side of the old man. "Don't worry, dog, it will be a couple of days before you can have one of those" the old man assured him as he opened the door wider so the pup could squeeze in between it and him. "We had some flea and tick medicine this morning didn't we dog" the old man explained at the look on Heather's face.

"How about some cake, dog" the old man said deciding that it was the only thing in the fridge that would rate high enough to be considered special. "A little cake and tea for all of us, sound good ladies" the old man asked as he pulled the cake platter from the top shelf, and stood up.

"I have tasted that cake ever since yesterday" Susie said smiling at him as she slid a drawer back into its slot below the counter beside the sink behind him.

"Give us some of those plates Heather" the old man said as he turned to the island, and let the fridge door swing shut behind him then slid the pile of drawers, and pans that were still stacked on that end of the island over with the platter.

"Cake" Angie said on the other side of Susie. "I haven't had cake since my sixteenth birthday."

"Strawberry with white frosting" the old man said taking the plates and cake knife that Heather was handing him. "I made it myself" the old man said proudly as he started to slide the pile further out of his way.

"Wait a moment" Heather said reaching quickly to catch a frying pan that was almost about to fall off the pile. "If you want cake then help me Angie" the older woman said steadying the pile then starting to put the items away while the old man stood holding the stack of plates with a grin on his face.

"Take the cake, and go sit over there, Albert" Susie said taking the plates out of the old man's hands.

"Yes ma'm" the old man said picking up the platter, and moving out of the women's way. At the other end of the island he pulled a stool out from under the counter top of the island, and sat down lifting the lid from the platter, and setting it on the stove.

"What's this" Angie asked picking up the metal box sitting on the island.

94

"That my dear is a lunchbox" the old man said motioning her to slide it over to him.

"Help, Angie, not talk" Heather said crisply to the younger woman, and in a few more minutes the three women had the kitchen back in order, and were sitting on stools of their own. The old man had divided the remainder of the cake into five equal pieces, and everyone including the little black pup was eating happily.

"Oh that was so good" Heather said with a deep smile as she pushed her empty plate away then took a drink of her tea.

"I had forgotten what cake tasted like" Angie said nodding as she cut another bite from her piece with her fork.

"It's better than I remembered that's for sure" Susie said scraping the last of the frosting up with her last bite.

"How about you dog, special enough for you" the old man leaned over on his stool to look past Heather and down at the dog who was still licking the last of his cake from his food bowl. "I'll take that as a yes" the old man said with a grin when the little pup paid him no attention.

"Let me have your plates" Susie said rising, and taking the old man's empty plate.

"Angie, we should start on the bedroom as well" Heather said handing Susie her plate.

"That can wait for the moment" the old man said reaching for the metal box sitting in front of him. "First, what kind of a plan do you two have for running off" the old man lifted the lid ignoring the gasps of the three women.

"How do you know about that" Angie asked with fear trembling in her voice.

At the same time Heather said "What do you plan to do about it" her voice was resigned as if she already saw the gallows waiting for her come Sunday.

"Someone who is a lot more observant than I expected told me" he said looking at Angie. "I plan to help you" he said to Heather as he pulled a cigar from the box one of his last four he noted with a grin. *Ironic that it should be so* the old man

95

thought absently as he offered it to Heather who took it, looking at it like she didn't know what it was.

"How many were you planning to take with you" he asked taking another of the cigars out, and offering it to Angie who took it as well.

"All but the twelve who the Magistrates have completely broken and use as informants" Angie said sniffing the cigar as she looked at the old man over it.

"And the men" the old man asked taking the last two out and offering one of them to Susie who had retaken her seat once placing the empty plates in the sink. To his surprise she took the offered cigar with a grin at the look on his face.

"The same except they have twenty informants housed with them" Susie said then put the cigar in her mouth holding out a hand for the old man's lighter.

"How many all together" the old man asked as he pulled his lighter from his pocket, and smiled at Susie before lighting his cigar.

"Twenty six hundred and fifty nine men and women" Heather said then put her cigar in her mouth tasting it then took the lighter when the old man offered it to her. He grinned around his when Susie stuck her tongue out at him.

"And your plan" the old man asked puffing on the cigar, and pulling the almost empty bottle out of the box.

"Four groups to start running in four different directions then…" Angie cut off as Heather began a fit of coughing.

"You have to take short draws girl" the old man said puffing on his cigar to show her how when the woman caught her breath.

"Then breaking down into smaller groups the farther away we get giving each a better chance of not getting caught" Angie continued, and took the lighter Heather pushed across the table. She tried taking the shorter draws on her cigar, and managed not to get choked.

"Won't work" the old man said unscrewing the cap from the bottle.

96

"Why won't it work" Susie asked taking the lighter from Angie and looking across the island at the old man as she lit her cigar.

"Those marks on your forehead are bio chemical transmitters" he took a sip of the clear liquid, and passed the bottle to Heather. "When that many are reported missing the Magistrates will track you down... got a kick don't it" he said grinning at Heather as sweat popped out on the woman's forehead. "... Using satellites and probably kill you all where they find you. A dozen or so can get away for a while, the Magistrates track them, hoping they will lead the Magistrates to larger camps of Citizens who have run before being Bonded" the old man grinned at Angie who was holding the bottle up, but looking at it doubtfully.

"So... so... what... what should...?" Heather was having trouble focusing on her words.

"That's enough for you girl" the old man said with a grin as he rose, and walked to the fridge, and got the containers holding the ham, lettuce, tomatoes and cheese. Picking up the loaf of bread he walked back to his stool, and set the containers on the table.

"You better eat something besides just that cake, or you'll get sick" the old man said nodding to the containers.

"What should we do then" Susie asked for the other woman, and took a sip from the bottle then passed it across to the old man.

"Well I'm thinking on that girl" the old man said. "Open one of them drawers behind you and get the green bowl out" the old man told her and pointed to the counter behind her. The third one she opened contained the requested bowl.

"What's that for" Angie asked trying to hold the cigar like the old man was but her finger weren't familiar with the task, and she keep having to catch it.

"For the ashes, and to hold the cigars" the old man said with a grin as she had to catch her cigar again. Putting his cigar in his mouth he puffed on it a few times to get the fire going good at the end then tapped it on the edge of the shallow bowl knocking the ash off, and laid it in the bowl leaning against the top.

Opening the containers and the bread he quickly made a sandwich and handed it to Heather who was sitting with her hands griping the edge of the counter top. "The room is spinning so fast" she said looking at him with fear in her dull eyed gaze.

"That's half the fun when you get used to it" the old man said with a grin. "Eat this girl you'll feel better in a few minutes" the woman finally released the counter with one hand, and took the sandwich.

Susie and Angie were both making them one and Angie gasped when she stood up to get a piece of ham, and her knees wobbled. She grinned over at the old man when he pushed the container closer to her then he made one for himself.

"You're finally corrupting me old man" Susie said around a mouthful of sandwich, and giggled.

"Girl when I was growing up we lived" the old man said. "We worked all day to earn a living through the week. Then when the weekend rolled around we'd eat what we wanted, drink beer, smoke cigarettes, do drugs, play music, dance and have sex if we were lucky till it was time to start a new week. Then somebody decided that it was better to live longer than to live, and laws started being passed that slowly whittled all that fun away. Then the Moralist stepped in, and went to the extreme with it, and the people let'em so we're all to blame for this world. Or I guess I should say that I'm to blame since I am probably one of the very few who was around back then. But those were the ups, and these are the downs" the old man raised his glass to Angie.

"But those were the ups, and these are the downs" she said raising her glass with him, cocking her head at him when he burst out laughing.

"You don't have to say it word for word girl" he told her when he got his laughter under control. "The ups and downs" he said nodding to her to raise her glass again.

Looking at him she finally raised her glass and with a smile said "to downs and ups" and took a drink.

"That's it girl" the old man grinned, and took a drink with her.

"Heather you alright" Susie asked suddenly as she looked at the woman with a concerned expression on her face.

"I think I'm going to be sick" the older woman said looking of into space.

The loud crack, of the old man's hand slapping the table made her jump, and turning her head she focused her eyes on him. "You are not going to waste my cake woman, take a bite like I told you" the old man said pointing to the untouched sandwich in her hand.

She slowly raised it to her mouth as if unsure that she could eat it, but managed to take a bite, and chew it slowly then swallowed.

"Make her a glass of water please Susie, with ice" the old man said as the young woman got up. "How about you Angie how you doing" the old man asked.

"My head feels funny but in a good way" the young woman giggled, and took another bite of her sandwich. When she swallowed it she picked up her cigar from the bowl, and puffed on it gently, smiling at the old man who was watching her and the older woman both now.

"How long before you all have to be back at the Compound, Susie" the old man asked wondering if the women had time to sober up before they had to leave.

"Magistrate Fines gave us an over night pass" Susie said at the sink.

"An overnight pass, when did they start giving those out" the old man asked in wonder.

"They have always given them for certain people" Susie said in an angry tone, and gave him a look over her shoulder that made it clear she did not want to discuss the subject further.

Understanding dawned on him, and he said no more, but inside he seethed with anger for a moment then turned his focus to the problem of getting so many Servants out of town. *Twenty six hundred and fifty nine, that would put a burr under someone's behind for sure, but how do we do it.*

"Here Heather drink some of this" Susie said setting the glass of ice water in front of the other woman who smiled up at her as she chewed on another bite of the sandwich.

"Thank you Susie, I am feeling better ah… Albert" she bowed her head a fraction before picking up the glass, and taking a long drink of the water.

"I'm glad Heather" the old man said giving her a pat on the shoulder and then looked at Angie who now had the cigar in one hand, and what was left of her sandwich in the other. "You'd do to run wild with on a hot summer night under a full moon girl" the old man said grinning at the younger woman.

"What's that mean" the young woman looked at him with a lost look in her eyes, and the wad of sandwich puffing out one of her cheeks.

"Wait till tonight, and we'll see if the moon's full" the old man said with a grin taking a bite of his sandwich.

"To full moons" the girl said after setting her sandwich down, and picking up her glass.

"Full moons" the old man said lifting his glass, and drinking with her.

"You said Magistrate Fines gave you the…" he changed his word at the last minute… "assignment. What do you know about the Magistrate" the old man asked thinking of their conversation earlier in the day.

"He's not like the others at the compound" Angie said popping the last of her sandwich in her mouth.

"He brought Shelia medicine for a week when she sliced her leg on a rusted piece of metal" Heather said looking at the other two women who nodded their heads at the memory.

100

"Where the other Magistrates beat, and abuse us at every opportunity, he has if not a kind word at least not a harsh one. I suppose in his position there are limits that he can't cross when interacting with us" Susie said, and the others agreed with her.

"Any chance he is an informant lulling you into a false sense of security with him" the old man asked. Taking a piece of the ham, and pulling off a chunk to give to the little pup who had finally finished his cake, and was up on his hind legs with his front paws resting on the old man's leg sniffing at the air. He took the chunk of ham, and dropped back to the floor chewing on it as if he was starving. "You ain't wormy too are you dog" the old man asked him with a grin.

"I don't think so" Angie said when the old man turned back to the women. "He's had plenty of chances to turn any number of us in for Punishment on Sunday but he never has that I know of" she was doing much better at holding the cigar now, and brought it to her mouth to puff on after speaking.

"Why do you ask" Heather said her face less pale now that she had nearly finished her own sandwich, and most of the water.

"We had a discussion today that has had me concerned ever since" the old man said picking his own cigar from the bowl, and relighting it while he thought.

"Well what did, he say" Susie asked when the old man didn't say anything further.

"What do you know about a man named Noah" the old man said around his cigar.

"Just rumors really" Angie said around her cigar immolating the old man the best she could which meant that she had to try, and catch the cigar when it fell from her mouth. She tossed it around a couple of times burning her palm a little then picked it up when it landed on the counter top of the island. "Sorry" she mumbled wiping the ashes up into a pile, and then over the edge of the counter into her palm, and dumped them into the bowl.

"Mostly just rumors and myths about him, that he's an old man who helps Servants escape their captivity" Heather said shaking her head at Angie.

"I think the most significant part of the rumors is that he is an old man" Susie said looking at the old man with a questioning look but a hint of suspension in her eyes.

"Magistrate Fines has figured out that I am Noah that is why he assigned you two to work for me" he pointed at Heather and Angie. "He knows about your plans to escape, and he gave us an opportunity to put our heads together, and plan something out."

"He said that he thought you were Noah" Susie asked with a shocked tone.

"No he didn't come out, and say it like that but I have no doubt about what he meant by what he said" the old man knocked the ash from his cigar into the bowl sharply looking at the three women in turn.

"You're Noah" Angie said with awe in her voice, and eyes as she starred across at him.

"Well honestly yes and no" the old man said putting the cigar back into his mouth, and puffing on it till the fire at the end glowed brightly.

"What do you mean yes and no, either you are, or you are not, which is it" Heather asked sharply a hint of anger at his answer in her voice.

"I am the old man who helps Servants, but the real Noah is a teenage boy who arrived here last night. Some how the two of us have been combined in the rumor mill but the Magistrates are hunting me specifically, and they think I am Noah" the old man said rolling the cigar in his hand, and watching the fire slowly dim.

"That was what they were here for today" Susie said looking at him with sympathy on her face now.

"Yes" the old man said putting the cigar back in his mouth, and picking up the ham to tear another chunk off, and hand it to the little pup that was on his leg again. "Dog you better not have worms, I don't want to make another trip to town this week" the old man said with a smile around the cigar as the black pup dropped back down chewing on the ham.

"Then if they've already searched here they won't come back" Angie said trying the rolling between the fingers trick, and managing not to drop the cigar this time.

"No, the man leading the search will be back" the old man spoke around the cigar then puffed on it a few times, and blew a smoke ring into the air. "He's something I've never seen before, he called himself a Servant to the High Chancellor, and he had the marks of the Servants, but his were golden where yours are black" the old man pondered the man for a moment.

"How can you be sure he'll come back" Heather asked when the old man didn't speak for a few minutes.

"Because he's not a fool, he's smart, dedicated, and thorough though. So eventually he will make the same conclusions that Magistrate Fines did. In fact he may have done so already, and is simply attending to other matters that he feels obliged to correct in the district. I am an old man, and I can't run too far without getting caught not that I would run anyway. I'm an old man, and I never expected to be on this Earth nearly as long as I have" he said with a grin to the women.

"We could kill him" Angie said looking across her cigar at the old man with eyes steady.

"Girl you're hard core under silk wrappings ain't yah, what I wouldn't give to be fifty years younger" the old man chuckled at the young woman's stunned expression.

"I don't know what that means, but we could still kill him" Angie said setting up, and leaning her elbows on the counter top, starring across it waiting for the old man's explanation.

"It means you're strong willed, and tough under that pretty face, but no we can't kill him" the old man said shaking his head and chuckling.

"I still don't see why we can't" the young woman insisted stubbornly.

"For one he's got a hundred soldiers with him, for another I would say he's a trained killer, and no one that got close to him would have much of a chance" the old man took a puff on his cigar looking at the girl, and seeing that she was still not backing down from the idea so he continued. "For another if he died here after the High Chancellor sent him personally, then she would send a million troops, or more if need be. They would surround this district in a circle, and that circle would start collapsing. They would drive every thing ahead of them men, women, children, animals, and beasts. They would kill anything that tried to escape, and when the circle had everything else penned they would start the killing in earnest. It would last for several days, girl maybe even weeks and I couldn't allow that just to save my own life. Do I make myself clear girl" he gave her a searching look to insure that she understood, and nodded when he saw that she did.

"So what do we do then" Heather asked looking at him with a pale face at his description.

"We get you and your people to some where safe" the old man said with a mischievous smile.

"And where is that" Susie asked with doubt that such a place truly existed clearly in her voice.

"Since you asked so confidently young lady" he gave her a sharp look for her tone. "After we finish getting the house straightened I'll show you" the old man said with a grin at their shocked faces.

"Really" Angie asked still a little skeptical.

"Really" the old man said rising with a grin on his face.

The Door

An hour later with the sun sitting low on the horizon Susie followed the old man with the other two women holding onto one of his arms across the back yard towards the old man's truck. She thought that if the old man had not insisted on telling his fantastic stories it would have only taken half the time to straighten up the rest of the house. Where he came up with his stories she had no idea, but he seemed to believe most of them, she wondered if it had something to do with his age. She knew that there was no way they could be true though, men could not walk on the moon, or see the edge of creation, let alone spend months under the sea. It was just impossible. But the old man insisted that they were true, and she didn't have the heart to argue with him about it, nor did the other two, they all just smiled and nodded in agreement.

Heather looked back at her now, rolling her eyes, and shook her head at the story the old man was telling about how they had once used metal, and plastic to replace the bones in old people. Unbelievable.

"Don't worry I don't think he's crazy yet" she told the little pup who was walking along beside her. Shifting the metal box the old man had insisted on bringing to her other arm she bent down, and petted the little pup's head then followed after the others.

"You don't believe that either do you" the old man was saying, and looking back and forth at the two women on his arm.

"Of course we believe you" Angie said patting his arm hers was wrapped around.

"You tell it with such conviction how could we not believe you" Heather smiled on the other side.

"I guess you don't believe me either Susie" the old man looked over his shoulder at her.

"I believe that you believe it, Albert" she said honestly. Knowing that the old man could tell that none of them really believed his stories of the things people had done when he was young. They were just too fantastical to believe.

"Well at least you're honest about it girl" he smiled at her then turned back to where his truck was sitting in front of the barn.

"Looks like this is the last mess, girls" the old man nodded to the truck. "I wouldn't worry about it, but there's going to be a heavy dew tonight, and I don't want my tools rusting" the old man pulled his arms from the women's grips.

"Climb up in there Angie, and just chunk it all in the box" the old man said leaning over the side of the bed, and looking at the stuff lying in the back. "Susie let me have my box" the old man said as Angie started climbing over the tailgate.

"There aren't anymore cigars in there Albert, I've already told you twice before" she said holding the box out to him as he turned towards her.

"I know what's in my own box girl" the old man said as he took it, and reached over, and pushed the hood of the truck closed then set the box on top of it. "Heather would you be nice, and put that stuff on the seat back into the glove box please" the old man asked while he opened the box, and took out his pipe, and faded little can.

"For you, Albert, I'd be happy to" the older woman said patting him on the back as she went by headed around the front of the bubble truck.

"How far do we have to go, Albert?" Susie asked as she looked in the cab of the truck wondering if they could all fit on the seat.

"Oh, not far, girl" the old man said dropping the little can back into the box, and closing the lid. "But then again farther then you would believe if I told you" the old man said with a grin as he handed the box to her.

"What does that mean" she asked arching an eyebrow at his chiding tone as she took the box.

106

"Well, you didn't believe me about men walking on the moon; I doubt you'd believe me about this till you see it with your own eyes." The old man smiled at her as he dug his lighter out of his pocket then held the flame over the bowl of the pipe still watching her as he puffed it alight.

"Done back here" Angie called as she closed the lid of the truck box then swung down on the far side of the truck.

"I'm ready" Heather said from inside the cab as she scooted over to make room for Angie to get in.

"Are you ready, Albert?" Susie asked as she opened the driver side door, and climbed inside. It **was** going to be as crowed as she had thought.

The old man stood puffing on the pipe, and looked at the three women starring at him through the windshield. "Come on, dog" the old man said glancing down at the little pup, who was looking up at him expectantly as well, hoping to go for a ride. "They'll figure it out soon enough" the old man walked past the open door with the little black pup trailing along behind, but looking back at the open door wishfully. He would have liked to take a ride.

"Where are you going, Albert?" Susie asked leaning over to stick her head out the door, and watch the old man walk towards the barn door.

"Some place safe, isn't that what you wanted" the old man called over his shoulder as he disappeared into the gloom of the barns interior.

"I am seriously beginning to wonder if he's really insane" Heather said twisting in the seat to look out the back glass at the old man's silhouette outlined against the light coming through the open doorway at the back of the barn.

"I guess we're not leaving yet" Angie half asked half said looking at the other two women.

"I don't know what we're doing" Susie sounded exasperated as she climbed back out of the truck, and slammed the door closed.

"I guess we're getting out" Heather said to the younger woman beside her, and Angie opened the door. The two women got out of the truck, and caught up to Susie at the barn doors. Ahead of them they could see the old man standing at the far side of the barn puffing on his pipe with the little pup sitting at his side.

"What are we doing, Albert?" Susie asked when the three women reached him. When he didn't say anything Susie stepped closer reaching out to put a hand on his shoulder, but something stopped her hand just inches from touching the old man. His gaze was intense as he stared ahead of him, and she followed his gaze. There was a dirt ramp leading down to a concrete block wall with a door set in the middle of it, and the old man was looking at the door.

"What is wrong?" Heather leaned forward, and whispered in her ear as they watched the old man.

"Nothing is wrong woman" the old man said turning his head to look at the three women. "I have another story to tell you, a story that I have never told anyone not even one of the many that have passed through this door" the old man waved his pipe in the direction of the door.

"It was the year of the Great Cleansing as you know it, the year that Hope Died as we called it. When the Wicked rose up against the High Chancellor, when we who knew what was coming tried desperately to stop it. It was the First Battle as the Moralist later called it only it wasn't a battle, in those days Citizens had the right to peacefully protest the actions of our government. My sons, their wives and my grandchildren went to Washington, Emerald City; tens of thousands of unarmed Citizens were slaughtered by the High Chancellor's soldiers including my sons, and their families."

The women were standing around in front of him seeing the pain on his face, and hearing it in his voice. The little pup was softly whining at his foot, the smell of hurt back again stronger than ever.

108

"We couldn't bury our dead, couldn't even put up a marker to remember them. The High Chancellor ordered the bodies burned like trash. Tizzy and I were heart broken, sick with grief. I came out here wanting a place to get away from the pain that was a living creature eating my soul away a little at a time. I wanted to curl up, and hide from what had happened so I went down to there" the old man pointed his pipe at the door. "I wanted so much to escape this world and I opened the door" he took his gaze from the door and looked at the three women one by one then smiled.

"Now it's your turns" he said pointing at the door once again with his pipe. "Open it and see where it leads Susie" he pulled out his lighter looking at her expectantly.

Frowning at him she looked over her shoulder at the door, and was suddenly afraid. Stuffing the fear down, she looked at the old man once more then turned, and strode down the ramp. Wrenching the door handle she pushed the door open her momentum carrying her through. On the other side was a dark room that was empty as far as she could tell. "What's this, Albert?" she asked angrily turning to see him lighting his pipe as he walked down the ramp.

"Close it Susie" the old man said when his pipe was going good. "Angie" he looked over at the young woman on his left. "Your turn, open the door girl" he motioned with the pipe for her to go ahead.

"What's going on, Albert?" Susie asked closing the door, and stepping back making room for Angie.

"Wait and see girl, you youngsters are always so impatient, ain't they, dog" the old man looked down at the little pup trotting along at his side.

"It's just a store room" Angie said when she opened the door, and looked inside.

"Heather" the old man prompted stopping at the foot of the ramp then puffed on his pipe while Angie closed the door back, and Heather walked forward.

"I don't understand what point you're tying to make" the older woman said looking inside the door at the dark room.

"I haven't been in here in years" the old man said stepping up beside the woman to peer into the room then stepped back. "Close the door please, dear" he said when Heather stood leaning against it, looking at him with a hint of anger in her eyes.

"What…" Susie started to speak then stopped when the old man pointed his pipe at her and gave her a look.

"Close the door Heather" the old man said turning his attention back to the older woman.

"I still don't understand" she grumbled, but swung the door shut, and stepped over to stand beside Susie.

"Sometimes when we really want something strong enough, or really need it bad enough the universe shifts things around to provide it" the old man said looking at the three women. "That's the only way I know how to explain it" the old man said stepping forward and putting his hand on the door handle.

"How to explain what, Albert" Susie asked concern evident in her voice.

"This, girl" the old man said, and pushed the door open.

Light filled the doorway, and shown into the gloom of the barn revealing their shocked faces clearly. The women stepped forward crowding around the old man to see through the door at what was definitely not a store room on the other side now.

"How" Susie asked in awe as she looked up at the old man.

"I really needed to get away from this world" the old man said stepping through the door, and then paused to look back at them. "Are you coming" he put his pipe in his mouth, and puffed it a couple of times before the women finally stepped through.

"Where are we" Susie asked as she stepped through the doorway looking around.

110

On this side, the door was set into a high rock face of dark gray stone that stretched to either side for about twenty yards, or so then was swallowed by the hillside. All around the cliff the hillside was covered in a thick stand of trees that she did not recognize; the ferns spread around them were familiar though. Where Susie was standing the ground sloped gradually away from the cliff face, the trees blocking the view of anything beyond a hundred yards or so though.

"Another planet across the universe I think" the old man said around his pipe as he stood looking back at them. "Are you two going to stand there all day" he sounded amused at the other two women standing on the other side of the door with their heads stuck through looking around.

"It's earlier in the day here" Susie said holding a hand over her eyes and looking up through the trees to where the sun sat about half way between its zenith, and the horizon to the west.

"By a little more than four hours" the old man said still watching the two women now hesitantly stepping through the door, their eyes wide as they starred around at the forest. "That's why I never bring anyone through during the day" old man nodded to the two women. "Scares people half to death, and you Susie are you scared" the old man asked looking at the woman's pale face, and wide eyes.

"Terrified" Susie said honestly. "Anything could be in these woods just waiting to attack us" she was trying to look in every direction at once after saying that.

"Most animals I've found are similar to ours, different coloring in their fur on some but mostly the same. Good tasting too huh, dog" the old man said grinning down at the little pup who was sitting beside him looking back at the two women as well. He was used to coming here now, this trip making his third since being with the old man.

"Come on you two, we've got a fair piece to go" the old man said loudly at the two women to get them moving. "And close the door behind you. Were you born in a barn, raised in a

111

shed, and grew up in a field that you don't know how a door works." All three women were looking at him then Susie burst out laughing at the old mans words as she realized what he meant.

The other two grinned sheepishly at each other, and Angie stepped back to close the door. Then followed Heather as she started towards where the old man, and Susie were waiting.

"Do you think his other stories were really true too" she asked the older woman when she caught up with her.

"I'm beginning to think that maybe they were indeed" Heather said with a nod.

"You girls over your little fright" the old man asked around his pipe then relighted it once again.

"You have to admit, Albert that this is a lot to take in all at once" Heather said holding her hands out to her sides, and looking around.

"Its cooler here" Angie said as a wind rushed through the trees around them.

"About mid September" the old man said turning to lead the way along the cliff face. The little pup bounding ahead stopping to smell around the ground till the old man reached him then taking off again.

"Mid afternoon or morning" Heather wondered aloud behind him but the old man continued on.

"Albert said that it was around four hours earlier here" Susie explained, and glanced at the older woman as the three walked side by side behind the old man. "He said we're on another world, can you believe it" Susie shook her head, and shifted the box to her other side to give her left hand a rest from holding it.

"Another world" Angie asked peering into the trees on her side. "Are there any dangerous animals here" she asked imagining some huge beast bursting out to kill them all.

"Albert said the animals were much the same as ours" Susie said shrugging her shoulders not really knowing that much about wild animals on her world let alone this new one.

"There are some that resemble bears, tigers, and snakes that can kill you, but they mostly stay away from around here" the old man said over his shoulder without stopping.

"Mostly" Heather asked hoping for more reassuring words, but the old man continued walking, angling up the hillside now that they were past the cliff.

"Better wild animals than the Magistrates, and the Councilmen" Angie said fiercely as she walked along fists clenched at her side from memories that would never leave.

"Think of it, a whole world where we'll be free of them and free to live our own lives how we choose" Susie's voice held wonder, and awe as the seeds of freedom took root.

"As long as they don't find a way to follow us here" Heather said. Head swiveling as she searched the forest for any sign of an animal that had decided today was going to be the day that it went where it **mostly** didn't go.

"But the door only led here for Albert" Angie said as if that solved the problem.

"What if they are waiting for us when we go back, and keep the door open after they arrest us?" Heather's voice carried fear at her own words, and of the things her imagination was conjuring up that was going to come running out of the trees any minute now.

"Woman you worry too much" the old man said over his shoulder. "Don't get too far ahead dog, you might get eaten" the old man flashed a grin over his shoulder at the three women. He gave the older woman a wink of amusement that she missed because she was looking into the trees for something that might eat her.

"Stop teasing her, Albert" Susie said taking the older woman's hand. "Don't worry Heather I'm sure we're safe."

113

"Safe, you people are too blind and deaf to be safe in your own beds" a male voice said from behind them making all three women jump, and spin around.

"You make enough noise to wake the dead" the old man said over his shoulder still not stopping.

"He's leaving you" the black haired blue eyed teenage boy who had startled them said to the three women. He walked towards them nodding his head beyond them to where the old man was still climbing the hill.

"Where did you come from" Heather asked returning to searching the trees even more intently. If the boy had sneaked up on her what else was doing the same at this very instant.

"From my mother's womb lady" the boy's tone was sarcastic as he strode past the three women, following after the old man.

"Did you see him" Angie whispered quietly to Susie as the women turned to follow the teenage boy.

"Not even a glimpse" Susie said shaking her head, and quickening her pace to catch up, dragging the older woman along by the hand. She added looking behind her as well now, and Angie kept even with her on the other side doing the same.

"You trying to give them women heart attacks boy." The old man asked when the boy fell in beside him, and glanced over his shoulder to see the women hurrying to catch up.

"Little fear now and then never hurts nobody" the boy grinned but didn't look at the old man.

"Words of wisdom from the mouths of babes, and it wouldn't hurt you to heed them yourself boy" the old man grinned as he saw the boys jaw clench for just a moment. "Yeah I got a tendency to make people mad as well boy."

"I've been scared enough to keep me on my toes for the rest of my life old man" the boy said lengthening his strides, and pulling ahead till he disappeared into the trees once again.

"Who was that, Albert" Susie asked when she caught up to the old man.

"That was Noah" the old man answered nodding at her questioning look when he glanced back at her. "Yeah that Noah" he confirmed for her.

"But he's just a boy" Angie said though in truth she was only a few years older herself.

"That boy has been through a lot in his short life" the old man said thinking of the reports he had read on the computer. "Maybe in some ways as much as any of us have" the old man said thoughtfully then looked over his shoulder at the three women. "Come on I want to show you something" he changed direction, and quickened his stride moving along the ridge line now that they were on top of the hill.

"Wait, Albert" Susie called as the old man started pulling away from them.

"Keep up girl, I'm an old man more than three times your age" he called over his shoulder, and quickened his pace once again. "Dog, it makes me fear for the human race" the old man said grinning as the little pup scampered out of the trees to trot along at the old man's side.

"Albert" Susie called again.

"Can't you girls move any faster than that" the old man called over his shoulder and speed up to a trot.

A few minutes later a break in the trees appeared with blue sky filling the gap, and the old man headed for it. Slowing when he reached another rock out cropping he tapped the empty pipe on the dark gray stone that rose almost waist high out of the dirt, and stuck it in his pant's pocket. Reaching down the old man picked up the pup that was waiting patently, familiar with the ritual now. Then he climbed up onto the huge slab, and walked to its edge to stare out at the landscape spread out before him.

There was a large river below him, and about a mile from the base of the hill he stood on. The valley it had carved appeared level, but actually sloped gently down to its banks. Spread across the valley were low ridges some tree covered, some with waist high grass growing on them. The flats that lay

115

between the ridges had the same grass except on this side of the river. There the rich flood plain had been taken over, and planted with crops that flourished in the dark soil, but now late in the season the fields lay empty their crops already harvested. Orchards of apple, peach, pear, and cherry trees had been planted along the base of the ridge that bordered the valley to keep them safe from spring floods. A bridge of heavy stone foundations, and thick wooden beams now spanned the river, and he could see cattle, horses, and sheep grazing on the far side of the river.

A village sat below, and to his left on top of a low wide ridge. The houses of worked stone, and wood planks circled around three long buildings of hewn wood and a single log cabin that bordered a large open grass covered area. The village Green as the residents called the area. The little village had four hundred permanent residents that lived in the houses, and the three buildings were barracks for those in transit. There were over two hundred of them there at this time, mostly the ones Michael had brought in the night before.

"It always lifts my spirit, dog, seeing this" the old man said rubbing the little pup's ear absently.

"Albert" he heard Susie calling from behind him in the woods.

"Those women are going to have to learn to run, dog" the old man said looking down at the little pup in his arms with its head turned towards the sound of Susie's voice.

"You don't think he's left us here in the woods do you" he could hear the fear in Heather's voice clearly.

"No, he wouldn't do that Heather, would he Susie" Angie's voice was strong and certain. The old man was sure that had he done as Heather thought that Angie would have no problem surviving. He was not so sure of the older woman however.

"Albert" Susie called not bothering to answer Angie there was just a hint of fear in her voice.

"You'd think you all were on a strange world, in a dark forest, with unimaginable dangers lurking at every turn the way you carry on" the old man said loud enough for them to hear him. "You're going to have to learn to run faster girls if you can't even keep up with an old man like me" he said when Susie appeared; walking out of the trees with the other two women in tow.

"Why did you leave us like that" Susie's fear was gone replaced with anger at the old man's behavior.

"There are some new lessons your going to have to learn here, girl, and it's better for you to learn them early and quick" the old man said simply unaffected by her anger. "One of those is to control your fear when away from the settlements" he looked pointedly at Heather who was still trying to watch every direction at once.

"Is it really that dangerous here" Angie asked curiously, and with no fear in her voice as she climbed onto the rock, and started across towards him.

"Falling and breaking a leg out here by yourself is just as deadly as a Hiss Snake's bite girl, but if you keep your wits about you then you can avoid both from happening" the old man said. "Come on you two you'll want to see this" the old man looked at the other two women standing beside the rock looking around on the ground for snakes. They looked up at his words then climbed up following Angie.

"Oh my it's beautiful" Angie almost whispered the words when she reached the old man's side, and looked out at the view drawing his attention, and he turned around to see it again as well.

"It really is" Susie said when she stepped up on the other side of the old man and looked out across the valley.

"Incredible" Heather said on the other side of Susie no fear in her voice now.

"Welcome to Shangri-La ladies" the old man said with a grin at the name, but the women paid him no attention, and would not have known the meaning behind it had they been listening.

"What are those" Angie asked pointing to the village.

"What are what" the old man asked not understanding what she was pointing too.

"Those tall things with the fan blades turning on them" she said looking at him and pointing her finger at them again.

"Those aren't fan blades girl, they're like them, though instead of pushing air these 'blades' act like sails that catch the wind, and turn a shaft, they're called wind mills. You never seen them before girl" the old man asked in surprise at the girls lack of knowledge.

"No, what are they for" her tone was curious as she watched the blades turning round and round.

"Those generate electricity for the village" the old man smiled as the three women looked at him with wide eyes of surprise. "What, you thought you were going to live in mud huts, and cook over a campfire."

"Something like that" Susie admitted with a blush rising in her cheeks.

"Nothing to be embarrassed about girl" the old man said when he saw her red face. "That's what many had to do in the beginning, and you may still have to for a while. Depends on what you want to do here" the old man turned with a grin at the shocked looks on their faces now. "Come on I'm hungry again, and looking forward to some of Martha's fine cooking" the old man started across the rock. "You too huh, dog" he smiled at the way the little pup had perked up at the woman's name.

"How long have you been bringing people here Albert" Heather asked as the old man slid off the back of the rock, and set the pup down.

"I really don't know for sure" the old man said reaching up a hand to help the woman down. "More than thirty years I suppose, there's grown men and women who were born here

118

with children of their own now" he reached a hand to help Susie off the stone.

"But I thought you said seven or eight hundred yesterday" Susie said stepping off to land on the ground beside him.

"So far this year that many" the old man said reaching a hand to Angie. "Too many at one time puts a strain on the resources of the community."

"Thank you" Angie said, and gave the old man a hug, her words obviously meant for more than helping her down.

"You're welcome dear" the old man said into her ear as he hugged her back.

Releasing the young woman the old man turned back to look at Susie. "That's one of the reasons why I'm concerned about bringing over twenty five hundred people here at once, especially with winter coming on." The old man started around the rock the women following him, and angled his path on as straight line for the village as the terrain would allow.

"But you are going to bring them" Angie said fiercely as if to make the old man do so with her words alone.

"Martha will take a liking to you girl" the old man said glancing over his shoulder, and giving the girl a smile. "And I'll bring every last one of your people here, or die trying" the old man turned his attention back to the path. "Now keep up" he started to trot.

The Village

A half hour later the old man was leading the three women up the hill into the little village at a slow trot now. The women were sweating, and breathing hard while the old man was breathing easy. During the trip down from the ridge the old man had occasionally voiced his opinion to the little pup running along at his side about the failings of the modern youth. Slowing to a walk the old man went around the corner of one of the houses on the outer circle, and turned down the main lane that led through the village to the Green.

"How you doing, Albert, I haven't seen you in a while" a voice called from across the lane.

The old man looked up to see Charles Patterson sitting on the porch of his house with his leg wrapped in a cast laid up on the railing. "Doing better than you looks like" the old man called to him. "That your grandson" the old man nodded to a three year old boy sitting beside the man starring at the little group.

"Growing like a weed ain't he" the man's voice carried the pride he felt for the boy as he eased his injured foot down to the floor, and sat up looking at the women standing beside the old man. "Why is it, Albert, that most times I see you, you've got pretty women following you around" the man said grinning, and nodded to the women in greeting.

"It's my charming personality Charlie" the old man matched his grin as he turned, and gestured at the women. "This is Susie, Heather and Angie. Ladies this is Charlie Patterson, the village harness and saddle maker and the little rascal beside him is Mark" the old man was looking at them expectantly, but the women seemed unsure what to do. "Say hello" the old man finally said softly for their ears only.

"Hello" they chorused together nodding to the man and boy.

"Hello ladies, welcome" the man was stilling grinning at them. "You'll get use to introductions in no time" he shared a knowing look with the old man. "Things are less formal over here than where you're from" the man looked back at the women with confused looks still on their faces.

"Where's everyone at" the old man asked looking around at the empty village, and drawing the other man's attention back to him.

"Up at the north fields" the man jerked his head back over his shoulder indicating the direction up river from the village. "They're harvesting the peanuts, took most of them folks that come in last night too" the man shaded his eyes, and looked to where the sun was sitting low on the western horizon. "They should be back before long."

"Mayor with them" the old man asked looking at Charlie.

"Naw, him and the Village Council" at the women's gasps he stopped and looked at them. "Sorry ladies I forgot what things are like over there, but you don't have to worry about our Council. They're good people" the man reassured them, and the old man nodded his confirmation of the other man's words when they looked at him. "Any way" the man continued. "They came back an hour, or so ago to figure out what to do with those that just came in. Reckon most will go out with the supply wagons next week" the man sounded as if it was the most logical conclusion.

"Them and a lot more Charlie" the old man said smiling at the man's questioning look. "I'm bringing another twenty five hundred and fifty nine over in the next day or two" the old man's smile turned into a grin at the shocked look on Charlie's face.

"Gees man that's a lot" Charlie rubbed his chin for a moment thinking. "How you going to do that without raising a fuss over there though" he asked with doubt in his voice that it could actually be done.

"Still working on that part, Charlie" the old man said honestly. "They at the Meeting House" the old man asked looking at a steeple tower that rose above all the roofs of the nearby houses.

"Nope" the man grinned again. "They're up at Martha's place, probably stuffed full and kicked back" the man's grin deepened. "I think the Mayor's gone sweet on her, he's spent a lot of time up there the last few weeks. She'd be good for him too" the man's grin faded and he became serious. "Been what two years since Cheryl passed, the man's mourned enough and Martha's still young enough to have children. Be good for both of them" the man's tone said this was only logical too.

"Yeah, they would be good for each other" the old man agreed. "Take care of that leg Charlie I'll see yah later" the old man turned to start up the lane.

"Albert" the man on the porch said pulling the old man's head around to look at him. "Don't go doing nothing foolish over there" the man tilted his head forward as if getting a closer look at the old man. "They'll kill you in an instant, and not think twice, and you ain't gonna help no one dead" the man nodded at the logic of this statement.

"I'll keep that in mind, Charlie" the old man said then started up the lane the women turning to follow after him.

"See you ladies" the man called to them from the porch with a grin.

"See you later Charlie" Angie said thinking of what the old man had said to the man. While the other two women just looked uncertainly at each other then nodded to the man before turning, and hurrying to catch up to the old man, and Angie who were striding along.

"Should we have said something like Angie" Susie asked the older woman as they trotted along.

"Probably" Heather said. "But I couldn't think of anything but 'good day Citizen' myself, and I don't think that would have been right to say here." Heather looked back over her shoulder at the man sitting on his porch with his foot once again resting on the railing grinning as he talked to the little boy who was smiling at his words.

"Neither do I" Susie agreed beside her as she turned back.

"How do they keep the grass so short" Angie was asking the old man when the two women reached them.

"Sheep" the old man said absently pointing to his right down the side lane where the women could see half a dozen of the dirty white fluffy coated animals grazing.

"What are those" Angie asked curiously looking down the cross lane past the sheep where she could see three large long building sitting on high stone foundations.

"Warehouses" the old man said after glancing at her then looking in the direction she was pointing. "You're like a county bumpkin come to town for the first time ain't yah" the old man said looking back at the young woman, and barked a laugh at the suspicious look that had appeared on her face.

"What's a country bumpkin" she asked him her tone verging on anger, feeling like the old man was making fun of her.

"A country bumpkin with a quick silver temper as well" the old man said grinning as her brows drew down in full anger. "Ah, keep that spirit, girl, and you'll do well here" the old man said warmly, and reached out an arm wrapping it around her shoulders. Pulling her close he kissed her on top of her head then smiling he released her. "A country bumpkin is someone who has spent their life out in the country" the old man waved a hand to the hills passed the village. "And are unfamiliar with the ways of city life" he lowered his hand and gestured at the village surrounding them.

"Where do you come up with these sayings," she asked, her brows raised as she smiled up at him.

"Our world was once wild and free like this one girl" the old man said his voice carrying a hint of sadness now. "We" he emphasized the word "were free, we could say what we wanted, live like we wanted, and be who we wanted to be. That type of freedom gives rise to all sorts of aberrations, and I'm old enough to know a few of them girl" the old man smiled at her as they walked around the end of a long low building, and entered the village Green.

"Are those the people you brought here last night" Heather asked stepping up on the other side of the old man, and nodding to the men, women, and children sitting at the tables in front of the building they had come around. "They look terrible" her voice conveyed her shock at the condition they were in.

Most of the faces looking at them were drawn, and pale with cheeks sunken from hunger, and hands shaking from weakness. But their eyes held hope now where the night before they had been filled with despair when the old man had looked into them. When they saw him whispers of "Noah" passed from lip to lip.

"They have a chance now at least" the old man said to the older woman without looking at her. He quickened his pace as he continued towards the cabin at the far end of the Green.

Along the two buildings on either side of the Green the people were turning their heads to see the old man leading the three women across the grassy area. Whispering the name "Noah" in awe, they dropped spoons into forgotten bowls of soup, and began to rise from the tables. Mothers carrying babies or pulling toddlers along beside them, men stooped with age or holding children of their own, all made their way towards the old man with looks of joyous thankfulness on their faces.

The old man slowed a little, and reached down scooping the little pup up. He was nervously eyeing the crowd of people slowly surrounding the old man. Turning to Heather he handed the pup to her, "Take him, and you three go on to the cabin I'll join you in a bit. Hurry before you get trapped here with me" the old man nodded at the closing circle of people.

Heather reached out, and took the little pup then led the other two past him, and towards the cabin. Angie hesitated looking at him then at the crowd, concern for him in her eyes when she looked back. "Go ahead girl I'll be fine" he assured her then nodding at his words she followed the other two.

The old man stood his ground waiting for the people to come to him now. He hated this not because of the people, but because he did not like so much attention. He usually tried to wait a week, or so before coming here after bringing people through the door so that most would be gone to the other villages.

A dark haired woman with a bandage covering the spot on her forehead where the sign of the Servant had been was the first to reach him. She was holding a two year old boy on her hip with one arm, and leading a small girl of about four with the other. "Thank you Citizen, thank you so much..." she kept repeating the words, and would have gone on if the old man had not raised a hand to stop her.

"You are welcome dear" the old man said reaching out with his up raised hand to pat the young boy on the back. "You make sure these little ones get plenty to eat, and you do the same." He smiled at her, and started to turn away, but the woman released the girl, and reached out to touch him on the shoulder turning him back to her.

"Thank you" she said once more, but now in control of her emotions, and smiled at him warmly then took the girls hand once more. "That was Noah the man who saved us" she said to the little girl as she turned leading her away through the growing crowd around the old man.

The next was an old man though still as much as thirty years younger than Albert, and he smiled toothlessly hoisting a young boy of three or four up into his arms. "Go ahead Will" he said to the boy.

"Thank yah, Noah, for saving us" the boy said loudly, and grinned at the old man.

"You're welcome son" the old man said reaching out, and patting the boy on the shoulder.

"Thank you" the toothless man said looking at the old man with gratitude in his eyes.

125

"My pleasure, Sir" the old man nodded at the boy. "Make sure you both get plenty to eat" the old man said resting his hand on the man's arm, and giving it a squeeze.

"Was that really Noah grandpa?" The boy asked the toothless man as he turned back into the crowd. "Sure was, Will" the man answered proudly as he walked away.

The old man had already turned to face another woman with two girls of eight or nine that had to be twins standing in front of her. All three looked worn and tired, but their eye shone with joy at seeing him.

"We just wanted to thank you too, Citizen, for helping us" the woman said a bandage on her forehead as well marking her as a former Servant, and the two girls both nodded then chimed together. "Thank you, Noah" they grinned, and reached out towards him.

"You're welcome" he said as he took their hands, and squeezed them warmly then looking up at the woman he smiled. "You don't have to call anyone here Citizen, we're all free people on this side of the door" he reached a hand out, and grasped her shoulder in assurance.

"Thank you, Noah" the woman said then turned the two girls around, and the crowd parted making room for them.

The old man turned to the next, a woman with a baby in her arms, then a man with a girl of two or three. They were followed by another woman with three children standing around her all about the same age indicating that they were not all hers by birth. They were followed by still more, and the old man spoke to each accepting their thanks graciously, and giving them a touch, and words of encouragement. The crowd did not press, leaving a space around him that only those who were next to speak to him entered, and he did not know how they were chosen. As one little group was leaving the old man would turn to find another waiting to speak to him.

The afternoon wore on, the sun slipping down towards the horizon, and the crowd slowly began to thin till only an older woman in her fifties stood in front of the old man. She had six children standing around her looking at him in awe, the youngest a girl about three looked up at him from in front of the woman. "Are you really the man who opened the magic door" she asked.

"Well I guess I am little one" the old man grinned at this.

"We all wanted to thank you" the woman said smiling at him.

"You are all welcome" the old man said in return. "Have you been getting enough to eat, you have to keep your strength up" he looked at each of the children who nodded back at him.

"I haven't eaten this much in for ever" a girl of about ten standing beside the woman said with excitement when he looked at her.

"You eat all you want there's plenty" the old man assured her.

"Well, we'll let you get back to what you were doing, we just wanted to thank you, Noah for helping us" the woman smiled at him. "Thank you, Noah" the children all said when she finished speaking.

"Your welcome children" he said holding out a hand to shake each of their little ones in turn. "You've done well" the old man said nodding to the children as he took the woman's hand in his.

"I've done what I could" she said simply then lead the children away towards the building on his right. The little girl looked back and waved at him with a smile on her face, and the old man lifted a hand to her waving it back and forth in the air.

"I should have been doing this all along" the old man mumbled to himself seeing the change in the people his time had generated. Where they had been listless and despondent before they were now energetic and animated, chatting to one another across the tables as they ate their soup enthusiastically. The old man now knew that he had done the other groups wrong by hiding from them for his own selfish need to avoid their attention.

127

"They think you're me, old man" Noah's voice behind him sounded amused at the idea.

"No, they know who I am boy, you just happen to have the same name is all" the old man said turning to see the boy standing with a dozen others, some teenagers and young men and women the old man noticed. All of them were looking at him.

"I suppose you think we are here to thank you as well" the boy's voice held such arrogance that it was obvious he wouldn't even if his life depended on it.

"A little humbleness would do you good boy, but I don't expect thanks from anyone that I help." The old man's tone carried a subtle hint that there was no doubt in his mind that he had helped the boy.

"I've been humbled old man" the boy said with bitterness in his voice that swamped the arrogance.

"Haven't we all, boy" the old man said sadly guessing at the boy's pain. "Where are you and the Wild Bunch off to" the old man asked waving a hand at the others standing behind him. They were all holding spears and unstrung bows like they knew what they were about.

"I thought we'd go make sure those soldiers weren't sniffing around your place old man" the boy said emphasizing the 'old man' as if he weren't up to the task.

"Itching to do some more killing then" the old man's voice sounded sadder than before.

"Killing" the boy's voice sounded confused at the word. "I ain't killed nobody old man" he sounded angry now at the old man's suggestion.

"That's not what I heard" the old man said now confused by what he had learned on the computer earlier in the day.

"What have you heard, old man" the boy's challenge was clear.

"About two years ago, a truck load of food and a man hanged to get it." The old man watched the boys face and caught the light in his eyes when the memory surfaced but there was no shame or guilt in them.

"We found that truck sitting on a bridge, and the driver had hung himself before we got there" the boy gave his explanation simply his eyes daring the old man to call him a liar.

"A camp about a year ago where some Magistrates were killed during a raid" the old man asked wondering about the accurateness of the report on this incident now.

"We were there" the boy nodded at the memory, and grinned at the old man. "Warned the camp about two hours before the Magistrates got there, had everyone gone too" he looked over his shoulder at the others, and his grinned broadened. "We were sitting on a ridge watching when the fools surrounded the camp. They went in firing, killed four of their own men, and wounded a dozen more before they stopped shooting" the boy shook his head at what he saw as obvious stupidity on the Magistrates part.

"What else have you heard, old man" the boy looked at him with a thoughtful expression. "Let's see the warehouses where we supposedly killed twelve, and cleared out four buildings worth of stuff. Do we look like we could carry that much even with help? Or the dozen other rumors I've heard where we killed, and robbed some of them hundreds of miles apart at the same time. You should know better than believing everything you hear old man" the boy shook his head in disbelief of the old man's gullibility.

"Maybe there's hope for you yet boy" the old man said thoughtfully looking over the others for a moment. "Why don't you let these youngins rest up a bit more? They still look a little gaunt behind the ribs, and come with me" the old man nodded behind the boy towards the cabin's roof just visible above the groups head.

"Why" the boy asked skeptically.

"You might learn something" the old man said his tone implying that it could be important.

"What about the soldiers" the boy sounded worried that they might indeed be back.

"If they were coming back, they would have already done so, and it's too late now to worry about. If they don't, you will have wasted a night. There is going to be a lot of work to do tomorrow night, so let'em rest now while they can" the old man advised.

"What sort of work" the boy asked considering, his tone implying that he might not want to be involved.

"We're going to bring twenty six hundred and fifty nine people through the door in one night" the old man said as if it were the simplest thing in the world to do.

"You're crazy, old man" the boy said astonished. "There's no way you could move so many with out stirring up the whole country side." The boy sounded as if he definitely didn't want to risk his friends on such a foolish endeavor, and the old man really couldn't blame him.

"We could with your help" the old man said his tone implying that the boy should want to help.

"Alright, old man" he said giving him an appraising look. "I'll listen to your plan, but I make no promises yet" when the old man nodded in understanding he turned to the others. "Jamie, if you don't mind, would you make sure that they get some more food and rest. I'd appreciate it if you'd all be ready just in case things change" the boy jerked a thumb over his shoulder at the old man giving Jamie, and the others a significant look.

"Sure thing, Noah" the freckle faced red headed young man in his early twenties said. Smiling at the old man seeming to say that if need be he'd kill the old man in a heart beat to save his leader from harm.

"What's your plan, old man?" Noah asked turning back to the old man as the others started walking off.

"Don't have one, just yet" the old man said honestly. He had nearly been convinced that the boy meant to refuse, and discarded the arguments he had planned to use to change his

130

mind. "Just some ideas so far" he knew that a lot was going to depend on what the Servant did, and that was still a mystery.

"Jen" the boy called and a young woman maybe nineteen or twenty dropped out of the group, and turned back towards him. "Would you care to come with us? She's good at planning things" the boy said to the old man in explanation, and turned towards the cabin. "You need some help old man" the boy said frowning as he glanced back over his shoulder at the old man who was still standing. "Maybe a crutch to help you walk" the frown became a grin of amusement as the boy hefted his spear in offering.

"I could walk you in the ground boy" the old man said starting forward with a sharp look at the boy.

"Don't let him get to you" Jen said when she fell in beside the old man. "He's just got a twisted sense of humor" she said louder for the boy to hear, grinning at his back.

"Better than a twisted sense of direction" he said over his shoulder with a laugh when Jen blushed, and her grin faded.

"Old joke" the young woman said when she saw the old man's confused look at the banter.

"Figured that" the old man said but did not question further, and the girl had no desire to explain so they walked on in silence till they reached the cabin door.

"Boy, you need to work on your manners" the old man said behind him when he reached for the door latch. "Knock first, and wait for an answer, or someone opens the door" the old man said stepping up, and rapping his knuckles on the door. "Like so" he said giving the boy a sharp look.

"Well, Heaven be praised, look who's come knocking at my door" a plump woman with gray in her otherwise black hair said after swinging the door open, and looking at the three standing outside it. "Albert, always a pleasure to see you dear" she said stepping back to let the old man enter. "You two are welcome, but leave the weapons by the door. Outside by the door" she corrected when they started forward.

The boy looked at her for a moment with hard eyes then leaned his spear against the wall beside the door jam along with his bow and quiver. Jen had started placing hers against the wall as soon as the woman had spoken.

"This the one I have been hearing all the talk about, Albert" the woman asked as she stepped back, and the two younger people entered the cabin. The boy glanced at her sharply at her words.

"It is" the old man confirmed from across the room where he was taking a seat at a large table with four other men and two women.

"Not used to being told what to do is he" the woman said smiling when the boy turned his head back to look at her again with a hint of anger tightening his eyes.

"He'll get used to it the same as the rest of us have, being around you Martha" the large man sitting across from where the old man had sat down said. He was broad shouldered and thick with the impression of being tall even while sitting.

"I don't know about that, Able" Martha was looking the boy up and down appraising him. "I don't think he'll get used to it, he's run wild too long, but as long as he does do what I tell him in my house we won't have a problem. Sit boy" she gestured to the chair at the head of the table next to Able and the old man.

"I'm not a dog to be ordered about in anyone's house" the boy said angrily looking at her with eyes now blazing.

"Told you so" she said looking at Able with a smile on her face. "You got spirit boy I'll give you that" she said turning her gaze back to the boy. "Please, won't you take a seat" her voice was mocking as she glided past him to pull the chair back, her head turned studying his face.

They were all studying him he realized just as Jen stepped forward a little, her hand behind her back signing 'test' quickly then dropping it back to her side. *Testing him for what though* the boy wondered. Getting a grip on his anger he walked forward and at the last instant turned to the side walking past the woman, and her chair to the far end of the table, and taking a seat there. Jen took the seat on his left watching the other men and women while placing her arms in such a way that he could see one of her hands, and the others could not. He was glad now that he had brought her along.

"Stubborn and prideful" she shook her head at the boys back. "Good traits for this side of the door boy, deadly ones on the other side though" the woman said taking the seat she had offered him herself. "I suppose, Albert you want to retire now, and move down south with all the other old people" she asked the old man beside her.

"Thought about it, but there is still much he doesn't know yet" the old man said nodding to the far end of the table where the boy was sitting watching them like a hawk trying to decide if they were a threat or prey.

"Of that I have no doubt" Able said across the table watching the boy as his blues eyes shifted to the large man anger flashing in them for a moment. "At least he can hold his anger in though he looks fit to burst with it" the man continued, watching the boy's reaction.

"Can he read and write" the man next to Able asked his tone wondering as he ran a finger along his jaw considering the boy.

"He can write his name at least, Jason" the old man's tone said he doubted that the boy could do much more than that. He looked over at the shorter bald head man beside Able and shrugged his shoulders.

"It would be unlikely, having been raised in the wild like he has" the woman next to the old man said shaking her head sadly. The thick locks of her blond hair falling over her shoulders.

"At least I can teach him to read and write more than his own name, Dianne, but it'll take a stronger hand than mine to beat that arrogance out of him" Martha shook her head at the boy. He reminded her of one of the stories in the old man's

133

books. He looked like a king sitting on his throne starring at them like criminals he was about to pass judgment on. Criminals that had killed by the smoldering anger in those blue eyes he looked at her with now.

"I think I could do it in a day or two then it wouldn't take so long to teach him to read and write. He'd sit up straight and pay close attention to you Martha" the woman beside Dianne grinned at the boy. Her blue eyes meeting his with a shine of anticipation, she was as broad and thick as Able though much shorter and there was no fat on the woman.

"Maybe that would be best, Harriet, I think he would cause no end of disruption in my class room the way he is now" Martha said in agreement with the larger woman.

Noah shifted his eyes back to the woman at the other end of the table. Out of the corner of his left eye he saw Jen's hand moving and just managed to keep up with what she was saying. 'They want something important. They're pushing to test you. Surprise them.' While she was signing her eyes were looking up the table watching the old man studying him, and Noah shifted his eyes to him when she was done.

"Let those who enter here know peace and joy that they may brighten the world with happiness when they leave" the boy said reciting the words embroidered on a cloth and hung in a frame above the mantle of the fireplace. "I don't seem to be getting either from you, which suggest that you are all liars" he looked around the table as he spoke, but his gaze settled on the old man who stared back at him his face unreadable.

"So he can read. That would suggest he can write as well" Martha said from the far end of the table.

"They know sign language as well" the man closest to Jen said with a smile for the girl when she looked at him. "She was signing away just before he spoke up" the man nodded to the wall past the girl where the shadow of her hidden hand could clearly be seen on it. "It was a good try" he assured her "most would not have noticed at all."

"Interesting, Michael what did she say" Martha asked watching the girl now.

"That we want something important, we're testing him, and surprise us" Michael said with an arched eyebrow questioning the girl if he had missed anything. Her quick look of failure at the boy was answer enough.

"Smart enough to have an advisor, and to listen as well, but does she make all your decisions for you boy" the man between Michael and Jason asked with a hint of sarcasm in his voice, but the boy ignored the question keeping his gaze on the old man.

"I don't think he's going to answer you Peter" the old man said watching the boy with a hint of a smile on his lips. "Well" the old man directed this question to the table of adults who now ignored the boy at the end of the table. Instead they looked at each other.

"I'm not going to live forever" the old man reminded them.

"It's a big responsibility for one so young" Martha said turning her attention back to the boy her tone questioning whether or not the boy was capable enough.

"All our lives will be in his hands" Able said beside her, his tone questioning whether or not the boy was worthy of the risk.

"One mistake and all we have worked for will burn" Dianne said studying the boy her tone suggesting the flames were already smoldering.

"Before you go any further" Noah said cutting off Harriet with her mouth open to speak. "What ever you want me to do for you" he looked around the room at all of their faces. "Forget it, I will help the old man get those other people across then we're going back to finish our business with the Magistrates" he stood up as if to leave.

"Sit down boy, please" Martha added the last word at the sharp look in his blue eyes. She moderated her tone as she continued once the boy had sat back down in his chair. "The problem is that there is no one else young man so whatever plans you had, this is more important."

"What is it exactly you want me to do that no one else can" the boy asked uncertain of what it could be.

"Why to open the door of course" Able said surprised that the boy did not know.

"What…" the boy asked really confused now. "It's just a door, anyone can open it" he said looking at them warily as if this was another tactic.

"Boy, I have been on this side of that door for thirty two years. I was one of the first that Albert here" she nodded to the old man "brought through it. Every man woman and child that has passed through it has been taken back up there, before they are allowed to go anywhere else, and asked to open it from this side. In all that time not one has ever been able to do so till you boy. Like Albert said he isn't going to be around forever boy, so that leaves you to take his place" Martha's tone said the matter was already decided.

"But it's just a door" the boy insisted. "How hard can it be to open a simple door" the boy asked still not understanding the problem.

"There is nothing simple about that door boy" Able said looking at him intently. "It is a door between worlds and you can choose anyone you want. Take them up there, tell them it's just a simple door all the way, and they still won't be able to open it. We've tried everything, even blindfolding people, and no one has managed to open it except you" the man gave him a pointed look.

"But, I don't want that kinda of responsibility, I've got other things that I want to do besides sit around, and open a door for people" Noah shook his head in denial. Refusing to accept what they were saying, or to allow it to interfere with his plans. Jen was feeling the same way her eyes darting around searching for a way out. In the years they had been together they had never stayed in any of the camps for long. As soon as someone told them they had to do something they were packing up and leaving. He always asked his friends to do things, never told, he hated being told, and he would not do that to others. Now these people were telling him he had to do something because he was the only one that could do it.

"Boy" the old man said drawing his attention. "We ain't the Moralists" the old man glanced around the table reminding them as well. "We won't try to make you do anything you don't want, but let's start here. With what you do want" the old man lifted his eyebrows in question, waiting for the boy to answer.

"I want to fight them, to kill them all for what they've done to us" the boy's voice was full of bitterness and hatred. He looked at Jen, and the girl nodded at him confirming that she felt the same way. He looked back at the old man daring him to try, and change his mind on this.

"I understand completely" the old man said rising, and waving his hand at Martha to stop her from speaking. "Have you ever heard of a place called Briton" the old man asked as he walked down the table.

"No" the boy said wary of what the old man was up to.

"It was an island nation with about sixty million people living on it" the old man looked at the boy sitting at the end of the table as he walked. "You know how many that is" the old man asked him stopping in front of the book case on the wall beside the boy waiting on his answer.

"A lot" the boy said not really understanding the number but knowing that it was significant.

"It's more than a lot boy, a lot more than a lot" the old man said picking a large book from the top shelf, and opening it at the front. "Think of the blades of grass in a large field and you will come close to the number I'd say" the old man said to give the boy a reference as he walked over, and laid the book on the table in front of him.

"This is Briton" the old man said pointing to a spot on the page he had opened the book too. "In just a few weeks time the High Chancellor's army killed everything on these islands. Men, women, children, animals, and even the plants

137

then they salted the earth so that nothing would ever grow back. This is Italy" the old man pointed to another spot.

"There were about the same amount of people living there when the High Chancellor's army arrived to wipe the Catholic Sinners from the earth. They left nothing behind except the dead" the old man looked at the boy who was starring at the spots on the pages.

"This" the old man drew a circle around several countries "was the Middle East nearly half a billion people lived here but refused to renounce their religions and embrace the Moralist. The High Chancellor had them sought out around the world not just in the Middle East and exterminated. Two whole races wiped from the earth never to rise again."

"These two" the old man pointed to two red dots on the map. "Were holy cities and now there is nothing in either place except an empty plain. The High Chancellor had her army force the residents to tear them down stone by stone and then break those stones into dust. When that was done they were forced to level the whole area where the cities stood so that never again would people look there for salvation. After they had finished, the people that still survived were chained so that they could not escape and left to die where their cities had stood, as a warning to others."

"These" the old man pointed again "were the largest populated nations at the time. Hope for the world rested with them, hope that they would resist and fight back against the Chancellor. The war lasted three days; the High Chancellor unleashed nuclear fire on them, wiping cities from the earth in minutes. As punishment for resisting those who wished to live had to present their sons and daughters then kill them with their own hands. Many thought to avoid the decree, and committed suicide leaving their children behind thinking they would survive. Instead this infuriated the High Chancellor who ordered all the orphaned children killed, from billions to a mere few million in the blink of the High Chancellor's eye."

138

"That, boy, was during her rise to power. Now she has a population born under her control that fanatically believes in her as a god. Those that don't won't lift an eyebrow at whatever she orders unless it affects them directly, and then it's too late to do anything. You still want to fight that boy, with spears and bows" the old man looked down at him waiting.

"There has to be a way" the boy said refusing to accept anything else.

"There is" Jen said looking at the boy for a moment. "We kill the High Chancellor then the rest falls apart" she looked at the old man.

"It has been tried before, but now it is impossible" the old man shook his head.

"What's impossible" Angie asked coming down the stairs at the far side of the room freshly washed, and now dressed in a red dress that made her look stunning. Behind her Susie followed washed as well, and in green dress that highlighted her hazel eyes, and Heather behind her, washed and in a blue dress that made her look radiant. The little pup raced down behind them, and crossed the room to jump up on the old man's leg.

"Killing the High Chancellor girl" the old man said smiling at the three women and reaching down to rub the little pup's ear for a moment. "I wondered what had become of you three" the old man said as they came across the room, Angie reaching out, and giving him a hug when he straightened from the little pup.

"Why can't we kill the old witch" she asked when she stepped back looking up at him with an arched eyebrow.

"Hard core under such a pretty wrapping" the old man said fondly giving her a pat on the shoulder. "Martha all this talking has dried my throat out woman, ain't you gonna offer an old man something to drink" the old man said looking down the table at her.

"I'm sorry, Albert, I didn't realize your leg was broke like Charlie Paterson's" she said grinning at the old man as she rose.

139

"I'll get you some tea" the woman said walking towards a wide doorway.

"I'll help" Susie said turning to follow the woman.

"Bring me my box too girl" the old man called to her before she disappeared through the doorway.

"Now as to why we can't kill the High Chancellor, girl" the old man said turning back to look at Jen while Angie and Heather took seats at the table listening closely to him.

"First is the Emerald City as the old witch calls it now. No one gets into the city with out an invitation from the High Chancellor herself. If you tried sneaking in you'll find there are more sensors and cameras around the perimeter than you could count. There are also constant flights of helicopters circling the city with cameras that can see your body heat, and micro phones that can hear your heartbeat. Now even if you could get past all that you still have to get across ten miles of city full of people that eat, sleep, and breathe the High Chancellor. People who know each other by sight, and strangers caught on the street are ripped to pieces if they can't answer what they are doing there. Sometimes even then" the old man looked at the boy and girl for a moment then glanced at Angie before continuing.

"Then if you happen to make it through all that, there is still the Chancellors Palace which is surrounded day and night by thousands of devout followers. Their only reason for living is to guard the High Chancellor, and keep her from harm. If you happen to get past those outside there are still a thousand more inside that question everyone not known to them personally. There is no way to get to her" the old man said shaking his head at the hopelessness of the idea.

"Could we draw her out some way" Jen asked looking up at the old man.

"I see now what you meant about this girl, boy" the old man said smiling at her with respect in his eyes. "The problem there is that she still has thousands that travel with her no matter where she goes. It's impossible to kill the High Chancellor" the old man said shaking his head to the question.

"Nothing is impossible" the boy said looking into the air in front of him.

"Didn't you say that you knew her" Angie asked looking up at the old man, and thinking of one of the stories the old man had told them while straightening the bedroom. One of the stories she had not believed.

"Yeah when I was about your age" the old man said smiling when Martha and Susie came back through the doorway with glasses, and pitchers of tea sitting on platters.

"Thank you, Susie" the old man said taking one of the glasses and downing most of it in one drink. "Between talking to everyone out there" the old man nodded towards the outside wall of the cabin. "And all the talking I've done in here my throat was parched" he took another drink then reached down absently patting the little pup that was trying to climb his leg again.

"So the High Chancellor is as old as you are Albert" Angie said taking the platter from Susie, and sitting it on the table before taking a glass from it.

"What are you getting at girl" Able said from the other end of the table. "Wait long enough, and she'll die on her own for us" he took a glass from the tray Martha set on the table smiling and nodding to the woman in thanks.

"I saw a live broadcast of the High Chancellor last week." Angie said giving the man a sharp look that brought a grin to the old man as he pulled his pipe from his pocket. He looked at Susie as she was about to set down, and she grinned knowingly at him, and started back towards the open doorway.

"Could you bring the dog a bowl of water too please, Susie" the old man asked smiling at her as she turned looking at the little pup at his side and nodded.

"The woman on the broadcast wasn't much over thirty" Angie finished saying rolling her eyes at the innocent look the old man gave her. "How is it possible that a woman Albert's

141

age can look sixty years younger" she looked around the table for an explanation.

"Body double" Michael said looking up at the old man his eyes questioning.

"Nope, I saw the same broadcast, and a body double can't copy the eyes. That was the old witch herself" the old man said taking his metal box and the bowl from Susie. Sitting the bowl on the floor at the end of the table he patted the little pup's side as he started lapping the water noisily. Grinning at the little pup's thirst the old man pulled the chair out, and sat down beside Susie, and at the boy's right.

"Maybe she really is a witch" Dianne said from up the table with a grin, and sounding like she didn't really believe it.

"Maybe she is" the old man nodded thinking as he opened the lid, and looked inside. "Bless you Martha" he said with a smile looking up at the woman at the other end of the table. "I opened a door to another world" the old man continued, and took one of the cigars from the box.

"You can get us the ashtrays Albert" Martha said pulling a cigar from her skirt pocket, and smiling at the old man with a shine of amusement in her eyes as she pointed to the mantle.

"I certainly can" the old man said rising once again, and walking down the room to retrieve three ashtrays from the mantle, and setting one on the table beside Martha's elbow. Then the old man handed one to Harriet as he passed, and finally set one on the table in front of him as he resumed his seat. The other men were grinning as they pulled out cigars or pipes from their pockets, and the women were sharing a look with Martha as they did the same.

"With all of us smoking would you be a dear Albert, and open the door to let the smoke out" Martha asked sweetly.

"Why..." the old man started to say.

"I'll get it Albert" Angie said rising and plucking a cigar from the box with a grin for the old man and giving Martha a sharp look as she stood. That made the older woman cackle with delight when Angie turned and started down the table.

"Now, boy since we have gotten something to drink and smoke. Back to you" the old man said after lighting his cigar. "How do you propose to fight an army of millions, enter an impenetrable fortress, and slay a witch? With a dozen companions, using nothing but bows and arrows" the old man sounded curious, and waited puffing on his cigar for the boy's answer.

The boy was looking at the book studying on what the old man had told him about what had happened so long ago. He raised his head slowly, and looked at Jen who understood his desire to fight most of all, but she shrugged her shoulders meaning she had no idea what to do. Finally he looked at the old man who was puffing on his cigar watching him, waiting for his decision, and already knowing what it was so he was in no hurry.

"I will find a way to defeat them" he said to the old man with conviction that defied logic, but he was sure of it none the less.

"Then until you do I would ask something of you" the old man said around his cigar.

"What open that door for you" the boy asked sarcastically.

"No I can take care of the door. What I would ask of you is a promise not to start your war till after I die. Until then work with me to bring people through the door" the old man said his eyes filled with understanding for the boy's struggle.

"I promise" the boy finally said after glancing at Jen, and seeing her nod in agreement.

"Good, now that that's settled, Martha what can you do with twenty six hundred and fifty nine more people" the old man laughed as the woman gasped at him.

"Twenty six hundred Albert" the woman asked incredulously looking at the old man to see if he was joking, and seeing that he was actually serious continued. "I don't know... we don't even have enough room for so many... I don't think" the woman was completely flabbergasted to the old man's delight.

"Well, you're going to have to find room Martha because they're coming tomorrow night" the old man said with a grin for the woman's disconcertion.

"Where are they coming from Albert" Michael asked with concern heavy in his voice.

"Town" the old man nodded to the three women beside him, and took a drag on his cigar.

"Haven't you always said that something like that would bring too much attention to you" Pete asked looking surprised at the old man's intentions.

"The attention is already on me, what we have to do is take it off me, and put it somewhere else" the old man said rolling his cigar in his fingers. "A Servant came to see me today" the three Servant women turned their heads sharply at the casualness of his tone. "He claimed that the High Chancellor sent him, and I'm pretty sure he knows who I am" the old man continued, and Angie reached out a hand to his shoulder her eyes filled with sympathy and concern.

"Then why risk bringing so many here now" Able asked from down the table raising his cigar to his mouth, and looking at the old man as he puffed on it.

"To lay false trails that take the suspicion off Albert" Noah said looking over at the old man with a light of understanding in his eyes.

"And put it where" Harriet asked looking at the boy over her glass of tea.

"On Noah" Jen answered nodding her head at the boy, but looking at the old man with understanding in her eyes as well.

"And how do we do this with out getting Albert strung up on Sunday" Martha asked the concern in her voice clear as she looked at the two with sharp eyes.

"Very, very carefully" the old man answered with a grin.

"That doesn't answer my question, Albert" the woman said testily looking down the table at him sharply.

"Well" the old man nodded to the boy. "Noah here is going to free the Magistrate, and his comrades in crime, and take them to a farm house north of town" the old man took a puff from his cigar.

"And the Servant will follow us" Jen said looking at the old man trying to figure out how that alone would help him.

"Correct" the old man nodded at her. "And he will find that you have given the Magistrate and his associates' new identities. As well as the equipment needed to do so, and other incriminating evidence that they instigated the Noah myth to cover their own tracks" the old man said looking towards Martha at the last.

"I think we might have a spare scanner and network laptop around here somewhere" Martha said finally seeing the old man's plan. "But what about the Servants, when they all disappear you know the Magistrates are going to be tracking them" she asked seeing a flaw in the plan.

"That is where Noah comes in again" the old man said turning to look at the boy.

"You want me to lead them where" the boy asked not understanding this part of the plan.

"South for three hours then back to my place" the old man said smiling at the boy.

"But what about the satellites you said they could track us with these" Angie asked leaning forward to look at the old man past Susie, and putting a finger to the mark on her forehead.

"They will develop a technical problem about three hours after the Servants have escaped" the old man said grinning at her. "But as a backup we have a chemical solution that when applied to the marks will disrupt the signal" the old man nodded to the symbol on her forehead. "And there are ways to avoid the satellites as well, and we will take every

145

precaution to get your friends here safely" the old man assured her.

"And all this will be blamed on the Magistrate" Jen asked skeptically looking across the table at the old man with doubt in her eyes.

"Hopefully it will girl" the old man said.

"If not" Noah asked looking at him. "What happens then" it was clear his concern was for his people more than anything.

"Then we are still in the same boat we're in now" the old man said looking at him with a hint of amusement in his eyes.

"Only we ain't in the boat with you, yet" the boy said smiling at the old man.

"If you want your war you are, boy" the old man said smiling back at him. "I have the tools you will need to master for when that day comes" the old man wasn't smiling now. "Are you in or out, boy" the old man's tone implied that there would be consequences if the boy backed out now.

"I gave you my promise, old man" the boy said his tone warning not to question his word further.

"Good" the old man said as if the matter were closed. "How about some supper Martha I'm starving." The old man rubbed his belly in anticipation of the smells that had been come through the open doorway leading to the kitchen for some time now.

Dancing

It was nearly full dark, and the sound of those returning from the field drifting through the open door had quieted. Now they sat at the table finishing the dinner that Martha had brought out after the discussion. A roast with carrots and potatoes as well as yeast rolls, peas and green onions. Angie had been the first to push her plate away; stuffed full she had risen, and now browsed the books in the book case seeing subjects she had never heard of. Sociology, Psychology, and World History as well as Physics Mathematics and Science with dozens of books under each subject; there was even a shelf marked Religion but with only three books on it. Now she studied the map hanging on the wall next to the book case.

The map was large taking up a considerable area of the wall, and depicted rivers, mountains, plains, as well as part of the southern coast line. Spread across it were dots with names written next to them showing settlements that had been established. Most were along the river systems that flowed out of the mountains to the east and north then emptied in the ocean to the south.

"Albert has made a nation here, though one wide spread, and sparsely populated so far" Michael said watching the younger girl as she scanned the map then directed a grin at the old man. He ignored them both and continued eating. Pulling off a sliver of the meat he passed it to the little pup sitting beside him.

"All these are towns" Angie asked him, waving a hand at the dots on the map hung on the wall next to the book case.

"Yep, there are more than a hundred of them spread out across the continent so far" Michael's voice was filled with pride at what they had accomplished.

"There are still survey teams out exploring" Peter nodded to indicate the empty space around the edges of the map. "It's a big world out there and it'll take time to map it all."

"How many people are here" Angie asked nodding at the dots on the map.

"Over forty seven thousand, plus how ever many have been born this year" Martha said rising from the table with her empty plate. "We take a census at the first of each year" she added as she passed carrying her plate through the open doorway into the kitchen.

"There are mines in the mountains over east of here" Able said from the table pointing a knife towards the map then returning to using it to smear butter on his yeast roll. "We've built a foundry there and have started producing good quality steel. We are starting to build a rail road that will join all the villages together" the man took a hearty bite of the roll and smiled around it with pride at what they were planning.

"All because of you Albert" Angie said smiling fondly at the old man as he forked a piece of potato and popped into his mouth.

"All I did was open the door, girl" he said over his shoulder after chewing for a moment.

"And gave us all a chance at a better life" Dianne reminded him of the words he had used so many times before.

"You have made your own lives better not me" the old man said pulling off another slice of roast and holding it down for the little black pup to take. Then the old man looked down in surprise when he didn't take it to find the pup already chewing on a piece that Noah had given him.

"He looked like he was starving" the boy said with a grin when the old man looked up at him then laid the slice meat back on the edge of his plate.

"Martha, once again you have surpassed yourself" the old man called loudly pushing his plate away and pulling a cigar from the metal box sitting on the table and smiled around the table at the heads bobbing in appreciation.

"It's always a pleasure" Martha responded reappearing in the kitchen doorway, and nodding her head slightly in gratitude for his complement.

"Now if you will excuse me" the old man said rising with the cigar in his hand. "Feed him good, boy" the old man nodded at the little pup, and gave the boy a sharp look before he turned from the table.

"Where are you going, Albert" Angie asked following him into the kitchen.

"Visiting, girl" the old man said opening the back door, and going out into the night.

"Visiting" the girl asked following him outside, and then across the lane to the next ring of houses when he didn't answer.

The old man strode along, feeling the cool evening air as he made his way through the village with the girl following. In a few minutes he was at the edge of the last ring of houses then passing beyond them into the darkness that surrounded the tiny village.

"Is it safe out here, Albert" Angie asked starring into the dark uncertain what might be lying in wait for them.

"Safe as anywhere, girl" the old man said continuing at a slower pace across the open ridge letting his eyes adjust to the darkness.

"That's not very reassuring" she shot him a frown that was missed in the dark.

"Did you ever hear the story of the man who tried to cheat death girl" the old man asked looking ahead a wooden slat fence beginning to take shape in the darkness ahead.

"No" Angie said looking up at the stars that sparkled in the sky looking for any familiar shapes, but found none. *We really are on another world* she thought.

"A Fortune Teller once told a man that on his forty fifth birthday he would die at his home at eight in the morning" the old man paused looking at a shape in the darkness that was slowly moving away from them across the ridge top. "Well at

149

seven o'clock on the morning of his birthday the man had a bag packed, kissed his wife goodbye, and was heading out the door planning to be far away from his home by eight" the shape had paused, and was watching them approach it's huge head up in the air sniffing their sent.

"Walking down the steps he slipped and fell breaking his back and for an hour he lay on the walk in pain and agony." The shape was watching them closely, but the old man was the only one aware. Angie still looked at the night sky. "When Death finally showed up he looked at the man then checked his clip board, and shook his head at the man. 'You were supposed to go peacefully in your bed sir what prompted you to try, and escape me' he asked the man. 'I thought if I could get away then I'd live longer' the man replied. 'My dear friend the hour of your death was set down at the moment of your birth, all you have done is caused yourself greater pain and suffering' and Death reached out a hand and took the man at eight in the morning at his home." The shape decided that they were not worth the risk, or that it was not as hungry as it thought because it turned, and continued across the ridge away from them.

"What is the point of that story, Albert" Angie asked then gasped when she saw the shape disappearing over the crest of the ridge.

"That death comes to us all, girl, in its own time and place, and to worry about it is pointless" the old man smiled into the dark as Angie starred at where the huge animal had disappeared.

"What was that" she whispered as if afraid her voice would draw it back to them.

"Bearcat is what I call them" the old man said for explanation.

"Bearcat" the girl put as much question in the whispered word as there was fear in her voice at the memory of the animal.

"Yeah, it has a head kinda like a cat, and it's claws are retractable like a cat but its body is more like a bear" the old man said as they reached the fenced area he had been heading for.

"That bear or cat or what ever, was as big as a horse" the girl whispered as she still stared at where the animal had been then bumped into the old man who had stopped in front of her.

"They're not that big, close though" the old man said feeling for the latch at the gate in the waist high fence then swung it open. "Still worried about dying, girl" the old man asked tapping her on the shoulder causing her to jump at the touch.

"Yes" she admitted still whispering and followed the old man through the gate quickly closing it behind her as if it was protection from the animal in the dark. "What is this place" she asked when she turned to see the dark shapes filling the fenced area.

"A graveyard" the old man said walking among the stone markers to stand in front of one then kneeled on the ground beside it.

"This is a fine place to be, after talking about death" Angie whispered looking around nervously.

"You superstitious girl" the old man asked with a smile for the girl that she couldn't see in the darkness.

"No" the girl whispered emphatically.

"Then come over here and I'll introduce you to Tizzy" the old man said patting the ground next to him.

"Your wife" the girl asked hesitantly as she knelt down beside the old man.

"My dead wife, girl" the old man's voice carried a humorous tone as he looked at the girl, her features shadowed in the darkness. "You would have liked each other I think, you are a lot like her in some ways" the old man said turning back to the grave stone, and running a hand over the rough stone.

151

"I wish I had known her" Angie whispered, respect in her voice now instead of fear, and rested a hand on the old man's shoulder.

"When I first opened the door we came here to this spot. We were sick with grief over the death of our sons and their families. So we dug these graves" the old man pointed to the line of stones beside the one he knelt in front of. "One for each of our dead and I built coffins for them. We placed some of their most cherished possessions inside the coffins and then buried them. It was a simple ceremony but it let us get past their deaths. So many never did and went mad, or committed suicide from the grief." The old man's eyes glistened with tears at the memories.

"This is all that is left of her now" the old man said slapping the stone and reaching down to place the hand on the grass covered earth below it. "This and the memories that haunt me constantly these days, I see her, my sons, my daughter in laws, and my grandchildren in my dreams, and when I'm awake like wraths that will not give me peace. My spirit is so tired" he turned his head to look at the girl; in the darkness his face was unreadable.

"I have a favor to ask of you girl" he finally said as if reaching a decision. "When I'm gone I need you to stay with the boy, to help temper his anger with reason" the old man's tone sent a shiver down her back.

"You'll be there to do that, Albert, better than I could for sure" she said lightly trying to shake the feeling of dread.

"No girl, the world has changed. You and Noah are the future while I am the past" the old man seemed to be looking into that future and judging by the gleam... she could see in his eyes even in the dark... was not happy with what he was seeing. "My ways are not what the world needs now and I do not have the courage to change" the darkness seemed to gather around him hiding him further from her eyes.

"You are the most courageous man I have ever known, Albert" she said gripping his shoulder tighter trying to draw him from his mood with her own strength.

"I think you for the sentiment, girl, but I have never lied to myself, and I'm not about to start now" the old man grinned at her in the dark but she could not see it only hear the sadness in his voice, and she wanted to weep for him.

"Now, girl if my old ears aren't deceiving me, the band is tuning their instruments, so why don't you head on back, and let me talk to my wife. With out having to worry that you'll think I'm going crazy" the old man said patting her on the hand that still held his shoulder.

"I'd never think that of you, Albert" she said rising to leave the old man in peace.

After a while the old man sat down with his back resting against the cool stone and began to speak. He told Tizzy of recent events catching her up from his last visit to present. Occasionally he would pause as if listening to a comment or question from her, and then continue in accordance. For so many years she had been by his side, and he felt lost with out her now. At a time when he needed her most this was the best compensation he could find.

The moon was its own height above the horizon by the time he finished speaking. Music drifted from the village, the sound of a woman's voice keeping time with the beat as she sang of a love that was lost then found once more in her darkest despair. The old man chuckled at the words wishing life could be more like songs and stories where the people got what they wanted in the end.

"Well Tizzy I'll see you in a day or two" the old man caressed the grass covered ground beside him as if it was the woman's hair. After a few minutes of fond remembering he stood, and made his way to the gate then exited the graveyard.

Standing in the darkness he felt a cool breeze on his face, and ideally wondered if the southern flow might bring rain in the coming days. Staring at the lights of the village while listening to the music drifting along the breeze, the old man felt a sudden desire for his home. Considering the emotion for a moment he realized that there was no need for him to remain here. The boy would be coming with the girls, and he could open the door for them. This realization brought a smile to the old man's face because for the first time he was not required for other people to cross through the door.

"I'm too old to be dancing the night away, and I'm ready for bed" the old man said to the night then turned, and started across the hill towards the ridge with the door on the far side.

Aware that on such simple decisions sometimes hangs the fate of so many, the old man headed for home and bed. Unaware that this was in fact such a time.

When Angie left the old man she walked quickly, watching the hill top for any other shadows that might threaten her. Reaching the light that extended past the first ring of houses she breathed a sigh of relief. Not even realizing till then how nervous she was to be in the darkness. Ahead she could hear the band starting a song that seemed familiar to her. Relaxing a little more she started slapping her thigh to the beat as she passed between two houses, and onto the open lane.

As she neared the cabin she noticed other people along the lanes heading for the sound of music. One pair were already dancing their way along, the older woman laughing as the man twirled her round and round. Their children walked behind them laughing at their parent's antics. Angie felt a burst of amusement at the scene that made her join in on the laughter.

Feeling truly free for the first time in her young life Angie started skipping towards the cabin laughing at the people who looked at her and smiled. They figured she was one of the new arrivals, and had seen such behavior before in them. As well as remembering when they had first come to this wonderful world free of the High Chancellor and her Moralist.

Rounding the cabin Angie slowed upon seeing the mass of people that now filled the Green. Most danced around a band that were in the middle of the open area, but many stood around the tables along the front of the buildings with their mouths hanging open starring. Angie realized suddenly that her mouth was open as she looked, and came to the conclusion that the others were the ones who had arrived the night before. Like her they had never witnessed anyone acting so with out the Magistrates quickly arresting them for indecent behavior.

Laughing and clapping with glee, Angie quit looking around for the Magistrates that were not going to appear here, and looked instead for Susie and Heather. The two women were sitting on the backside of the nearest table in front of the long building on her right. With them were Noah and Jen who seemed as nervous about the people's behavior as the two women did. Martha and Able were sitting across from them facing the crowd, and twisting around to talk over the sound of the music to the four when Angie reached the table.

"You're going to have to jump in some time" Able nearly shouted at them but his voice was still barely audible against the music, and people clapping in time with it.

"Just grab someone" Martha cried then lifted a mug to her lips and drank deeply. As she set it down she saw Angie standing at the end of the table. "Where you been dear, the fun is already started" she called even louder, and lifted her mug to the young woman.

"Visiting" Angie yelled back with a grin for the older woman. "What are we drinking" she called to Susie who had shoved a mug across the table towards her.

"They call it beer" Susie cried back at her, and made a face that suggested she did not like the taste of this particular drink.

Lifting the mug Angie took a sniff of the liquid inside then a sip that was followed by a deep drink as she found the taste appealing. "This is good" she cried back with a smile for Susie's frown and shaking head. Taking another deep drink she set the mug down and looked at Able who was grinning at her. "Come on show me how to dance" she yelled at the man, and reached a hand out to him.

After a quick glance at Martha who nodded back with a smile, Able took a drink from his mug then set it on the table before rising and taking her hand. As he led her towards the crowd surrounding the dancers she heard Martha's yell behind them. "See that's how you do it, just grab anyone, and get in there" the sound of her laughter was lost as they passed into the crowd.

Breaking through the people standing and clapping to the music Able swung her around in front of him then lead off in time with the music. He was stiffer than the old man had been, but the experience was still thrilling as they swirled along with the circle of dancers. In the center was the band with three guitarist, two bassists, and a man beating on a set of drums, and another with an odd instrument she had never seen before. It had what looked like a bellows on one side that the man worked with his hand while playing a set of keys with the other, and the sound produced was haunting and melodious at the same time. Two women played fiddles with wide grins enjoying themselves as they worked their bows in harmony with the others. Angie had never experienced anything like this before, and was laughing joyfully as Able twirled her along in step to the beat.

They made two revolutions around the band, Able guiding her through the other dancers gracefully despite his size. He seemed preoccupied with other thoughts besides the dance however as he kept glancing in the direction of the table they had left, yet his steps never faltered. Then the band finished the song with the fiddle players drawing the last note out then dropping it to a resounding round of applause from everyone.

The band members paused for a moment taking mugs from the table they surrounded and drank deeply. Able led her back to the table where the others still sat, and took his mug from Martha with a gracious smile, and took a swallow. Angie grinned at Susie and Heather as she picked up her mug, and had a drink of the beer enjoying the warm feeling it was giving her.

"Aren't you two going to dance" she asked the older women with a grin as she set the mug down. The band was plucking strings, tapping drums, and the odd instrument was wheezing as they were getting ready to start the next song already.

"I don't know, there's so many people" Susie's voice was half dread, and half excitement at the prospect.

"Come on" she cried taking the woman's hand and pulling her from her seat. Leading her to a pair of men who had been looking at them, one apparently was trying to convince the other to agree with asking them to dance.

"Which of you wants to dance with my friend" Angie asked boldly when they reached the two men the hesitant man who was actually a year or two younger than Angie held up a hand. "I guess that means I get to dance with you then" Angie said turning to the older man with a smile on her face.

"Anthony" the dark haired man said. Reaching out a hand to her then leading her after Susie, and the younger man as the band started up another song.

The drummer started with his bass drum beating the rhythm, *boom, boom... boom, boom... boom, boom....* In the pauses between the two beats the crowd began to add a clap, *boom, boom, clap... boom, boom, clap.* The pulse set Angie's heart racing in excitement as she passed from the crowd into the dancers. Now instead of pairs dancing a circle around the band there were three circles of dancers, each stepping to the beat of the drum, and clapping with the crowd. Anthony lead her into the center circle and side by side they fell in with the pair ahead of them, *boom, boom, clap... step, step, clap.*

"Yeeeeeeah" the drummer cried and changed the rhythm. *Boom, boom, boom, boom...* and the crowd clapped along with each strike of the drum. Anthony smiled at her as she faltered at first, but she adjusted quickly following along as

157

the other dancers stopped in place, and spun quickly each step landing with the beat of the drum, hands clapping in time.

"Call'em girls" she heard the drummer cry and the rhythm dropped back to the *boom, boom, clap*. As Angie caught up to the change the fiddlers joined in working their bows quickly to produce a sound that indeed resembled some one calling out. Laughing Angie became caught up in the dance *step, step, clap, step, step, clap* and beside her Anthony laughed with her.

"Yeeeeeeah" the drummer cried again and changed the rhythm once more. *Boom, boom, boom, boom...* and the fiddlers changed as well their instruments wailing. The sound was driving Angie's pulse faster as she spun around and around clapping in time to the beat of the drum.

"Run'em boys" the drummer cried louder than ever but maintained the beat this time. *Boom, boom, boom, boom...* and the guitar players began working their fingers on the strings. The sounds they produced were a rush that drove Angie and the other dancers into a twirling run around the band. Anthony was the anchor as they hooked at the elbow and he spun her around and around while stepping forward in the same motion making her feel like she was flying. She threw her head back laughing she felt so thrilled, and so alive it was intoxicating. She had never suspected that what she was feeling was even possible for a human being to experience.

Suddenly Anthony pulled her in close, and grasped her by the waist lifting her, and for a moment she was truly flying. Then as he lowered her back to the earth the music ended abruptly almost the instant her foot touched the earth as if she had called the dance to a halt.

"You dance wonderfully" Anthony cried above the sound of laughter and clapping going on around them. "Can I have the next dance as well" he had to nearly yell to be heard.

"I'll dance the one after if you will dance the next one with my other friend." She cried leaning into him, and placing a hand on his chest so he could hear. Then pointing in the direction of the table where they had left Heather.

"Of course, I'd be happy to" Anthony said with a smile, and led the way weaving through the dancers then the crowd to reach the table.

Picking her mug up and taking another drink of the warm beer Angie realized that a number of young men had followed her and Anthony. There were four of them standing together in a small group looking at one another with frowns on their faces. Two more were circling the little group on either side when Susie came running past them stopping at the table laughing merrily.

"That was so much fun" she cried taking up her mug, and downing a drink. Then a sour look chased the smile from her face as the taste of the beer hit her. "Oh, that's just nasty" she shook her head disgustedly, setting the mug back on the table. "Haven't you got anything else to drink Martha" she asked the woman as Able led her to the table to join them.

"Of course, dear" Martha responded with a laugh taking Susie's mug, and downing the last of the beer herself then picked up one of the pitchers sitting on the table. "Try some of this Apple Wine, child, you might find the taste more to your liking." She filled the cup then passed it to Susie before sitting the pitcher back on the table.

"Much better" Susie nodded after taking a sip then took a deeper drink. "Now which one of you wants to dance" she asked looking at the six men over the top of the mug using it to hide a mischievous smile that she shared with Angie.

"Getting in there now aren't you, girl" Martha laughed at the grin the younger woman directed at her. "Come on, boy, your turn to give it a try" she said looking across the table where Noah and Jen were still sitting watching the others in silence. "And I bet Johnny here would be happy to dance with you, girl" she said to Jen. Giving the youngest of the six men a shove towards the end of the table to get him started.

"And I think I'll dance with you this time" Susie pointed at a man a year or so older than her with blonde hair and grey eyes then took another drink from her mug before sitting it down. "How about you Angie" she called over her shoulder as she reached out a hand to the man, and started to follow after him.

"Better hurry girl, the band's starting up again" Martha yelled as she led Noah away with Johnny and Jen following them. Anthony had already disappeared with Heather ahead of them all.

"Want to dance with me" she called to a younger man little more than a teenager. He had been approaching her before the others had cut him off. He was turning away certain that she would not choose him when she spoke, and glanced over his shoulder perhaps to see who she had chosen, and was surprised to see her looking at him.. She took his hand after she passed the others pointedly ignoring them, and led him into the now thinning crowd as more of the people began dancing instead of just watching. "What's your name" she called glancing over her shoulder at the blushing younger man.

"Maaa... Mark" he stuttered, and blushed even redder as he followed after her.

"I'm Angie" she called pulling him into the ring of dancers as the band started once again. "You'll have to bear with me for a bit, I'm still learning" she said taking his other hand that he offered then blushed when he placed the other on her waist.

"I, I ... I'm... not, not... so good either" he admitted stuttering through the words as he led her jerking through the steps of the dance.

"Do you have a speech problem, or are you just nervous Mark" she asked picking up the steps quickly... two steps forward then one back followed by a spin, and back to two steps forward... and taking the lead from him instinctively.

"I, I... stut... stutter" he managed dropping his head a little to avoid her eyes.

"Really" step, step. "I've never known"... back and spin... "anyone who stuttered before" step, step. This music was more formal, and constrained than the previous music had been, but allowed a more intimate exchange between the dancers she decided. Some around them were holding one another very close, closer than she would feel comfortable doing in public.

"Were you" back and spin. "Born this way" step, step.

"Ye... Ye... Yes" he sounded so determined to get the word out, and yet had so much difficulty in doing so that her heart went out to him.

"What do you do here in the village" most of her attention was focused on the steps, and keeping her toes out from under his feet. Which he seemed to be intending to crush in his clumsiness, derived she thought mainly from his nervousness.

"I... I'm... a... a... express ri... rider" his head lifting and his eyes brightening he actually managed to stay off her feet as his nervousness faded.

"What's that" she did the back step and spin with a smile on her face at the young man's pride shinning in his eyes.

"We... car... carry... ma... ma... mail... be... betw... between the villages" he sounded enthusiastic, and struggled against his impediment to explain his duties. Evidently he had a circuit that he traveled continuously carrying letters and small packages. His travel took him from here to several of the surrounding villages then back, and kept him constantly traveling which seemed to be something he really enjoyed.

"Where do you live" she asked when he finished his explanation, and almost regretted it at the pained look that passed across his face at the question.

"I was... bor... born... in Lyon" he stammered out, but would say no more, and she remembered seeing the name on the map in Martha's cabin. It was far to the east almost all the way to the mountains.

"Why don't you join us" Angie asked as the music ended. "I'd appreciate it if you'd dance with my friends too, we're new here, and don't know hardly anyone yet" she looked into his eyes hopefully.

"Ye... Yes" he managed with a grin appearing on his face at the invitation.

When they reached the table the others were already standing around drinking from their mugs. Angie introduced Mark to Susie and Heather then nodded to Noah and Jen. "Let me try a bit of that Apple Wine please" she said to Martha after draining her mug of beer.

"Careful child" the older woman said sliding the pitcher towards Angie. "Mixing drinks like that can have disastrous consequences" she added with a grin.

"Just a little then" Angie asked pouring some into the mug to try the taste.

"That'll be fine" the older woman assured her.

"I wish Albert was here" Susie said taking a piece of bread and a chunk of white cheese from a pair of platters that had appeared on the table during the last song. "I would have liked to dance with him" she took a bite of the cheese then looked at the piece in her fingers as she chewed. "This is good, what kind is it" she looked at Martha with a curious expression on her face.

"Goat cheese" the older woman replied and reached for a piece herself.

"I like this too" Angie said setting the empty mug down. "It's got kind of a tart taste to it" she reached for the pitcher of beer though to refill the mug heeding the older woman's advice.

"It goes good with the cheese" Martha said around her bite. "Angie why don't you dance with Johnny this round" she gave the young woman a smile that said she was in for a treat.

"He is a good dancer" Jen said from across the table. She had a grin on her face as she looked at the young man with a shine in her eyes that suggested she might want to do more than just dance with him.

Looking at the younger man Angie decided that he was indeed handsome bordering on pretty with a smooth angular face, and bright eyes with light brown colored hair that was full of curls. Even standing still he looked like he was dancing. The only thing about him that wasn't appealing Angie decided was the fact that he knew just how good looking he was, and the effect it had on women.

"No, I think I'll dance with Noah this time." She took a drink of her beer to cover her smile of amusement at Noah's look of shock mixed with a little fear at the suggestion. Johnny seemed as shocked that she didn't want to dance with him, and his face nearly set her to laughing.

"I... ah... I don't... I'm not... sure I can" he stammered worse than Mark ever had while talking to her.

"I think we can mange" Angie assured him as she set the mug down. The drummer had started pounding his bass drum as an indication that the next song was about to start. They seemed to take a short break between each song to take their drinks from the small table set among them the same as everyone else.

"Ain't nothing to it boys" Able said setting his mug on the table as he grinned at Mark and Noah in turn. "Just got to get in there" he had been speaking with Mark quietly to the side since the young man had reached the table. "It's just like life boys ain't no wrong way or right way to do it" he grinned broadly as he held out a hand to Martha.

"I don't know about that" Martha said frowning at the man's comments, and looking at his offered hand. "There's a lot of wrong ways to do both" her tone suggested that the man had managed to make one of the more grievous errors with his words.

"Well, there you go boys one of the best lessons you can learn. God gave us two ears, two eyes, one mouth and women to insure that we listened and watched twice as much as we speak" Able said shaking his head in mock despair.

"Now, that gentlemen is the best advice I have ever heard out this man, and I would recommend you heed it" Martha grinned at Angie and Susie before taking Able's hand, and allowing him to led her away from the table.

"Well, Noah, ready to give it a whirl" Angie asked with a smile for the boy who still looked unsure of the proposal.

"There ain't no wrong way" he asked her as he came around the table, and took her hand.

"Nope" she said. "Just try not to step on my toes please" she said leaning in close and speaking lower for his ears alone as they started away. She didn't want to hurt Mark's feelings by letting him hear her words.

This time the song was started by the bassists slapping the strings on their large wooden instruments to a steady rhythm that the drummer picked up with a lower back beat to. Then the guitarist added their harmony, and the fiddlers picked it up making their instruments sound blend in smoothly so that they were almost missed in the music.

"It's a waltz, just follow us" Martha said as Able took her in his arms, and started off.

"What's a waltz" Noah asked with a puzzled look on his face.

"Just follow them" Angie said with a grin, and held out her arms for him to take hold of her the way Able had Martha. "Don't worry it looks pretty simple" she added nodding to where Able was leading Martha in a circle that was slowly taking them away from her and Noah.

"It might look simple, but I'm not sure it really is" the boy said glancing at all the people who had joined this dance including a number of the people who had arrived the night before. Gritting his teeth as if determined to try something that he was sure could not be done, he took her in his arms then led her off after Able and Martha.

"That wasn't so bad was it" Angie asked him after they had stepped through their first circle, the steps were really simple, but Noah felt stiff as he held her his muscles almost trembling at the tension in him. "Haven't you ever danced before, I'd suppose that growing up in the wilds you'd do this all the time" she was surprised that he seemed to be having such a difficult time with dancing.

"I never even heard music till I got to the old man's house yesterday" Noah replied, and had to step quickly when his foot almost came down on top of hers because of the distraction of speaking.

"Really" her tone conveyed her surprise at this revelation. "Just relax, this is meant to be fun not a chore" she said. Then laughed at the look he gave her, which said he thought it was supposed to be the other way around.

"Now you're getting it" she said a few circles later with a smile as Noah fell into a rhythm with the music. "Smile, this really is fun once you get used to it." He gave her a smile that was mostly teeth, and little humor bringing another laugh from her then grimaced when he stepped on her toe.

"Sorry" his face went crimson in embarrassment. "I told you I wasn't very good at this" he said reminding her that he **had** given her a warning. He was quite happy watching instead of participating in this dancing that everyone else seemed to think was so much fun.

"Its fine you just need more practice that's all" she said trying to wiggle her toes to make sure they weren't broken while not falling out of step with him. "And remember that this is fun" she laughed again at his look, and squeezed his hand. It felt so warm she was surprised she had not noticed it before.

"Do you really mean to start a war with the High Chancellor when Albert dies" she was curious as to how someone actually started a war.

"She needs to be stopped" he said grimly not even noticing that he was doing a fair job at the steps now that his mind was diverted.

"What if she dies before Albert" Angie asked noticing his improvement.

"Some one else will take her place, and nothing will change." He shook his head at the images the old man had conjured when telling him what he was up against. The prospect of defeating so many seemed impossible, but he knew that it was something he had to do.

"Even knowing what opposes you, you'll still try" she asked echoing his thoughts.

"I'll still do it" he said confidently, believing that it was still possible no matter how impossible it might seem.

"Then I will help you" she said thinking of what Albert had asked of her in the graveyard, shivering a little at the thought of him sitting up there now talking to his dead wife.

"Why" he asked more curious than suspicious.

"Why" she repeated confused by the unexpected question.

"Why would you be willing to help when you don't believe it can be done" he looked into her eyes as he spoke searching for an understanding. In his past experiences no one had ever helped beyond a self-serving point, and he wondered what she expected to get in return for her aide.

"I never said I didn't believe it could be done" she answered her tone a little short at his assumption. "I believe that we can run and hide, but it will only be a matter of time before they find us even if we are on another planet" she emphasized the last still a little awed by the thought. "You are right about the High Chancellor, no matter who it is they won't change anything, and wrong is wrong no matter what planet we're on." She was thinking of what Albert had said to her, and she knew that she could refuse him nothing now after what he had given her, but it was not just that. Noah was right in what he wanted as well she felt certain about that, and she knew that she had to help him. She just hoped that he would wait till Albert had passed on, she would not jeopardize his safety for anyone nor would Albert stop just because Noah was here now.

166

All this flashed through her mind while the boy was looking into her eyes, and it seemed as if she could see him reading her thoughts.

"Do you think you can fight" he asked still looking her in the eye. Both of them still dancing and neither missing a step lost in the rhythm of the music.

"I didn't know how to dance till this afternoon, and I learned it pretty well. I suppose I can learn to fight just the same" she said after considering her abilities from what she considered an objective view point.

"Do you think you can kill" he asked watching, and seeing the shock and revulsion that flashed through her eyes.

"I don't want to" she said honestly as she reconsidered her abilities from a new view point. "But that is what we will be doing isn't it" she said more than asked as she thought about what a war really was about. "I think I understand now why Albert wants you to wait till he dies. No one as caring and compassionate as he is could stand killing another human being" the thought of Albert hurting anything was so foreign she could not even imagine it.

"Can you" Noah asked pushing the issue.

"I am not Albert" she said thinking of the last few years as a Servant, and the things they had forced her to endure just to survive. "I have suffered enough to loose all my compassion for the Moralists and the High Chancellor, I can learn to kill" the last was said in a voice that was firm, and hard leaving no doubt that it was true.

"Good enough then" Noah answered with a nod that confirmed his belief in her. "You know this dancing might not be so bad after all" he said with a grin as he realized that he was indeed doing a fair job at it now. It was fun to feel her in his arms, her body moving at his direction, and knowing that she was enjoying the same experience. He wondered if this was what sex was like. Jamie had tried explaining it to him, but he had finally said 'until you experience it, words are just meaningless.'

167

"What?" Angie asked when she saw his face suddenly turn crimson.

"Nothing" he said quickly banishing the images of her that had surfaced from his thoughts.

"Are you ok" she asked concerned for him as she stepped quickly to avoid his sudden clumsy feet that seem to seek hers out intentionally.

"Fine... really... ah... sorry" he stammered. Trying to correct his movements, and find the place he had been before his thoughts had off balanced him.

"Are you sure" she asked as he regained his rhythm. She searched his face for some clue of what was going on inside his head, but it revealed nothing. The red fading quickly and his blue eyes empty except for a twinkle of something that was gone before she could recognize it. Replacing it was his usual expression of smug amusement, and he continued dancing as expertly as he had been a moment before.

"You were right this is kinda fun once you get the hang of it" he said grinning at her as they danced into another circle.

"I told you" she said with an answering grin though she was still wondering what he had been thinking that embarrassed him. She thought he had been embarrassed but if he didn't want to talk about it she was willing to drop the subject. "Wait till they play a faster song then you can twirl me around and around" she said laughing at the thought, and missed the flash of concern at the thought that passed through his eyes.

"I can't wait" he said with a grin. While silently vowing not to dance with her again tonight, but finding himself strangely wanting to dance every song with her for the rest of the night.

As they danced he wondered about her, she was about the same age as Jen, in her early twenties. She had the soft appearance he associated with those who lived in the cities, but there was strength in her gaze, and bearing that most he had met did not posses. He knew the symbol on her forehead meant that she was a Servant, but he really had no idea what that really meant. He assumed her life had been hard as one, which was the reason for her being here in the first place.

Angie, he liked the sound of her name, it fit her in some way that he could not explain. She was a short woman, the top of her head barely reaching his chin, and he was not overly tall himself. He could smell the soap she had used to wash her hair with, the soft light brown color shimmering in the bright light of the lamps that lit the area. Her eyes were hazel, but at the moment they were almost completely green except for a thin ring of brown around the outer edge.

When the song ended he found himself reluctant to let her go, but forced the feeling down. Only to have a longing to feel her hand in his once again rise in its place. She smiled at him as she turned to lead the way back to the table, and his heart seemed to lurch in his chest startling him.

"Have you tried that Apple Wine Martha has" she called over her shoulder, and glanced back at him.

"No, she said I was too young for it" he said fighting for control of his thoughts as his awareness of her continued throwing up unexpected images and observations. He had never experienced such a thing before, and was struggling to deal with what he did not understand.

"How old are you" she asked pausing to look at him intently for a moment as if trying to judge his age.

"I don't know" he said honestly. "My mother died when I was little, I don't even remember her. I was taken care of by the whole camp we were in for a while then it was raided. An old woman escaped with me, and two other children, but she died a few months later. We lived for a long time on our own in the wilderness before a man found us, and took us to another camp. They thought I was eight or nine then but we didn't stay there long before moving on. Jen said the men were too touchy, and that was about ten years ago more or less" he shrugged his shoulders at her his age was no real concern to him anyway.

"If you're old enough to start planning a war then you're old enough to try the wine" she said turning to led the way again.

He followed her, his brain in a fog, unsure why he had told her about his past. Before when some one had asked him his age he would just grin, and give some off hand comment about age being irrelevant in his world. For some reason it didn't seem right to do so with Angie. He found himself wanting to share other details of his past, but stomped the urge down immediately.

Dreams

Have to keep moving, can't stop now he thought franticly. They were still out there closing in on him now. He looked at the dark forest surrounding him hiding his pursuers from sight, but he knew they were close. Dodging around a tree his foot caught on a root that seemed to hump up as he passed to trip him intentionally. Jagged thorns dug into his flesh as he landed on the ground, the vines that bore the thorns wriggling around limbs trying to bind him for those pursuing.

Kicking and waving his arms drove the thorns deeper, but broke him free of the restraints, and he struggled to his feet, and began running again. An unnatural terror drove him as the sound of pursuit began to close in from behind, and both sides. Too many to fight, though he knew that fighting was impossible with out weapons, only escape was an option, but they were so close now. Their footsteps scattering the dry leaves, and breaking the dead limbs that covered the ground under the giant oak trees, that were impossibly tall and thick. There had to be hundreds chasing him now, and those trees were so close that he constantly had to weave around them.

She was back there, driving his pursuers; he could feel Her like hot breath on the back of his neck. She wanted him, and it seemed he had been running from Her his whole life, but now She nearly had him. The terror of falling into Her hands spurred him on even faster, only those following kept pace. Deep down, he knew that She would never stop hunting him, sending more and more pursuers after him till She had him. The pain would be endless.

Another root caught his foot, and the vines reached for him even as he was falling, their thorns digging deep once

171

more. He tried fighting free, but he was exhausted, and weak from running for so long. His pursuers were so close that he knew this time they would catch him, and there was no one to save him. Struggling to his knees with the vines still wrapped around his arms and legs he saw hands reaching out of the darkness. They had him.

The vines became ropes that bound him tightly preventing his escape. Out of the darkness the faces of friends, and people he knew appeared attached to the hands that held him. Jamie and Jen looked at him accusingly as if it was his fault for them having to do this to him. Martha with her mothering face now twisted in hate, Able who had been so supportive now had an expression of disgust on his face. So many others he had met were grinning with manic glee in their eyes, or loathing contorting their faces as they surrounded him.

Jamie and Jen had him by the arms turning him to follow Martha and Able when the forest changed to a city. In the distance was a tall golden palace where She waited and they were taking him to Her. The streets were lined with people shouting in anger and hate at him, their faces undefined except for the disgust and loathing on them. The walk seemed to take forever, and at the same time only seconds seemed to have passed, and he was before the door leading into the palace.

"You wanted this boy" the old man was standing in front of the doors looking at him accusingly with a sneer on his lips, and hate in his eyes. He swung the doors open a huge hall, its ceiling and walls lost in indistinct distance. It was filled with people who were looking at him, laughing and clapping at the fool who thought he could escape Her. "She's waiting for you, boy" the old man said waving him forward.

His bonds were gone, but there was still no escape now so he started forward the crowd parting for him then filling in behind as he passed. They called taunts and jeers at him as he passed. Above this was the sound of insane laughter that seemed to echo in the huge room. At the far end above the

172

heads of the crowd he could see a golden light like the sun rising on a glorious day while he walked in gloom.

Then the crowd parted, and She was there bathing him in Her glow that seemed to be as painful as the thorns, and digging even deeper. She was sitting on a throne of gold on a raised dais waiting for him in all her glory and power. She was dressed in a pure white gown of shimmering silk with Her hair braided in an intricate pattern. A network of precious stones sparkled in the light brown locks as if a part of her instead of woven into the braid. Resting on the silky strands was the golden band of crown. Her attention seemed to be to the side because She was looking away from him Her face hidden from his sight.

He started climbing the steps of the dais, and behind him the crowd's taunts turned to a rage filled roar that climbed in volume with each step he took. The sound echoed in his skull, painfully hammering at him, and driving him to his knees, but he had to go on. It was too late to stop now. He was crawling by the time he reached the top, the pain an agony in his head, and still he could not stop. Reaching out a trembling hand he touched the hem of her gown, and looked up at her in hopes that She would end his torment, but knowing it would only become worse.

"What is it" Angie asked looking down at him from the throne with a concerned look on her face.

He opened his eyes, and sat up in a bed soaked with his sweat grabbing his head that seemed to be full of little men trying to pound their way out with hammers. He felt his heart racing with fear in his chest, and wondered if it was trying to escape as well. He had lost track of the number of times he had had the dream over the years. It was never been the same at the beginning, but always in the end he had faced the High Chancellor, and been crushed with agony when she looked at

173

him. *Why had Angie become the High Chancellor this time, and what did it mean* he asked himself, but had no answers.

"The Dream again" Jen asked looking over at him from the next bunk the darkness of the room revealing only her outline as he looked at her.

"Yes and no" he said as the pounding eased to only a dozen little men with hammers, and dropped his hands to the soaked blanket. Jen knew about his Dream, but it was a mystery to both of them, and for him it had become a normal occurrence in his life. He did not know what she thought of it, and at the moment did not wish to tell her of the sudden appearance of Angie in it.

"What time is it" he asked throwing the blanket back, and swinging his legs over the side of the bed to sit up. His head lurched as more men joined in the escape attempt, and he held himself still for a moment till they eased up once more.

"It's about time to get up anyway" Jen said sitting up as well then rising to make her way across the darkened room to the table. Picking up an empty mug she poured water from a pitcher, and carried it back to Noah. Handing it to him she sat back on the edge of the bed, and picked her pouch up from the floor.

"I'm about out of these" she said taking a bottle from the pouch. Opening the lid she shook out two pills, and handed them to him. "I wonder if Martha has something for headaches" she popped the lid back on the bottle, and returned it to the pouch.

"We can ask her before we leave" Noah said after washing the pills down. With out them the headache would last for days, and it was not something he preferred to endure if there was a way to avoid it. At times the pain had left him unable to even move, and once Jen had risked capture to steal some more pain medicine for him.

"Would you wake the others, I want everyone to have something to eat before we leave" he said fighting his head to

174

reach down for his pile of clothes lying on the floor beside the bed.

"Wait a bit" Jen said placing a hand on his shoulder to halt him. "Give the pills time to work" she stood, and walked down the room returning with a basin of water, and a cloth.

Kneeling she set the basin on the floor then reached over to turn on the small lamp that was sitting on the low table between their beds. "Noah" she gasped looking at the boy sitting on the edge of the bed. He was covered in blood from shoulders to ankles, the white cotton underwear he had on blotched with red where blood had soaked them.

"What's happened to you" she whispered with fear filling her voice. She grasped a hand, and soaked the cloth to wash away the blood, and reveal several small perfect round holes in the cleaned area. "How did you do this" she asked releasing his hand, and throwing back the blanket to inspect the bed.

"Thorns" Noah said his voice distant in his own ears as he remembered the thorn covered vines in the dream.

"There aren't any thorns in here" Jen said still searching the blankets. Martha had warned her about several bugs that inhabited the area. Their bites could kill if they were left untreated, but nothing the woman had described resembled Noah's wounds.

"They were in the Dream" he said absently as he looked at the holes in his skin. They were puckered, and surrounded with red inflamed skin. The center was dark almost black where the blood still seeped from the torn flesh.

"That's not possible" Jen said stopping her search to look at him with fear and concern on her face.

"There were vines with thorns on them, and I felt them digging into me" he said holding out the arm for her to see the wounds they had produced.

"But how can a dream do this" she nodded to the wounds, and moved back in front of him. Taking the cloth she began washing the blood away revealing more and more of the round holes that still seeped.

"I don't know, but that's where they come from" the pounding in his head was easing as the pills began to work, but he was feeling light headed now, and the room was growing hot. "I'm not feeling right Jen" he said realizing something else was wrong as well.

"You're burning up" she said after placing a hand on his brow. "A fever and maybe infection though both are coming on really fast" she turned back to her pouch pulling more bottles from it. "Take these" she handed him a half dozen pills this time, and retrieved another mug of water for him.

"Jamie" she called sharply to the man sleeping in the bed on the other side of Noah's from hers. "Go get Martha quick" she added when the man raised his head.

"Lay back now Noah it'll be alright" she said to him, but her voice was so far away that he barely heard it as she eased him back down on the bed.

"What happened" Jamie asked pulling his pants on, and looking at the boy lying on his bed covered in blood.

"Just get Martha" Jen hissed at him, and began washing the blood away to see how badly Noah had been hurt.

"Go now" she barked when Jamie started to reach for his shirt, and at her tone he glanced once more at the boy then jumped up, and raced from the room.

"Hold on Noah" she checked his pulse, and found it weak and erratic. "I won't let you die I promise, but you have to hold on" she felt real fear that she might not be able to keep her promise.

"Brenda" she called over her shoulder to the woman already sitting up in the bed past hers, and when the woman reached her side had her take over the washing. "I don't know what else I've got in here that might help" she sounded frustrated as she searched the pouch reading the labels on the bottles then tossing them on her bed. By the time she finished Jamie was coming back through the door leading a procession

176

of people headed by Martha followed by Able, and with the three Servants bringing up the rear.

Unnoticed by anyone the little black pup slipped into the room, and trotted over to crawl under Jamie's bed, and watch what was happening. He had been upset when they had all left him in Martha's cabin; he had liked the sound of music he heard outside. They had not returned to let him out till after the music was over, and he had been in serious need of doing his business. The old man was not among them but the little pup knew that he would be waiting at home for him. So he had spent the remainder of the night with the young woman with the light hair and eyes that the old man liked so much knowing she would take him back through the door.

"What's happened" Martha asked arranging her woolen robe as she knelt on the other side of Noah, and began inspecting the now puffed circles in his flesh. "How did this happen" she asked looking across the boy at the two women staring back at her expectantly.

"Thorns" Jen said not sure how to explain that they had been in Noah's dreams, and hoping that she wouldn't have to.

"Thorns" the older woman's tone questioned the word, but she looked back at the boy lying on the bed his skin pale, and his breathing shallow. Reaching a hand out she felt for his pulse, and almost couldn't find it, it was so weak. Thumbing back an eyelid she looked into the eye then waved a hand across it checking the pupil response. "Able go wake the Doc, and tell him to bring a full kit with him" she said looking over her shoulder at the man with an expression that said she really didn't think it would do any good, but they'd try anyway.

"Everyone else out" she said turning back to survey the room. Everyone was awake, sitting up in their beds, and turning on lights to look at Noah with concerned expressions on their faces. "Get your clothes and dress outside" her tone was sharp when no one moved. She swept a glare across the room that set them all to grabbing their possessions, and head for the door.

"You three" the older woman turned to the three women who had followed into the room. "Take them to my house and feed'em" she turned back to the bed as if the issue was closed.

"I'm staying here" Angie said walking over to stand beside Martha, and stare down at the boy. His face looked dry to the point of nearly crumbling to dust, and his breathing was a dry rasp.

"We'll go" Heather said when Martha started to speak, and then urged Susie out the door after the others.

"What do you think you can do here girl" Martha asked testily as the girl knelt beside her, and placed a hand on the boy's forehead.

"I don't know" she said giving the older woman a frown at her tone. "But Albert asked me to stay with him, and help him. Which is what I intend to do now" her tone was frosty, and she ignored the older woman's frown. Rising she glanced around the room then crossed over to another wash stand picking up the pitcher, and pouring water into the bowl. Taking a wash cloth from the shelf she returned to her place beside Noah's bed, and soaking the cloth laid it across his forehead.

"Do you think that's going to do any real good girl" the older woman shook her head at the girl's aide.

"Do you think it's going to hurt" Angie snapped back.

"Enough you two" Jen said harshly from the other side of the bed drawing the other two women's eyes to her. "Brenda you go ahead with the others please" she said glancing at the woman, and moderating her tone for her. Turning back to the other two her eyes hardened, and her jaw set in determination.

"I am not going to let him die so either help or get out" she said nodding to the door that Brenda was heading for.

"I'm not sure he can be saved" Martha said sadly looking down at the boy. "There appears to be some kind of poison in his system, and it is working quickly" she turned back to look at Jen. "I am curious though how the boy got into thorns while

178

sleeping in his bed" she arched an eyebrow waiting on the woman to answer.

Jen looked back at Noah lying on the bed slipping further away with each breath by all appearances. Only Jamie and she knew about the Dream, since they had been with him since he was a little child, and he had never wanted to tell anyone else. She could not blame him for that. Her view of him had changed because of knowing though in her case it was a good change in others it might not be so. But he was dying, and every bit of information might aid in his survival.

"Noah has a Dream sometimes" she looked at the older woman before continuing. "It started when he was a little child" the memory of the first time he had awakened screaming in terror and pain intruded on her thoughts. "He says the first part is not always the same, but that it always ends the same" she decided not to tell the details unless the woman pressed. "When it happens he has headaches or is sick for a day or so after, but this time" she paused trying to decide how to continue. "This time he dreamed of vines with thorns wrapping around him, and this happened" she nodded to the boy's wounds.

"You're telling me that this happened to him in a dream" Martha asked incredulously as she stared at the woman like Jen had lost her mind. "That's not possible" she mumbled more to herself.

"We're on another planet because we walked through a door in Albert's barn" Angie said dipping the cloth in the bowl of water again. Noah's flesh was sucking the cloth dry in minutes. "If that's possible why can't thorns in a dream hurt the living flesh" she looked at the older woman as if it made perfect sense to her. "How does his dream end" she asked turning her head to look across the bed at Jen who hesitated for a moment before answering.

"He is captured and taken before the High Chancellor" Jen reached out a hand to take Noah's limp one, and looked at his bloodless face. "She hurts him badly in some way he won't

179

talk about, and then he wakes up usually screaming in pain" she laid his hand back beside him on the bed. The memories of waking up to the boys screams so many times in the past brought tears to her eyes, but she refused to shed them instead she blinked them away. Tears would do him no good.

Any further questions were cut off as Able entered the room with the doctor right behind him. Both men crossed the room quickly Able helping Martha to rise giving the doctor room to start working on the boy.

"What in God's name has happened to this boy" the doctor asked looking at the dozens of puncture wounds visible now that the blood had been washed away.

"Thorns Doc" Martha said behind him. Giving Jen a look that said she should not tell anyone else about the Dream.

"Poisoned" Doc asked turning from his inspection of the boy, and opening the large satchel he had brought with him.

"I think so" Martha said looking over his shoulder at the boy.

Jen watched anxiously as the doctor quickly ran an IV into a vein in Noah's hand then filled a syringe from a bottle, and injected it through the IV. Returning the bottle he took another, and filled the syringe once again then injected the clear fluid through the IV. Returning that bottle to the satchel the doctor took Noah's wrist, and watched the boy's face for any reaction to the medication.

"Hum" was all he said before turning back to the satchel, and pulling out a clear plastic bag filled with another clear liquid. Connecting the end of the line that ran out of the bag to Noah's IV the doctor hung it from the bed post, and stood for a moment looking down at the boy.

"I don't know Martha" the doctor finally said turning to look at the woman. "I gave him a shot of adrenaline and epinephrine, but without knowing what poison is in his system..." he shrugged his shoulders saying he couldn't do any more. "I got a saline solution going now; maybe if we can keep fluids in him, he'll live long enough for his body to filter the

180

poison out. If it doesn't shut his kidneys down first" his tone said that he doubted there was much hope for the boy surviving that long.

"There's nothing else you can do for him" Jen asked anguish tingeing her words, and drawing the doctor's eyes to her.

"I'm sorry" he said sounding like he really meant it.

"He's not going to die" Angie said her voice sounding like she meant it as well.

"I can't promise that" the doctor said looking down at her as she wet the cloth again.

"I wasn't asking for a promise Doc, I was telling you" she wiped Noah's face gently with the cloth, the water sinking into the dry skin as soon as the cloth released it.

"You two" Martha said with a tone that she would stand no argument as she fixed each of the younger women with a look. "I want to talk to you" she turned so sharply she almost stepped on Able. "Why don't you go check on those rascals they've probably eaten me out of house and home by now" she said to him with a sweet voice that did nothing to disguise her anger, and patted the larger man softly on the cheek.

"Yes dear" he said with a grin seemingly unaffected by her tone, and turned to walk away. His steps were a little too quick however to hold the pretense that he truly was unaffected as he escaped out the door.

"Doc you've done all you can. You might as well go too" she glanced over her shoulder at the man who bowed his head, and quickly followed after Able. "Come with me" her glance swept between the two women who were still on their knees looking up at her with identical expressions of defiance on their faces. They both rose however, and followed the older woman across the room, and out the door.

Once they were outside the older woman turned to face the younger two. "Now you listen to me" she started her tone sharp. "What ever has happened to that boy" she gave Jen a look that said she still did not believe it had happened in a

181

dream. "Is killing him, and if it has affected him this much in so short a time then it is unlikely he will survive." Both women's eyes hardened as she spoke, and Jen started to speak out but the older woman rode right over her. "You have to face the truth no matter what you want to believe to the contrary. Now before long you two are going to have to go, and follow the plans we made last night because more than that boys life is in the balance, and Albert will need you both..." she continued explaining what her tone said should be obvious.

Inside the room the little pup heard her voice, but it was in the back ground as his main attention was on the boy lying on the bed. The little pup could smell the boy's pain, it was sharp and deep. The little pup knew he was hovering on the edge of life, and he whined at the thought of loosing his new friend. He knew it would hurt the old man too if the boy died, and he didn't like it when the old man hurt.

Crawling out from under the bed the little black pup looked at the door, but the women were not paying attention to anything, but themselves. Reaching the boys bed the little pup rose on his hind legs, and rested his fore paws on the edge of the bed sniffing the boy's scent. The pain was strong and intense, and the pup knew the boy had little time.

Whining the little pup dropped back down then tried to jump up on the bed with the boy, but failed in the first attempt barely managing to land on his feet. Trying again he caught the boy's leg with his forepaws, and used his hind legs to climb the rest of the way up onto the bed. Standing between the boy's knees the little black pup sniffed at the inflamed wounds smelling the source of the boy's pain.

They smelled wrong like the people in town smelled, twisted, and filled with hate that was one of the reasons he liked the old man. His smell was clean and pure. The wounds were different though it was almost like they weren't really there, but the little pup could see them, and knew that they had to be cleaned if the boy was to survive.

Gently the little pup began to lick the nearest wounds. The taste on his tongue made his stomach turn, but for the boy and the old man he would do anything. He knew the two of them were linked in some way. Their smells were so similar, more so than any of the other people. The little pup worked his way down one leg making sure to get all of the wrong smell out of each wound before moving on. The pup stopped occasionally to wipe his tongue off on his fore leg when he could no longer stand the taste then went back to his ministrations; anything for the boy and the old man.

"Stop it, dog" the woman who ran with the boy said drawing the little pup's eyes, but he continued licking the boy's wounds. "Get down" she said crossing the room towards him as the little pup started making his way up the boy's other leg ignoring her.

"I said stop it" the woman reached a hand out, and the little pup knew she meant to stop him, but he wasn't done yet, so he growled warningly at her, and bared his little teeth then continued his work.

"What is it Jen" Angie asked coming into the room, and seeing her standing at the foot of Noah's bed. She had sent Martha back to her cabin mumbling angrily about the stubbornness and foolishness of the two younger women.

"This dog is licking the wounds" Jen said stepping to the side so Angie could see the little black pup between Noah's legs. "He'll get them infected, but he keeps growling, and nipping at me when I try to pick him up." She sounded frustrated as she reached for the little pup again, and it growled warningly again.

"Let me try" Angie said reaching the side of the bed. "Come on sweetie I know you want to help, but you'll only make it worse" her voice was soft and coaxing.

The little pup looked at her, but continued his licking. He knew the old man liked her, but if she tried to interfere he would bite her, he decided. The old man might get mad about it, but if the boy died he would be hurt more. The little pup

183

knew he couldn't take much more of that kind of hurt. She reached out to take hold of him, and he knew she meant to stop him so he growled a warning that she ignored. When her hands were almost on him he stopped licking long enough to snap at her hand biting the fingers, but not hard enough to break the skin. The little pup didn't want to hurt either woman, he like them both, but he couldn't let them stop him.

"What's wrong with you" Angie jerked her hand back looking at it to see if she was bleeding while the little pup went back to licking Noah's wounds.

"See, the little sucker nearly took my finger off" Jen said angrily shaking her head at the little pup.

"Grab that blanket, Jen" Angie said nodding to Jen's bed. "We'll cover him with it so he can't bite us then take him outside" she didn't want to hurt the little pup. Albert was so fond of him she knew it would hurt him if anything happened to the little fellow.

The little black pup finished with the boy's leg getting all the wounds he could reach. There were more underneath, but the little pup couldn't get to them so he climbed over the boy's leg. Then started licking on the boy's stomach, and arm lying beside him on the bed. The little pup was watching the two women warily so when the one the boy ran with picked up the blanket from the bed he raised his hackles, and growled another warning.

When the woman tried to throw it over him the little black pup scampered across the boy's stomach feeling bad for the pain it caused, but managed to evade the blanket. As soon as he was on the other side of the bed he began licking the nearest wounds. He knew that he could not avoid the women much longer, and that there was still too much pain in the boy for him to survive.

"What is the deal with this dog" Jen asked picking the blanket up and holding out one end to Angie so they could catch the little pup under it.

"He seems pretty determined doesn't he" Angie answered her tone puzzled as she took the blanket. Instead of spreading her side out like Jen she was watching the little pup. His little dark eyes were flicking back and forth between the two women, but his licking had intensified as if rushing to complete before they could stop him.

"Wait" Angie said tossing her end of the blanket back across the bed.

"What?" Jen asked confused, and eyeing the little pup warily as she considered trying by her self once more to catch the little demon.

"You're just not going to quit are you dog" Angie said watching the little pup. "What can it really hurt Jen. If what Martha and the doctor said is true" her voice carried the anguish that was in her eyes as she looked across the bed at the other woman.

"They're wrong" Jen said vehemently starring at the little pup as if it was his fault. The pup growled at her when she lifted the blanket again considering trying to catch him by herself once more. "Go ahead you little mongrel" she said as if surrendering, and tossed the blanket back on her bed, and sat down on it to watch the little pup.

"I know they're wrong too Jen" Angie said sitting on the bed on the other side of Noah's, and watched the little pup.

When the two women sat down the little black pup took a moment to clean his tongue on his fore leg. The taste was so thick he was becoming sick from it, and hoped the two women would not try to interfere again. Moving more slowly he took greater care in making sure he had all of the smell of wrongness out of the wound before moving on to the next.

The women said nothing further just watched him, and the little pup relaxed a little more, but still keep his eye on them in case they tried to interfere again. The little pup worked his way down the boy's side licking carefully around the thing the one man had stuck in his hand. When the taste became too strong on his tongue he cleaned it, but the little pup could

185

already feel it coursing through his body. Anything for the old man and the boy, to his last breath if need be.

Finishing the last of the wounds the little pup could get to he made his way to the foot of the bed, and sat looking back and forth at the two women. He gave a sharp insistent bark when they remained sitting staring at him then pawed at the boy's foot pulling it to the side. The little pup gave the woman the old man liked a pleading look, and whined trying to convey his desire for them to turn the boy over.

"What's he doing now" Jen asked cocking her head to look at the little pup in puzzlement. The little pup whined again, and pawed at the boy's foot once more.

"Honestly I think he wants us to turn Noah over" Angie said starring at the little pup in amazement.

"Really" Jen asked in disbelief at the idea.

"I think so" Angie said rising from the bed, and stepping over to Noah's to kneel down, and inspect his wounds. "Do these look better to you" she asked nodding to them. She thought they were a little less inflamed. She reached up to feel his forehead, and thought that maybe his fever was easing as well.

"There does seem to be less redness around them" Jen conceded. "How's his fever" she looked at the other woman.

"I think it's starting to come down a little, but I'm not sure" Angie said honestly not wanting to give any false hope pinned on a little pup licking Noah's wounds. "Help me" she gently took the boy's shoulders, and pulled the upper half of his body to her side of the bed while Jen pushed the lower half. Together they rolled him over, and back to the center of the bed. As soon as he was in place the little pup started licking the wounds they had exposed.

"I guess that was what he wanted" Jen said watching the little pup work.

Dropping to her knee Angie began rummaging through the satchel that the doctor had left till she found a digital thermometer, and sleeve for the probe. "Here let's check his temperature" she said rising, and turning to bend over Noah's head. "Open his mouth, and put it under his tongue" she slipped the sleeve over the probe, and handed it to Jen then hit the start button when the other woman had it in place.

"One O three" she said when the monitor beeped and the display showed one hundred and three in large black letters on the gray screen. "We'll check it again in few minutes to see if it drops any" Angie said taking the probe from Jen, and setting the device on the table beside the bed.

"I wish we'd taken it earlier so we could tell if it had dropped any" Jen sounded angry at the failure, and resumed her seat on her bed. Watching the little pup that had started licking on the back of Noah's other leg.

It only took the little pup a few more minutes to finish cleaning the rest of the boy's wounds, and he was thankful when the job was done. Working his way carefully to the side of the bed he tried to jump down, but it turned into a fall that left him sprawled on the floor. The woman the old man liked knelt down next to him when he didn't get up, he just didn't have the strength to do so. She lifted him into her arms, and laid him on the bed where she had been sitting. The little pup could feel the warmth from her body in the spot, and was glad for it because he felt so cold.

"What's wrong with him" Jen asked coming around Noah's bed to kneel down beside Angie who was looking the little pup over.

"I think he's infected with what was in Noah's wounds" Angie said turning to the satchel once more, and pulling out a pair of sterile rubber gloves. Slipping them on, she turned back, and opened the little pup's mouth. There was a dark greasy film on the inside of it. Taking the cloth that was lying in the basin of water she began washing the little pup's mouth, and he was so weak he did not fight her efforts.

"I'm sorry for calling you a mongrel you beautiful little darling" Jen said tears glistening in her eyes as she stroked the

187

little pup's side gently while Angie continued cleaning his mouth out.

When the water in the basin had turned a sickly grey color Angie took the basin outside, and dumped it on the ground. Back inside she refilled it with fresh water and retrieved a clean cloth then returned to kneel beside the bed. The little pup's eyes seemed glazed and unfocused to Angie as she set the basin beside her, and dipped the cloth into it. The little tongue hanging out its mouth was dry, and still covered in the black greasy substance hiding the natural pink color. The little pup was panting hard and fast trying to cool itself even as the fever continued rising.

"Is he going to die" Jen asked a tear escaping from her eye, and she quickly wiped it away.

"No" Angie said emphatically. "I'm not going to let either of them die from this" she opened the little pup's mouth, and continued wiping the filthy substance away as quickly as she could. "Check Noah, and see if his temperature has come down any" she said to the other woman after a few minutes. "Then bring me another basin of fresh water, and a cloth" she wrung out the cloth in her hand, the filth already darkening the water in the basin.

"Hang in there, dog" she said softly to the little pup. She had never heard the old man call him anything else so she didn't know if that was his name or not. The little pup whined in answer though, the sound was just barely louder than his panting. She wiped his little tongue, and for a moment she could see the pink flesh then it was filmed over again the black substance seeping out of the flesh like a puss.

"His temperature is down to a hundred, and his breathing is easier" Jen said behind Angie wonder filling her voice. "How this can be I don't know, but I am grateful to that little pup for what he did" she paused to look at him over Angie's shoulder. Then went around Noah's bed to retrieve the basin used to wash his wounds, and carried it outside to dump the bloody water.

188

"I'm grateful too, dog" Angie said softly. Wiping the roof of his little mouth and seeing the dark flesh for a moment there as well before the oily substance covered it once more.

"How's he doing" Jen asked when she returned with the basin filled with clean water, and a fresh cloth.

"I don't know for sure" Angie answered. The little pup was still panting heavily, but she thought that his eyes seemed a little clearer than they had been, and she was seeing more flesh in his little mouth. She dropped the wet cloth that was stained black now into the dark filmy water, and took the fresh cloth Jen held out to her.

"What are you two doing now" Martha's tone was half exasperation and half surprise. She looked at the two women kneeling beside the bed with the little black pup lying on it, and Noah now lying on his stomach in his bed.

"Well" she asked again as she walked briskly across the room to check on the boy. Shock opened her eyes wide as she found the boy breathing normally, his flesh only slightly warm to the touch, and his skin a more natural color instead of the chalky white he had been when she had last seen him.

"What has happened" she looked sharply across Noah's bed at the two women who were still focused on the little pup.

"This little pup saved him" Jen said turning her head to look at the older woman for a moment before returning her attention to softly petting the little pup's side.

"What?" Martha's voice was nearly a screech as her shock ratcheted up another notch. She walked around the end of Noah's bed to stand behind the two women, and look down over their shoulders at the little black pup. The little pup was still panting, but not as heavily as he had been, and he turned his eyes up to look at the older woman as Angie continued wiping his mouth out.

"He licked Noah's wounds, and got that stuff out of them" Jen rose and stepped around the woman to pick up the dirty watered basin. "Now we're trying to get it out of him" she

189

walked past the older woman, and went outside to dump the water.

The sun was just beginning to brighten the horizon to the east making her aware of just how long they had been up already. The houses that she could see had lights shining in the windows as the people inside were preparing to start their day. Able had assigned them the end room of the long barracks building next to Martha's cabin. The light was bright enough now for her to clearly see the table they had sat at the night before during the dancing. She had enjoyed dancing more than she would have considered before actually doing it.

Dumping the water out on the ground where she had poured the previous basins she could see in the growing light that the grass there was dead. Intuitively she knew that it would be a long time before the grass grew back in the spot.

A stiff breeze was blowing from the south, washing over her, and refreshing her, but also making her realize that she had still not dressed. She was wearing only the long shirt a woman had given to her when they first arrived along with other clothes. The woman had called it a night shirt. The breeze became a gust whipping the thin material of the shirt around her form, and she looked to the south where a line of clouds stretched across the horizon. The massive thunder heads were rolling over one another in their haste to reach the village. The villagers would have called it a chilly morning, but for Jen who had spent most of her life living outdoors the morning air was merely brisk, getting her blood flowing properly.

Turning she walked back inside, filled the basin with fresh water, picked up another wash cloth then carried them over, and set the basin beside Angie. She was sitting on her hip the wet cloth in her hand lying in her lap, an elbow resting on the bed its hand propping her head up. Martha was sitting on the edge of Noah's bed dividing her attention between the boy and the little pup.

"How's our little hero doing" Jen asked as she knelt down to look at the little black pup.

"I think he's sleeping now" Angie said nodding to where the little pup was lying with his eyes closed. His breathing was still rapid, but no longer the panting it had been. "I got as much of this stuff out" she held up the nearly black cloth in her hand "but I think there is still some in him. I've been waiting a few minutes to see if it would build up in his mouth" she tossed the cloth into the filmy water. Then took the fresh cloth from Jen and opened the little pup's mouth washing the tongue, and roof finding that indeed it was once more coated with the black oily substance.

"I don't think I will ever understand just exactly what I've seen here tonight" Martha said starring at the wash cloth in Angie's hand. "Dreams that can kill a boy as healthy as Noah, and a little black dog saving him by licking that filth out of the wounds" the older woman shook her head at impossibility of the idea.

"I never thought that I would travel to another planet by stepping through a door either" Jen turned her head to grin at the older woman. "Yet here I am" she rose and, walked around to the other side of Noah's bed looking down at him briefly to see that he appeared to be sleeping peacefully. Pulling the night shirt off she began dressing in the clothes she had been wearing when they first arrived in the village. A pair of thin cotton socks that had nearly worn through in the heels and a pair of soft leather pants made from tanned deer skin. She pulled on a short sleeved cotton shirt that fit her form tightly then sat down on the bed to pull her knee high boots on, and lace the strings up. The boots were one of Noah's creations; they were thick leather made for the sole purpose of preventing the snake bites that were a common problem in the wilderness. She had seen several people die horribly from them over the years.

"Did Jamie and the others leave on time" she asked Martha as she picked up her pouch, and began replacing the medications that were lying on the bed.

"Yes" the older woman turned her head to look at Jen over her shoulder. "If Albert realized that something happened, and opened the door for them then they should be well on their way to town by now" she sounded as if she had no doubt that the old man had, and they were.

"I hope everything else goes like we planned" Jen said laying the pouch on the bed, and turning to put a hand on Noah's forehead. "I think his fever has broken" she said feeling the thin sheen of perspiration that covered it.

"That's good" Martha flashed a smile over her shoulder at the younger woman. "How about the pup" she asked turning her head to look at Angie.

"I think he's fine now too" she answered dropping the now blackened cloth into the basin. "I don't think there is any of that stuff left in him" she nodded towards the basin.

"That's good too" the older woman nodded to emphasize her words. "Surprising on both accounts, but still good" her nod became a shake at the events of the night, and she stood up. "Now that they both apparently are out of danger why don't we go get you two some breakfast" she leaned down, and picked up one of the basins. "You both look like you could use it, and maybe a few more hours of sleep yourselves" she turned to start for the open door.

"Breakfast does sound good" Angie agreed picking up the other basin as she rose to follow the older woman, but looked at Jen questionably.

"Go ahead Angie, I'll stay, and watch them" Jen said in answer to her look, and waved a hand towards the door, and the older woman walking towards it.

They were all looking towards the open door when Jamie came trotting through it. His face was flushed red, and he was breathing heavier then normal indicating he had been running to get there.

"The old man didn't show" his voice was filled with worry.

192

"What" Martha asked surprised by his appearance, and by his words.

"The old man didn't open the door for us" he said again looking past her at Noah lying on the bed. "How's he doing" he nodded at the boy, but looked at Jen for an answer.

"He'll be fine" Jen said glancing at the sleeping boy. "Why didn't the old man open the door" she looked up at Martha meaning her question for the older woman.

"If I knew that I wouldn't have sent them up to the door in the first place." Martha's voice was testy as she stared at Jamie, her mind whirling through all the possibilities, and none of them were good.

"Something's happened to him" Angie said fear dominating her voice. "It has to be that Servant he told us about, I just know it" she sounded certain that was the case, and her voice was filled with fear at the prospect.

"We don't know anything" Martha snapped. "Another explanation could be that Albert just slept late" she moderated her tone, but she did not sound convincing.

"What do we do" Jamie asked looking at Noah laying on the bed his tone saying he was at a loss.

"We can't do anything till the boy wakes up" Martha said glancing over her shoulder at him sleeping on the bed.

"Should we try to wake him, Albert may need help" Angie seemed ready to try if it would get them to Albert.

"After what that boy's been through I'd doubt anything could wake him" she gave the younger woman a look that said she had better not try either. "If something has happened to Albert then it is already done. If not, then there is no rush, either way there is nothing we can do right now but wait." She shook her head at the situation, and turned back to look at Jamie.

"Where is the rest of your little bunch" she stepped around him to the door, and tossed the dirty water from the basin as he answered.

"I left two of them at the door, and the rest are at your house" Jamie said turning as she passed to watch her.

"Well at least you can think on your feet, we'll make something of you yet" Martha smiled as the young man flushed with anger at her condescending tone. She set the empty basin on the bed by the door, and turned to look at the two women in turn. "You two come with me, you need to eat something then get some rest" she turned without giving them a chance to argue, and went out the door.

The wind was cold chilling him further when he was already half frozen, his flesh feeling stiff slowing his progress. But at least the wind was against his back now. For so long it had been hollowing in his face fighting him for each step, but now as if seeming to finally give up it was pushing him. Driving him forward, but at the same time hammering against the thin exposed flesh of his back sucking the warmth out of his body as it passed; in the sound of its passing he could almost hear it laughing at him, taunting his efforts to oppose its will.

The wind had an almost feminine quality to it, but a woman filled with malicious joy savoring every drop of warmth stolen from him. The image of a woman with a face so perfect, the skin so smooth that her features seemed like polished marble come to life, and beautiful beyond belief. He knew her face from so long ago, but she had never looked as she did now except maybe in her dreams. She was dressed in a pure white gown of shimmering silk with Her hair braided. The long thick strand hanging over Her shoulder, Her eyes staring at him with Her chin pressed against the silky locks. She had always envied Tizzy's hair.

She had a crown upon Her head, a delicate center piece of laced gold threads in an arch imitating rays of light rising from the large diamond representing the sun on the golden band. The piece rested on her brow above eyes that seemed to bore into his soul drawing his life as the wind was drawing his warmth. She laughed and he heard it in the wind as She watched him suffer under the attack.

He shuffled a foot forward his shoulders hunched, his hands fisted, and tucked up in his armpits trying to keep them from freezing faster. For all it's ferocity the wind did not stir a single particle of the dust his feet stirred up. The terrain was a barren plain of powdered soil, and small fist sized rocks with jagged edges that sliced the skin of his bare feet if he didn't watch his step. His shirt was long gone if he had ever had one. His pants were rags, exposing his withered flesh, and barely hanging around his shrunken waist.

She laughed and the wind whipped him harder ripping a few more strands of cloth from the pants, a little more heat from his body, and She sucked another drop of his soul. Then Her head turned away from him, and he staggered forward as the wind died around him leaving with Her attention. Warmth began to soak back into his frail body with its passing, and the old man lifted his head a little.

Whether it was day or night he could not tell, the sky overhead was covered with a thick layer of clouds that hid any sign of the sun, but it was still bright enough to see clearly. Everything had a blue tint as if it was night with a full moon shining brightly in a sky filled with stars instead of the clouds. The old man shuffled forward, and far on the horizon a brilliant light began to crest like the sun rising, but getting closer with each of his steps instead of brighter with time.

Then as things happen in dreams he was suddenly there on the banks of a wide river. His side was still the barren plain with its powdered soil, sharp rocks, and heavy clouds. On the other side were green fields, tall trees giving shade from the bright sun in the deep blue sky, and gentle breezes that wafted pollen through the air while gently rustling the leaves in the trees. The sound beckoned the old man to take a rest under their protective cover, and let the worries of life slip away.

Between him, and their comfort was the river, its surface smooth, the water not flowing in either direction. The still water gave the appearance of an easy crossing for anyone who could swim, but the old man knew that the first touch would suck him deep into depths that were endless. Death waited in the reflection of himself that appeared on the glassy surface. Stretching away from him like a shadow as he stood on the shore. His toes were inches from the still water, the boundary between soil and liquid definite and unyielding. He felt that the boundary was the same below the surface, a line stretching to infinity separating the two elements forever.

Just as the river its self separated him from the far shore where he could see Tizzy, and the boys standing together in the thick grass on the bank. Tizzy was standing behind them with her hands resting on their shoulders. On either side of them were the boys' wives and his grandchildren, all of them of the same age now. They were all looking across the river searching for him it seemed. He cried out to them, but his throat was so dry the sound came out a croak around a tongue that was shriveled with thirst, and across lips cracked and raw.

Raising a thin hand in front of him then waving it at them slowly he realized it was in farewell because the only way to reach them was to plunge into the water. Death was not something he could embrace yet. There was still too much that had to be done, and he was the still the only one who could do it. Tears falling from eyes that stung with grit the old man turned away from the river, and started back across the plain.

The old man opened his eyes slowly surprised at how much pain the simple movement caused. The dream was still vivid in his mind, the anguish at leaving his wife and children still sharp, but he couldn't die yet. Not yet. Idly he wondered what time it was, he knew that he had slept after the dream, but for how long he did not know. Rolling his eyes he tried to fight the pain, and see around him.

He was still tied to the chair in his living room. One of the three troopers the Servant had brought with him was visible through the dining room doorway. He was standing at the island in the kitchen eating a sandwich. Next to him Marcy was still unconscious in her chair. Blood covering the flesh of her face that he could see through the hair hanging from her drooping head.

The Servant was nowhere to be seen, but the old man could hear the younger man's voice behind him out on the porch giving a report to someone.

"We apprehended the Servant shortly before dawn at the home of Citizen Albert Jenkins, and have been questioning them both. The Servant has not explained why she is here" his tone implied that this was only temporary, and that she would soon tell him what ever he wanted to know. "Citizen Jenkins has denied understanding why the Servant came here, or knowing the location of the three Servants assigned to him" his tone held a hint of doubt as to whether this was true or not.

"Continue with your questioning, and see that the Sinners are exposed Servant" the voice was scratchy as it came through the speaker on the Servants phone.

The old man smiled a bare hint of movement at the corners of his lips making him want to cringe from the pain it caused, but didn't, knowing it would only generate more. They had beaten Marcy because she was a Servant, and it didn't matter but he was a Citizen so on him they had used their Shockers. Sending what felt like thousands of volts of electricity coursing through him over and over again until the Servant began asking his questions in the same even tone as the day before.

The Servant and his three troopers had shown up only minutes after Marcy had wakened him with frantic pounding on his front door. All she had had time to tell him was that she had killed Adam Durum, the owner of the hardware store in town. Then the Servant had entered the door like the house belonged to him, and they were intruders he had caught.

One of the men had brought chairs from the dinning room table into the living, and they had been strapped in. The men had started their work until the last thing he remembered was passing out from the pain. Now if he judged correctly, by the light outside and the heat that had him sweating, it was nearly noon, and the men were about to start again.

"You are awake, Citizen" the Servant said coming around the old man's chair to look down at him for a moment before continuing. "You wish something to drink perhaps before we begin" his tone was courteous as if the old man was a guest, and all his needs were to be taken care of.

"You know I wouldn't mind a glass of tea." The old man tried to make his voice casual as he spoke around teeth gritted in pain at the movement of so many protesting muscles.

"Bring the Citizen a glass of tea" the Servant called over his shoulder loud enough for the men in the kitchen to hear, but never took his eyes off the old man. "And bring some water to clean up the Sinner" he added still starring at the old man as if trying to decide things about him through observation.

A couple of minutes later the trooper who had been using the Shocker on him came into the room with a glass of tea in his hand. Standing beside the old man he held the glass to his lips, and the old man began to drink. The man was careful not to pour more than the old man could swallow so as not to choke him. The old man noticed that he had the same indifferent expression on his face as he had had when pulling the trigger on the Shocker. Neither animosity nor sympathy showed if he felt them, just a soldier doing what he was told. When the old man raised his chin a little the man dropped the bottom of the glass, and pulled it away careful not to spill any on the old man while doing so.

"Citizen" the Servant's voice drew the old man's eyes to him. "No one has ever been able to lie to me. Yet your story has almost convinced me that you are without Sin. Except that it requires far too many coincidences to have transpired for it to be true. I could accept one or two, but so many events you claim are mere chance are impossible for me to accept." The Servant did not seem angry with the old man though there was a touch of anger in his voice, it seemed more directed at himself for some reason the old man could not fathom.

The other two troopers had arrived with two large pots from the kitchen filled with hot water, wisps of steam rising into the air and disappearing, and dish towels. One of them was holding Marcy's head up while the other used one of the towels dampened in the water to wash away the blood from her face. The old man watched out of the corner of his eye while his main attention was focused on the Servant.

"Perhaps, so many coincidences are at the direction of someone who wishes to avoid notice by implicating another" the old man said trying to put as much consideration in his voice as the painful muscles would allow. He looked up at the soldier, and the man held the glass for him to take another drink. The tea slacked his considerable thirst, and distracted from his desire to have a cigar.

"You suggest that someone is trying to hide behind you" the Servant asked though he seemed to be considering the possibility.

"Servant I **know** I am without Sin, I only offer explanations of events that make sense to me." *And hopefully continue confusing you* the old man thought. The man was right he could sniff a lie better than the little pup could food. So the old man had been careful to tell only the truth, but in such a way as to misdirect the Servant's reasoning. That was his one chance to come out of this alive, the man was analytical in his reasoning, but he relied on finding lies then focusing on finding the truth behind them. The old man had kept him running in circles so far hoping to set his focus on some one he already suspected.

Marcy was his only true weakness, his source of two lies already, but delivered in questions that had set the Servant's thinking towards the Council in search of a culprit. The girl had managed to hold her own so far, following the old man's quickly whispered warning before they were taken, about not telling a lie to the Servant. But now she was hurt. A slip of the

199

tongue in a moment of weakness, or just giving in to the pain, and revealing all she knew to escape it, either would be fatal to the old man. He couldn't die yet there was so much left to do, he prayed the girl could hold out a little longer.

"What of the Sinner, Citizen, she has not explained why she came here after committing murder" the Servant asked as if reading the old mans thoughts. Then nodded to where the two soldiers were still cleaning the blood from Marcy's face and hair. This was where the questioning had ended earlier. Marcy refusing to answer, and one of the soldiers beating her till the Servant asked the question again then the beating continuing when she didn't answer.

"Who can say why a Servant so deeply involved in Sin with a Councilman suddenly decides to kill him. Maybe the guilt was too much for her" the old man avoided the question, and hopefully once again sent the man's thinking back to the Council in search of a culprit. Evidently from what the man said most of them were in his custody now along with several of the Deputy Magistrates.

"Yet that was not the question I asked Citizen" the Servant said a glimmer of suspension in his voice.

"If I can not understand the one, how could I know the other Servant" the old man said crisply trying to cover the lie while not appearing to be trying to do so.

"So you know of no reason why this Sinner would come to you Citizen" the man thought he finally had his lie, and nothing would distract him.

"If the Sinner had not produced a reasonable explanation for being here, I would have phoned the Magistrate's office, and recommended her hanging tomorrow when I found out about the murder of Citizen Durum." The old man refused to lie outright, the man would catch it instantly, but if he could just continue seeming to answer the question with out actually doing so he might have a chance.

"And the three Servants that have disappeared" the Servant asked seeming to accept the old man's words for an answer.

"As I said when I woke up they were not here" lying by omission was nearly as bad so the old man held to the only part of the story that was the whole truth. The women had not been here when he woke up, and it had actually been a surprise that none of them had appeared yet. He half hoped that they would show up, and save him, but feared the eventual consequences of such an action.

"Very well then shall we see if the Sinner has anything new to say?" The Servant walked over to where the soldiers were picking up the pots, and quickly stepped back to give the man access to the now cleaned Marcy.

The soldiers had left her head leaning back over the low chair back, her bruised and swollen face pointed towards the ceiling. Her lips were split in several places, her nose appeared broken the tip pointing sharply to the left. Both eyes were puffed to the point that she probably could not open them if she was awake. Reaching out a hand the Servant grasped the woman's bent nose and with a quick pull and twist reset it in place. The sudden pain caused the woman to cry out, and shake her head for a moment before trying to look around through narrow slits between her swollen lids.

"You are awake then Sinner" the Servant said taking a step back, and motioning to one of the soldiers. The man quickly took one of the damp cloths, and stepped to the side of Marcy's chair to hold it against her nose, and staunch the fresh flow of blood. After a few minutes he pulled the cloth away to see that the bleeding had stopped. The Servant had stood impassively waiting during this time.

"Shall we begin where we left off Sinner" the Servant's tone said he was not really seeking her permission.

"What do you know about Noah, Sinner" the Servant asked softly, and in that moment of pain and confusion when

201

he did not ask the question she expected Marcy glanced at the old man through her swollen lids.

"Nothing" she managed to mumble through her swollen lips, but the lie was clear in her words even to the old man. He knew that it was too late anyway the Servant had him now.

"So you are the one they call Noah, Citizen" the Servant said conviction in his voice as he turned to look at the old man. "I have suspected as much from the time I first met you, but you hide yourself well in plain sight. You almost had me convinced I was mistaken" his tone said he found this a surprise.

"And now what Servant" the old man asked, and glanced up at the soldier who held the glass for him to drink from again since not being told to do otherwise.

"Now retribution for your Sins will be exacted Sinner." The Servant did not sound satisfied or displeased with this announcement just that it was what would happen next to the old man. He was no longer Citizen but Sinner now the old man noticed.

"You mean I'll be hung" the old man grinned considering the implication, and what the experience might be like. He had so much left to do, but it was up to the boy now, and that was that.

"Yes" the Servant walked over to look down at him. "In the Square tomorrow at noon you will be hung by the neck until dead, the ceremony broadcast world wide to show that the High Chancellor's will can not be thwarted. Your body will be burned to ash then the ashes scattered so that nothing shall remain of you" the man seemed no more excited about this than the old man was about a grocery list.

"What about you, Servant" the old man asked looking at the man with sympathy shining in his old eyes for the Servant's empty life. "What will you do after I am gone from this world" he wanted to scream at the man that he was wrong in his fanatical beliefs in the High Chancellor, but it would be of no use. But perhaps a little doubt could be given root, and maybe grow giving rise to questions as it spread.

"I will await my next assignment from the High Chancellor." The man showed anticipation for this, perhaps the first real glimmer of emotion the old man had seen in him so far.

"I feel sorry for you son" the old man said the sadness thick in his voice. "You have such talent, but you waste it serving a woman who is not worthy of your loyalty" the old man shook his head in regret.

"You will not speak of the High Chancellor as a mere woman" the Servant looked at the soldier holding the glass of tea. The man used his free hand to hit the old man square on the temple causing pain to go shooting through his head as it rocked. "The High Chancellor is a goddess showing us the way to life with out Sin" the man sounded as if he could not understand why the old man could not see this simple truth.

"Boy, you should be chasing a pretty girl, and thinking about starting a family not praising a woman who has become..." the blow sent his head reeling and dark spots appeared in his vision. "...the living embodiment of true sin" the old man continued as he blinked the spots away.

"You would be advised to keep your opinions to yourself" the Servant's tone was a warning, but he was indifferent to the old man's comfort now. The guest had insulted his host, and was no longer to be cared for. "I would not have you beaten beyond recognition before tomorrow" he waved a hand at Marcy's swollen face.

"Ignoring the truth won't change it, boy" the old man said with a grin waiting for the next blow, but it did not fall so he continued. "What your faith has done in the name of that witch" the blow landed harder than before. The old man's upper plate of teeth flew from his mouth and slid across the floor. "Will be punished with fire and death" his words sounded jumbled, his breath whistling without the teeth, but they were distinguishable enough for the soldier to swing another fist into the side of his head.

The Servant walked over, and picked the false teeth from the floor, turning them over in his hands as he inspected them while walking back to the old man. His eyes rose from them to study the old man for a moment before he held them out, and inserted them back into the old man's mouth. "Gag him so that he can not continue his blasphemies then call for transport" his words were meant for the soldier, but his eyes stayed on the old man as he worked the teeth into place once more.

"I am disappointed that you were not the righteous Citizen I thought you might actually be Sinner." He turned away walking around the old man as the soldier followed his orders producing a gag from one of his many pockets. He was neither gentle nor rough in tying it around the old man's mouth just doing as he was ordered. Then he pulled a phone from another pocket, and made the call for transport then replaced it, and stood in place awaiting his next orders.

"I'm so sorry" Marcy mumbled between swollen lips. Her bruised and puffed face turned towards the old man, and tilted back as she tried to look at him through the slits of her swollen eyelids.

The old man tried to smile, but the gag only allowed the corner of his lips to stretch a little wider. He did not think she could see the assurance in his eyes that said he knew it was not her fault. They had never really had a chance at escaping the Servant the old man knew that now.

"When the transport arrives take them to town, and secure them with the other Sinners" the Servant said from the doorway behind the old man. "Burn the house and barn" the man's voice was empty giving no evidence to his feelings on destroying two lives, and the home of the old man.

Fire

Tears were filling the old man's eyes as the soldier released the ties on his arm, and cuffed it to the other before releasing it from the chair. After removing the bindings on his legs the soldier pulled him to his feet. With a strong grip on his arm the man led him outside behind Marcy, and the soldier holding her. The Servant was backing his car down the drive as they walked down the steps of the porch, and he paid them no attention as he started down the rode to town.

The tears started to fall as the old man stood in the yard beside Marcy, and smoke began to billow out of the windows of the house. The third soldier was quickly completing the order to burn the house. In minutes fire was taking the place of the smoke, licking up the outside walls, and spreading across them quickly. The old man saw the soldier cross from the back of the house to the barn as the glass in the windows began to shatter from the heat, the sound like gun shots in the still hot air making the old man jump at the startling bursts.

Disappearing through the barn door the old man could still see the soldier in his mind walking across the dark bare earth that was cool in the barns shadow. Searching the number of containers in a cabinet on the far wall across from the door till he found the red metal one holding fuel oil. Then opening the lid, and smelling the contents before sloshing it on the walls around the inside, and over the door then coming back outside trailing a line of the flammable liquid. The soldier appeared a few minutes later doing just so leaving a line of the thin oil on the ground till he was a good distance from the barn. Then tossing the nearly empty can back through the barn doors he produced a packet of matches from one of his pockets.

Striking one of the paper matches on the coarse strip along the back of the packet the soldier dropped it to the trail. The old man could see the flames racing along it, and into the barn then there was a whoosh of air as the fumes and fuel oil inside suddenly burst into flame. The concussion was powerful enough to blow the back doors open, the old man could hear them slap against the walls. Fear gripped the old man's heart as the thought that the fire might destroy the door entered his mind.

All is in your hands now boy, I'm sorry I won't be there to help you see the truth the tears continued to fall, and the old man did not try to stop them. Sometimes it was right to cry for what is lost, and can never be again.

By the time the transport arrived to take them away the house was a raging column of fire shooting high into the air. The barn was covered in flames, and was on the point of becoming a fire storm like the house when the old man was pulled away. The soldier half dragged, half carried the old man to the back of the van, and up the steps. Sitting the old man down in one of the hard plastic seats the soldier secured the seat belt around his waist while another brought Marcy in, and set her opposite him. Just before the door slammed shut the old man thought he heard the roar of the barn fire finally reaching the point where the flames shooting skyward were sucking the needed air into the base of the fire to create a fire storm.

As soon as the soldiers had strapped themselves in one of them pounded on the wall and the van immediately started backing out of the drive. The old man felt it lurch a little as the driver turned onto the road then the force of it starting down the road made him lean against his seat belt. The old man began feeling the first signs of motion sickness, he had always hated riding in the back of a vehicle, and his stomach never let the trip be an easy one.

By the time they reached town he was just short of vomiting, and desperately wanted out of the van. When it finally came to a stop he was impatient to have his seat belt off, and the door open. With the gag he feared he might get choked on his vomit and die before they had a chance to hang him. He considered the option for a moment both forms were suffocation, and hanging was probably the more painful, but dying with the taste of vomit in his mouth was not all that appealing.

His line of thought was interrupted by the door swinging open, and the blast of fresh air quelling his stomachs threat to expel its contents. The soldiers removed their seat belts then led them out the back of the van, and the old man took a look around surprised at where they were.

He had expected the Moralists Square and the Magistrates Hall instead they were in the residential district on the north side of town in front of the former Magistrate's home. The soldiers led them up the walk to the front door as the van pulled away then into the front room of the large house where all the furniture had been removed. Sitting on the floor along the walls around the room were the Magistrates and Councilmen the Servant had taken into custody.

"You may speak to ask for water, or to use the restroom, otherwise say nothing, or you will be punished" the soldier holding the old man's arm said as he released him, and started removing his gag. Then he unlocked one of the cuffs around the old man's wrist, and holding it stepped around in front of him grasping the free arm before the old man could even shake a little feeling back into it. Securing the cuff around the wrist once more the man nodded to the room, and stepped aside to allow the old man to choose a sitting place.

Working his jaw and lips where the gag had been the old man looked at his options for a moment then turned his head to the soldier. "I could use both a drink and the restroom boy" the old man said expecting a blow for his tone. But the soldier just nodded, and took his arm again leading the old man through a door that led into a large room that had been the dinning room. Now the table was pushed against the wall and the furniture from the living room filled the area.

"In here" the soldier motioned with his free hand to a door that led to a small room with only a commode and sink.

"Do not close the door" the man warned, and released the old man's arm, but remained standing beside the door as the old man shuffled through it.

Like there's anything I could do if it was closed the old man thought looking around the room. No window to escape through and nothing, but a set of plastic shelves that held toilet paper, towels and wash cloths. After relieving himself the old man took one of the wash cloths from the shelf, and turned the hot water tap on letting the water run till it felt warm to the touch. Soaking the cloth the old man washed his face, arms and chest. He had thrown on a pair of pajama bottoms before answering the door, but had not had time to dress before the Servant had arrived. Wringing out the cloth the old man laid it across the bottom of the sink to dry, and went back out to look at the soldier expectantly.

The soldier took the old man's arm once more, and led him back into the living room where he released his arm. The old man smiled at Marcy now trying to reassure her that it was not her fault they were there as the other soldier led her past on the way to the restroom. Looking around the room the old man chose a spot near the window so he could at least see outside, and walked across to it dropping down to the floor.

James Baker the old man's neighbor was sitting across the room starring at him though he had a feeling the man was not really seeing him. James's eyes were black, his nose appeared broken, the lower half of his face was covered in dried blood, and he looked defeated as he sat with his shoulders slumped, and drawn in around him. None of the others appeared in any better shape, they had all been beaten their faces swollen, and bruised with dried blood covering most of them.

After all the pain you have caused it is the least you deserve the old man thought looking at them. *Now we're all going to hang, and you look as if you're already dying. You sorry bunch of fools* the old man could find no sympathy for any of them. *Now all we can do is wait for the moment* the old man turned his head and attention away from the men and women who only a day before had been the most powerful in the district.

Out the window he could see the leaves of a large oak that was in the front yard, and a sky that was pale blue in the summer heat. It was afternoon, but the sun was out of his view as he was looking mostly southwest by his estimation. *Now all we can do is wait Tizzy* he thought once more. Using that thought he started a conversation with the woman aware of everything happening around him, but withdrawing into pleasant memories of life with his beloved wife.

Angie was mad, frustrated, and worried which was why she was pacing back and forth in front of the open door of the barracks. Noah was still sleeping on his bed, and the little pup still slept on the other. This was the source of her frustration. She wanted the boy to wake up so they could go through the door, and find out what was happening to Albert. The old man was the reason for her worry, she knew something bad had happened to him, and she wanted to go help him. The source of her anger was sitting on Jen's bed next to the woman, and occasionally Martha would give the girl a look that said she was being foolish wasting energy that she would need later.

Noah's little band was sitting on their beds, or on the floor sharpening knifes or spear points. Four of them in a little group at the far wall were rolling dice. Their calls after each toss subdued, and they all were constantly looking in the direction of the older woman sitting next to Noah. She had lit into them when they had raised their voices higher than a whisper.

Outside the open door the rain had started again, a heavy down pour that nearly hid the barracks across the open grassy area. She hated the rain; it was cold and darkening the already late afternoon to the point that it looked more like night had fallen. She wanted to douse the boy with a bucket of that rain water to wake him up. She knew Albert needed them, but the older woman insisted that the boy needed his rest. She had caught Angie by the head of the hair and pulled her away from him when the older woman thought Angie was going to try waking the boy. In truth she was, but the woman didn't have to pull her hair out to stop her. Since then Angie had been pacing in front of the door.

She had been there hours earlier when the boy Elmo had come running out of a shower, and through the door nearly colliding with her. The boy was barely a teenager, and was one of the pair that Jamie had sent to the door to relieve the two there after the first rains had come. He had stepped quickly to avoid her, and looked embarrassed at nearly running her down then had walked over to give his report to Jamie and Jen.

"The paint started bubbling on the door, then caught fire and burned off. The metal was glowing red like it was about to melt, but the rain started in cooling it down some. Kat was dousing it with what she could catch in her hands when I left" the boy had spoken loud enough for the whole room to hear.

Jamie had given a quick look to Jen then over at one of the young men now dicing, and a half dozen of them had followed him, and the boy Elmo back out the door. When they returned later Jamie said the door was still getting hot. Though not enough he thought to melt, but he had left four people there collecting, and pouring water on it to keep it cool.

Maybe the rain was a blessing Angie considered, but she still didn't like the way it weighed on her. She felt like it was trapping her in this room and in a sudden burst of defiance she turned abruptly, and went out the door into the down pour. The rain striking her upturned face was cold, but it felt good on her hot flesh as it soaked into her hair and clothes. She had not realized she was so hot until the rain cooled her, and being out in it now reminded her of when she was a child. The memory spurred her to stomp in the puddles around her helping her vent her emotions as well. When she finally began to feel a chill she turned back to the door, and grinned at the startled looks on everyone's faces who were watching her display. Until her eyes fell on Martha the older woman was looking at her as if she was a child in need of a spanking for her foolish behavior.

"Did the rain cool your temper child" the woman asked when Angie passed back through the door. Her tone was mocking, and Angie's anger cranked back up to full in an instant.

"My temper is just fine" Angie said tartly. Though she thought the heat of her anger should have been steaming the water she was soaked with.

"Children and their tantrums" the older woman said with a shake of her head as she returned her attention back to the afghan she was knitting.

Stomping her foot in frustration, and leaving a muddy print on the wooden floor boards she resumed her pacing; from the bed on one side of the door across the boards to the bed on the other side leaving a trail of water droplets now, and mud from her shoes. Her mind whirled with all the possibilities her imagination could conjure about what was happening to Albert, and they did not ease her worry. But she could not stop the thoughts from coming if she had wanted to, and she did not want to. She lashed her self with them, punishment for leaving the old man alone.

The sun had sunk below the horizon long since, Angie as well as the floor boards were dry, the mud gone back to dirt, and the dirt pounded to dust under her shoes when the boy finally roused. He opened his eyes to see Martha look over at him with eyes that seemed to bore into him seeking signs of something in the depths of his eyes. Satisfied she smiled at him.

"Welcome back to the land of the living boy" she said sitting her knitting to the side, and rising to step over to the boy's bed. "How are you feeling" she asked as he turned himself over, and looked at Jamie and Jen sitting together on the other side.

"Weak" he answered honestly. Lifting the hand with the IV still in it to look at the line connected to it. Then he followed the line with his eyes to the bag hanging from the bed post.

"Not surprising after what you have been through" she reached a hand out taking his upraised wrist in it. "Any dizziness or nausea" she looked at the watch she had pulled from a pocket then back at him as she silently counted heartbeats.

"No just weak" he said looking at his arm where the wounds were still visible. Though the holes were now beginning to scab over, and looked like they would heal quickly. "What happened" his voice squeaked a little as the memory of the dream, and the thorns flashed into his mind as he spoke.

"You nearly died" Jen said on the other side of him kneeling to rest a hand on his shoulder, and look him over as well. "If it hadn't been for this stubborn little pup you would have." She leaned back for him to see the little pup still asleep lying on the bed behind her.

"He saved me" his voice carried more doubt than question.

"He did boy" Martha confirmed as she released his wrist seeming satisfied with his heart rate. "Can you set up" she asked looking down at him with an arched eyebrow.

"What time is it we have to go" he said looking out the open door seeing the darkness, and started to hastily sit up, but Jen held him down for a moment.

"You have been asleep all day Noah" she took her hand away when she saw the information register.

"Why didn't you continue with the plan" he looked at Jamie his tone questioning, but not blaming simply wanting a report.

"Something has happened to Albert, and we have to go find out what." Angie answered from the foot of the bed her tone urgent as if she wanted him to go now.

The boy looked at her for a moment seeing the fear in her eyes then looked back at Jamie waiting to give his report. Nodding to the young man to begin the boy swung his legs over that side of the bed, and managed just barely to sit up with the two women's help.

"Something has happened to the old man, we don't know what" Jamie was saying. "Earlier the door caught on fire, but we have the fire out, and Marshal has his squad up there now" Jamie looked at him with concern in his eyes as the boy hung his head fighting the dizziness that now swamped his senses.

"The door was on fire" the boy mumbled as he reached up with both hands to hold his head for a moment.

"I think the barn caught fire" Jamie's voice said it was the only explanation he could think of.

"Does it still work" the boy looked at him through tear filled eyes as his head started pounding. Those little men were back in full force again, and determined to get through his skull in minutes.

"We won't know that till you try to open it, boy" Martha said behind him. "Is your head hurting" she asked motioning for Jen to hand her the satchel still lying on the floor beside her.

"Just a tad" his tone was thick with sarcasm as he moved a hand to glance at her over his shoulder.

"We have to go find out what happened to Albert" Angie nearly screamed from the foot of the bed as if volume would lend weight to her words.

"Give him some time girl" Martha's sharp tone did nothing to squelch the urgency in the younger woman's eyes. "Here, boy, take a couple of these" she said pulling out a bottle from the satchel, and shaking out two pills then handing them to the boy. Jen held out a cup of water for him to drink with them. "I'd give you a shot of something more powerful, but I don't think you'd want to be loopy for a few hours do you" she grinned at the boy as she returned the bottle to the satchel, and set it down on the floor beside her.

"No, not really" he answered looking at the large white pills in his hand. "How is the pup doing" the boy asked after downing the pills, and all the water. He felt dried out, and when he handed the cup back to Jen he gave her a look that asked for more.

"He'll live though I doubt he'll be in much better shape than you when he wakes" Martha said as Jen refilled the cup, and passed it to the boy. "Could you eat something solid boy" she eyed him as if trying to determine the answer herself.

"I'm just weak not sick" the boy gave her a haughty look to accompany his sarcastic tone.

"With a headache" she said letting his tone and look both roll off her.

"And a headache" he agreed in a more moderated tone. The little men had to be nearly through his skull by now, but their pounding had certainly not slackened any.

"Girl, since you don't mind getting wet" Martha looked at Angie standing at the foot of the bed, and her eyes sharpened when the younger woman started to protest. "You can run over to my house, and fetch the boy something to eat." Martha watched the girl turn, and a wicked smile bloomed on her face at the stiff backed way she walked away from the bed. "Bring those other two and Able back with you when you come" Martha's tone held a mocking quality to match the grin on her face.

"You shouldn't treat her like that" Jen's tone held as much disapproval as her eyes that were fixed on Martha's face.

"The girl's got good metal in her, but it needs tempering yet" Martha said looking across the bed at the younger woman a warning in her eyes that said not to interfere with her again. "Now, boy let's get this out of you" she placed a thumb on the IV, and ripped the tape away in one quick movement. The boy looked at her, and started to say something when she pulled the needle free of the skin, the jolt of pain shutting him down. Putting a cotton ball over the bleeding hole she used another

214

piece of tape to hold it in place. "Didn't hurt a bit did it boy" she smiled at him as if daring him to say otherwise.

"Felt like you took half my hand off" the boy said accepting the challenge, and grinning at her, waiting to see if she would throw a jab in return.

"Would you help me get dressed Jen" he asked when the older woman seemed to have lost the desire to spar further. The young woman nodded smiling past him at Martha triumphantly then gently began to help the boy get dressed.

"So you're the one who saved me" the boy said as he shrugged into his shirt with Jen's help looking over at the other bed where the little black pup's eyes were open looking back at him. "Can you break up one of those pills in some water for him" he asked over his shoulder to Martha who had retreated to her knitting. "If his head feels anything like mine he could use it" he was still considering asking for that shot. The little men had gone into a frenzy of pounding with his dressing.

"I'll give him half of one" Martha said sitting the knitting aside, and reaching for the satchel. "Has your headache not slackened any" she sounded surprised.

"Not a bit that I can tell" the boy admitted, as he turned standing up into sliding off the bed to his knees. Unfortunately Jen saw his face, and was not fooled even when he made his way on his knees over to the little pup. "Thanks for the help" he said softly to the little pup who tried to lift his head and lick the boys hand, but failed in his effort, and let his head fall back to the blanket. "Take it easy" the boy said gently stroking the little pup's ear knowing how much he liked it. "We'll get you fixed up in no time" the boy assured him though he hoped the little pup wasn't suffering any more than he was, or else it might drive him insane. Those little men and their hammers were doing a fair job of it for him.

"Can I have some more of that water Jen" he asked the young woman who was watching him with alert eyes ready to reach out and catch him if need be. She nodded though and poured him a glass full then passed it to him still managing to keep one eye on him the whole time.

"Hand me that cup, boy" Martha said coming around his empty bed with the satchel in one hand, the other stretched out for the cup. Taking the already empty cup Martha sat on the bed behind him, and pulled a small wooden bowl from the depths of the satchel. Taking the bottle of pain pills she dropped one into the bowl, and took out a stone awl then began grinding the pill up. Dumping the powder into the glass she took out another pill only this time she left half of the powder in the bowl. "Fill it" she said to Jen and held out the cup.

"Drink it all, boy" she said giving him a look that said he wasn't fooling her, and that she could tell he was lying against the bed more than sitting on the floor while Jen filled the cup, and passed it to him. "If that doesn't help we'll go to something a little more drastic" she patted the satchel with her free hand then held out the bowl for the young woman to fill with water as well. "Stir it up, and make sure it's all dissolved before you give it to him" she advised nodding to the little pup.

"Ugh, you ain't gonna like that dog" the boy said after downing the glass of water, and grinned at the little pup as Jen poured water into the bowl, and stirred it with her finger then passed it across to him.

"Come on, boy, drink this, and it'll make you feel better I hope" the boy said holding the bowl next to the little pup's mouth, and helping him raise up to drink the bitter liquid. The little pup was either extremely thirsty, or knew that it would help because he drank it all down before lying his little head back down.

"So you're finally awake, boy" Able said loudly as he came through the door followed by Susie and Heather. "We'd about decided you'd sleep for a week" he grinned broadly, and shook the rain from his hair causing the two women behind him to grimace as the droplets struck them in the face.

216

"Do you mind" Heather said testily as she stepped around the large man, and walked over to look down at the boy. "Well, you're out of the bed how long before we can go to the door" she sounded as if she would carry the boy if need be.

"As soon as I can stand up" the boy said grinning at Able around the woman. "How's the weather out there" he asked looking at the man's soaked coat and trousers.

"Wind's changed, and the temperature is dropping" the man said pulling his coat off, and shaking it out. "We'll have snow before daylight I figure" the man shook his head at his own predication. "Early in the year for snow, but it is still coming" he looked at the boy seeing him lying against the bed. "Boy you alright or not" he tossed the coat across the foot of the empty bed.

"He's weak as a new born" Jen said when she saw that the boy was about to give an off handed comment that would be far from the truth, and giving him a look that said not to argue.

"Well, maybe Jen's right" the boy said making it sound like he didn't agree, but you couldn't argue with a woman when she thought she was right.

"I'd say she probably is boy, just by looking at you" Able gave the young woman a nod of agreement.

"What if we carried him up to the door" Susie asked her voice anxious as she stepped to the side of Able to look down at the boy.

"The boy is just out of his death bed, and you girls only want to put him into the grave" Martha shook her head at the younger woman disapprovingly her tone saying they were being foolish.

"We are just concerned about Albert" Heather said stepping over to stand on the opposite side of the bed the little pup was lying on. "How is your savior doing" she asked the boy as she leaned over to take a closer look at the little pup.

"About the same as me" the boy said with a grin looking up at the woman as she reached out a hand to stroke the little

217

pup's back, and seeing the concern in her eyes that he felt was for both of them, and the old man as well.

"Could you help me, Able" the boy said holding out a hand to the large man. When his own attempt to rise had resulted in the leg he was sitting on nearly putting him on his face in the floor.

"Are you sure, boy" Able asked his eyes doubting as he took the boys hand. "Maybe you should get back in that bed" he added when the boy didn't seem to make any effort to rise, and he had to pull him to his feet.

"Been there big man" the boy said with a tight smile. Leaning his weight against Able for a moment as his vision swarmed with flashing lights, and those little men intensified their efforts to break out of his head. "Don't care to go back" he added his smile stretching into a grin as he forced his knees to lock, and take his own weight.

"Don't drop him, Able" Martha said as she strode past, her anger at the boy evident in her tone, and the force of her feet striking the floor boards with each step. "Bring him over here" she ordered briskly striding to the end of the room where Elmo and three others were sitting around the room's one table. "Make some room for the boy" she ordered waving them away from the table. "Sit him down here, Able" she commanded turning the chair that Elmo was barely out of around, and giving the boy an agitated look as the large man half carried him over.

"Thanks" the boy said sincerely to the larger man after he eased him down into the chair. He wanted to hold his head in his hands it might cushion the blows of those little men's hammers, but instead rested them on his knees, and focused on clearing his vision of the flashing lights.

"Do you really think it's going to snow" he heard Jamie ask the big man.

"Afraid so, it happens sometimes, this time of the year. The wind'll blow hard out of the north, and freeze everything, but it won't last long. Once the storm is past the sun'll melt it all again" Able said absently watching the boy as he seemed on the verge of falling out of the chair, or just sliding out of it. The boy's body seemed to barely have enough strength in it to hold its own shape.

"Where is that blasted girl" Martha said to no one in particular as she looked at the open door. As if the question summoned her, Angie walked through the doorway. A heavy coat draped over her with one arm pulling it past her head to add another layer of protection from the rain for the cloth covered tray she held in front of her with the other arm.

Shrugging off the coat, letting it fall to the floor, she took a better grip on the tray as she crossed the room, and set it on the table next to the boy. "Eat, Albert is waiting on us" she said simply jerking the cloth away to reveal a plate of fried ham, mashed potatoes, carrots, peas, and a bowl of the same. She picked up the bowl, and turned away walking over to drop down beside the bed with the little pup, and held it out to him. He lifted his head sniffing at the aromas then slowly began to nibble at the food.

"Thank you" he called to her, and picked up the knife and fork lying on the tray beside the plate. Cutting a piece of the ham off he stuffed it in his mouth looking up as he started chewing to see most everyone looking at him. The exceptions were Angie feeding the little black pup, and Jamie who was giving instructions to Elmo and Kat. Probably on the coming weather change for those up at the door the boy decided as the two youngsters started gathering their things, and headed out the doorway. Glancing after them the boy saw that indeed the wind had changed direction and was blowing fiercely now driving the rain downward at a sharp slant. The temperature was falling too he noticed feeling the chill gathering in the room. He was thankful to see that Jamie was starting to build a fire on the hearth that was in the center of the room.

Rolling the peas and carrots into the mashed potatoes he took a fork full, and popped it into his mouth chewing as he cut another slice of ham off. "What do you think Jen" he asked before putting the ham into his mouth, and waved the fork with the piece of ham on the end of it at the chair on the side of the little table next to him.

"I think that we are going into a real fight if we cross that door, and you don't need to do so till you have your strength back" the young woman said crossing the room to sit down in the chair. Resting her elbow on the table, and setting her chin in the palm of her hand, she looked at him with deep resolve on her face.

"I'd say you were right" the boy agreed around the piece of ham in his mouth before continuing to chew.

"What do you mean" Susie asked angrily as she crossed the room to take the seat opposite Jen. "Albert needs us now" she added her tone pleading and demanding at the same time.

"The old man has been captured, and as long as he keeps his mouth shut nothing will happen to him till they hang him" Jamie said across the room, rising from the now blazing fire on the hearth, and starting across the room towards the open door. "The Magistrates fired the house and barn. It's something they always do when they take someone who has caused them as much trouble as the old man has" he swung the door closed, and turned towards the table. "There will be a number of soldiers on the other side of the door waiting, and watching for who ever comes to investigate including us" he crossed over to the table as he spoke looking at Susie with a meaningful expression. They were going to have to kill the soldiers.

"Are you ready to kill to get the old man back" the boy asked Susie with a wondering in his tone as if considering whether she could or not. He took another bite of the vegetables while looking at her, most of the flashing lights in his vision were gone, and he could see most of her shocked face.

"Kill" the young woman said the word with revulsion and fear as she stared wide eyed at the boy.

"You don't think they are just going to hand the old man over because we ask nicely do you" Jen's tone was sarcastic as she looked at the frightened woman. "Or maybe you expected us to do all the killing for you" her tone was scathing this time.

"How about you big man" the boy turned his head to look over his shoulder at Able. "Do you or any of your people want the old man back enough to kill for him" the boy's tone said he doubted that there were.

"I'd kill a hundred soldiers for Albert" Martha said when Able hesitated, her voice and expression leaving no doubt that she meant what she said.

"There are a few I could call on" Able agreed giving the woman a sharp look for jumping in ahead of him. "Most would be too scared to be of much use though" he looked back at the boy who had returned his attention to the food.

"I'll kill for him" the woman's voice drew all eyes around to look at Heather kneeling down beside the bed across from Angie. Her face looked as frightened as Susie's, but her jaw was set, and a look of determination was edging the fear out of her eyes.

"We'll see" the boy said taking the last bite of ham, and chewing on it as he looked at her for a moment before turning to drop the fork onto the now empty plate. His vision was clear now, but the little men were still hammering at his skull though most seemed to have given up in their endeavor. His body felt stronger, but still too weak for him to want to try standing up just yet. "Could I have some more water Jen" he asked politely smiling at the young woman as she rose, and retrieved the pitcher and glass that Angie passed to her when she reached the bed the little pup was on.

"He looks better" the boy nodded to where the little pup was licking the last of the potatoes from the bowl sitting on the bed in front of him. The little pup looked over at him as if hearing the words, and knowing they were about him then returned his attention to the potatoes.

"Thanks Jen" the boy said taking the glass of water she offered him. His insides felt as dried out as an old piece of leather even after downing the whole glass, and drinking half of another. Finishing the glass he held it out, and Jen filled it again then using the table, and chair he managed to make it to his feet. The lights flashed for a moment, and the little men pounded ferociously then after teetering for a moment his vision cleared, and the men resumed their normal rhythm.

"Are you ok" Jen asked standing beside him holding his arm with both hands, and looking into his face intently.

"Just dandy" the boy answered with a grin as he stiffened his knees to keep from sinking back into the chair. "Just a little dizzy from standing up so fast" he assured her seeing the worry in her eyes. He really did feel better now that he was on his feet he realized feeling his heart pounding rapidly, and the blood flowing back into his limbs.

"Ain't we a pair dog" the boy said with a grin at the little black pup who was looking at him with eyes nearly as worried as Jen's had been. Downing the glass of water the boy handed the empty glass to the young woman. "Well let's go see what's going on up at the door. Everybody that wants to come, better get ready" the last was directed at Able and Martha.

"Are you sure you're ready, boy" the large man asked eyeing him still standing, but weaving instead of standing straight.

"I'm sure" the boy said taking a hesitant step towards his bed, and then a more confident one when he didn't fall flat on his face. "By the time you get your friends gathered I'll be fine" the boy assured him nodding towards the door for the man to go get his people.

"You girls come with me" Martha said sweeping a look to the three younger women. "You'll need better clothes than you've got on" she explained when they all started to protest. Then the older woman led them from the room without a backward glance for the boy, or Able who followed after them.

Reaching his bed the boy sat down on the edge, and looked over at the little pup. "How you doing, dog" he asked as he leaned down, and picked up a boot. The little pup's tail slapped against the blanket, but he made no effort to rise as he watched the boy. "Yeah I feel the same way" the boy said as he straightened up holding the boot in his hand for a moment while his vision cleared, and the little men eased up on their hammering.

Struggling through the next round of flashing lights, and pounding hammers the boy got his boot on, and laced up then reached for the other one refusing to wait on them to subside. Lacing it up after getting his foot in it he sat for a moment letting his head ease then reached for his deerskin over shirt, and pulled it on. Leaning over once more he retrieved his pouch, and weapons belt then rose to settle his shirt into place, and slung the pouch's strap across his head pulling it around in place, the pouch resting on his right hip. Swinging one end of the belt around him he caught it with practiced ease, and slid the wide leather up under the pouch, and buckled it in place settling it on his hips comfortably. On his left hip his full quiver rested easily, his long knife's sheath was just in front of the pouch, and behind it was his hatchet. He felt much better being dressed in the familiar outfit, and reached for his unstrung bow and spear leaning against the wall beside the bed.

"Take a minute, and think about it dog" the boy said with a grin directed at the little pup who was now standing on the bed with his head hanging so low his nose was pressed into the blanket. "You look worse off then me" the boy said walking around the bed to retrieve the pitcher of water from the table, and returned to pour some in the bowl still sitting on the bed in front of the little pup.

"If you can't walk any better than that maybe you shouldn't be going" Jen said reaching out a hand to take the pitcher from him, and actually pour some into the bowl.

"I'm walking fine" the boy protested drawing himself back up from leaning over the bed before he fell across it.

"You didn't put one foot in front of the other even once" Jamie said reaching out a steadying hand that turned into a supporting hand for the boy.

"I still got where I was going didn't I" the boy looked at him through the flashing lights, and wished those little men with the hammers would take a break. How long could they swing those darn things with out a little rest?

"Just barely I'd say" Jen said with a grin as she watched the little pup lapping up the water thirstily.

"Huh" was all the boy said as the lights slowed, and a few of the little men took a break finally.

"You're gonna want these Noah" Elisa said walking over to him with a bundle in her arms. "It's already started snowing outside" she added tilting her head back towards the door.

"What are they" the boy asked eyeing the bundle as he leaned his bow and spear against the edge of the bed.

"A coat" the girl said with a grin as she shook the heavy wool out, and handed it to him. "And the man who gave us these called them ponchos" she shook out the other bundle, and waved a hand at the one she was wearing as he shrugged into the coat.

"A poncho" the boy said his tone curious as he took the offered item. It was made of sewn leather making it one piece with a hood in the center covering an open hole where his head went he assumed looking at the one Elisa was wearing. Lifting it over his head he settled it into place over his coat, and worked out the folds to get comfortable.

"They work good to keep the rain and I suppose snow off" Jamie assured him as he patted the one he was wearing.

"Definitely warm" the boy said already feeling his body heat building underneath it and the coat as he picked up his spear and bow. "Are we ready then" he asked looking around at the others who were looking at him with a mixture of worry for him, and determination to see that he was kept safe on their faces.

"We're ready, but are you" Jen asked rising to take the coat and poncho that Jody held for her.

"I'll be fine" the boy assured her, and started to turn towards the door when the little pup whined drawing his attention back to the bed. "Are you sure" he asked the pup who was trying to walk across the bed towards him, but was stumbling more than anything. There was a determination in him though that struck a chord with the boy. "If you're sure then" the boy said as the pup continued towards him, and started to reach out to pick the little pup up.

"I don't think so" Jen said looking at him with a disapproving expression. "You can't walk any straighter than he can" she nodded to where the little pup was wobbling back and forth on the edge on the bed his little head hanging low. "I'll carry him" she conceded seeing the determination in both of them, and reached over picking the little pup up. "You should be staying here for sure" she said to the little pup as she rested him on her hip, and covered him with the poncho to protect him from the weather. "Stop that" she exclaimed surprise in her voice. "He's licking my hand" she explained in a gruff tone to the others who were staring at her questions in their eyes. "Lets go if we're going" exasperation and agitation both in her voice at the grins the others had on their faces now.

"I'll carry those for you, Jen" Jody said picking up her bow and spear with only a small smile on his face when she started to retrieve them herself.

"Thanks Jody" she said her tone sincere. "At least there's one gentleman among this bunch" her tone was back to agitation.

"Yeah, only rogues, thieves, and soon to be murderers here Jen" the boy said looking at each in turn making sure that they all understood what was coming. He saw no hesitation in any of them, and gave a satisfied nod then turned towards the door once again. "Let's go see how Able's doing, I bet he ain't got a dozen men" the boy said with a laugh as he wobbled across the floor till Jamie and Elisa reached his side, and held out hands to steady his meandering walk. He gave them each a sharp look, but settled on accepting their aid since all the little men were pounding away again, but at least the lights weren't flashing as much.

Outside the wind was whipping the heavy snow around, and the boy pulled an arm free from Elisa long enough to cover his head with the poncho's hood then let her take it again. The wind was still cold against his face, and he was glad for the coat and poncho both. Since the large wet snow flakes were quickly covering him as they made their way towards Martha's cabin. The ground was still soggy from the rain beneath his boots, but he could tell that it would not be long before it was frozen solid, then the snow would begin piling up quick.

"Looks like you didn't miss it by much" Jamie said pointing with his spear to Martha's cabin where Able stood with six men and four women. Each of them had a poncho on, and as he got closer the boy could see rifle butts poking up the leather covering their shoulders.

"Looks like they're better armed than us too" the boy said nodding to the bulges.

"Don't mean they can shoot" Elisa said on the other side of him her tone and words making it clear she did not think too highly of the villagers abilities.

"We'll see before long" the boy said noticing that the little group stood in a tight formation that suggested training and discipline.

As they neared the cabin Able turned when the man he was speaking to nodded in their direction. Before he could say anything though the cabin door opened, and Martha led the three women outside all of them covered in the ponchos. Martha had a rifle in her hand, and the three girls had the conspicuous bulges above their shoulders.

"You ready boy" Martha asked tucking her rifle up under her poncho, the barrel holding the bottom up in a bunch just above her knees.

"They know what's expected of them" the boy asked Able ignoring the woman's question.

"We know" the man Able had been speaking to when they walked up answered, his tone indicating he for one had no problem with it.

"Not many considering all the people at the dance last night" Jamie said nodding to the little group.

"Albert told me once that a few lions were better than a whole flock of sheep when it came to fighting boy" Able's tone could have meant that he was looking at the sheep as his eyes surveyed the boy's little band while he spoke.

"We'll see who the sheep are before long big man" Elisa said catching the insinuation apparently, and not liking it by her tone.

"Times wasting boy and it's not getting warmer out here" Martha said looking at the boy from the hood of her poncho with a sharp glint in her eyes.

"Well, then let's go before you freeze" the boy said with a grin, and bowed his head directing the woman that he would follow her led with a wave of his hand.

"Figures, you'd want me to block the wind for you" the older woman snipped as she walked past the boy leading the three younger women who smiled from their hoods at his expression when they pasted.

"Got a tongue like a file don't she, boy" Able said after the woman was gone making sure to keep his voice low so the woman wouldn't hear. "Come on, boy, or she'll leave us behind" the large man grinned from his hood at the boy then nodded to the other man, and led his little group in orderly files after the four women.

"You sure we can't leave them here" Jamie asked his tone mostly joking, but a part of it was serious.

"No I reckon we can't" the boy said answering the serious part then turned, and trailed after the others his little group following.

The trip to the door was uneventful, the snow and darkness hiding the surroundings from view as the two groups marched. The ground became hard from freezing, and snow was beginning to pile up on its surface by the time they started climbing the ridge. The boy struggled to make the climb, but Jamie and Elisa managed to keep him from falling though they both slipped several times in their efforts. When they finally reached the door the boy was surprised by what he saw.

Marshal had three large fires going around the door. Lighting the area brightly which showed his troop standing around the fires trying to stay warm in the blowing snow. The door itself drew the boy's eyes, the paint gone leaving bare metal that was discolored from excessive heat that had to have come from the other side. Martha and the three younger women were standing beside the door, and Able had led his group to the other side all of them waiting on him.

"You're feeling a little better then" Marshal said his tone serious as always, the young man hardly ever joked or smiled. He had noticed the way Jamie and Elisa were nearly holding the boy up though.

"I'm fine, Marshal" the boy said but did not shrug off the aide of the other two, that was his first instinct at the young man's words. His legs felt like jelly again, and he was not sure if he could stand alone.

"What's happened" he nodded at the door.

"Nothing much since we got here, it was hot then, but I don't think there was ever any danger of it melting." He looked around at Elmo who was sitting next to the middle fire. As the man's eyes settled on him, he dropped his head down. "But it's still hot enough to burn so I wouldn't touch it with bare hands" the man advised his tone still serious not trying to make a joke out of the last only offering a warning.

"Good man" the boy said acknowledging the man's efforts. He was a good man in the boy's opinion though many of the others in the group did not see it. The man might not laugh and joke with them, but he was tough, smart, and did not know the meaning of the word quit.

"Shall we see what's on the other side then" the boy said starting towards the door with Jamie and Elisa more or less carrying him along.

When they reached the door the boy could feel the heat radiating off it. Glancing at Elisa who released his arm he

228

reached out a hand still covered with the leather of the poncho, and grasped the handle. Pushing it down and pulling he swung the door open wide, and was hit with a blast of hot air. Then the cold air rushed in as the fire on the other side drew it like a furnace, the force was so strong it nearly pulled the door closed, but Able managed to catch it with a booted foot, and hold it open.

The ramp leading up from the door on the other side was filled with timbers, and boards that were now a raging inferno. Beyond them nothing could be seen, but the boy doubted that much of the barn was left to be seen anyway. Stepping back he looked at Jamie, nodded to the nearest fire, and with his help walked over to plop on the ground beside it. The relief of being off his feet was instant, the lights had quit flashing, but those little men were still hammering away, and his muscles were like wet strings.

"Your head still hurting, boy" Martha asked as she dropped to a knee beside him.

"Like it's about to come off, and I don't know for sure if that wouldn't feel better" the boy answered with a grin that highlighted the pain in his eyes.

"Keep that smart mouth going boy, and I might oblige you" the woman said throwing the poncho back to get at the satchel hanging at her waist. "We'll try these this time, and see if they don't help your head, wish I had something in here for you mouth, but some things just have to be endured don't they, boy." She held out two small capsules that were bright red, and when the boy took them from her she produced a small ceramic jug from a large leather bag on her side. "They'll probably make you feel a little strange" she passed him the jug. "Slow your thinking, maybe slur your speech" she paused tapping a finger against her chin. "Maybe I do have something for that smart mouth of yours after all" she grinned at him as she reached into the pouch once more, and produced a cloth wrapped bundle. "Eat one of these and drink all of that milk" she nodded to the jug as she unwrapped the cloth and handed him a ham sandwich with thick pieces of bread and ham both. "I'm going to check on my other patient, now boy if you start feeling sick you tell me right away you understand." She gave him a sharp look before rising, and walking around the fire to where Jen was sitting with the little pup in her lap.

"How's he doing" she asked dropping to a knee once more beside the young woman.

"He's alive that's about all I can tell you" Jen said looking down at the little pup who was hardly moving his eyes flicking to look up at her for a moment before returning to watching the boy. The boy was filled with pain, the little pup could smell it, but he was no longer worried, the pain would pass, and the boy would live. His own pain was what consumed him at the moment everything hurt as if he had been beaten for hours. He wanted to sleep, but the pain would not allow that any longer, and they were going to the old man. He wanted to see the old man again, feel his soothing hand and quiet words once more to ease this pain away.

"I don't know much about treating dogs" Martha admitted to the younger woman. "But we'll give him another pain pill, plenty of water, and some more food" she threw the poncho back digging in the pouch for a wooden bowl. "I'll give him a whole one this time" she said taking the pill bottle from the satchel. Crushing one of the white pills to powder in the bowl then filling it with water from another jug she had in the large leather bag. "Feed him this" she unwrapped another cloth bundle and handed Jen a piece of ham. "And let him drink as much as he wants" she set the water jug at the young woman's feet.

Returning everything to the bag and satchel she stood up looking at the door where Able and Stephen were starring at the burning pile of timbers on the other side. "I guess I'm going to have to take care of this as well, or we'll be here all night shivering in the cold. You three come with me" she looked at three young men sitting around the fire. They all looked at the boy when she spoke waiting for his command she assumed.

230

"Do they only jump when you command it boy" she asked looking at him as well.

"They don't jump for anybody woman" the boy's tone was angry as he looked at her before continuing. "We don't do anything someone **commands** us to do, but if you **ask** nicely they'll do anything you want them to" the boy explained moderating his tone only a little; more aggravated than angry.

"Would you three be as kind as to accompany me please" her tone was mocking and childish.

"I said nicely" the boy said when the three started to rise then sat back at his words.

"Could you please come with me" her tone was courteous with a sullen undertone this time.

"Now, that wasn't so hard was it" the boy asked grinning at the three young men as they rose ready to follow the woman where ever she wanted to go.

"You're not very grateful boy" she said looking at him across the fire with eyes shining more from her anger than the firelight.

"I'm very grateful to you for your treatment, and I am sure that in the future I will ask the same of you again, but I will ask not demand it of you" the boy gave her a significant look at the end.

"I'll remember that boy, but you remember something too, when you ask someone they can always refuse" she matched his look.

"That's the whole point woman" the boy said with a grin, and took a bite of the sandwich as she huffed, and walked away from the fire over to the door. The three young men grinned at him as they passed following after her.

"Use those sticks of yours to rack that stuff out of the way" she ordered when the young men reached the door. "Please" she added when they looked at her with grins still on their young faces.

"It would be our pleasure" one of them replied, and the whole bunch burst out laughing when the woman growled in anger, and stomped over to stand next to Able. The man was wise enough not to say a word, or even look at her as the three young men began stabbing burning chunks of wood, and dragging them through the door.

"I'd say you made her angry, Noah" Jen said from across the fire loud enough for the woman to hear.

"They've all got to learn how we do things, and that that is the way things are going to be when dealing with us. Our way" the boy continued eating his sandwich occasionally looking over his shoulder to check the progress of clearing the door, and to check the woman's temper. One went quickly while the other barely changed.

It still took more than an hour for them to clear the doorway enough to pass through. The last timbers being shoved away from the opening on the other side to clear a path. The heat coming through the door way was intense making the boy thankful again for the poncho which shielded him from the worst of it as he stood in front of the door surveying the other side.

"Elmo, Kat you two want to go first" the boy asked over his shoulder as he leaned on his spear.

"Those kids" Able asked quietly after stepping over to stand by the boy, and the two youngsters trotted through the door.

"Those kids have **killed** before" the boy said turning his head to look at the older man with a hard expression on his face that hid the boy in him completely. "Angie, Susie, Heather if you don't mind would you go next please" he looked past the big man to where Martha still stood her face blank, but almost quivering with her anger.

"What do you want us to do" Angie asked stopping beside the boy and looking through the door hesitantly.

"You're the bait" the boy said his face still hard but not harsh as the woman turned her head to look at him surprised by his words. "Just walk over to the house and around front. We'll do the rest" he nodded to where Jody and Elisa were

232

stringing their bows while waiting on the three women to go through the door.

"Bait" Heather said the word with a little tension in her voice as she stepped up beside Angie.

"If you don't wish to do it I will ask another" the boy tilted his head back towards the rest of his group.

"We'll do it" Susie said putting a hand on each of their shoulders, pushing the other two women ahead of her towards the door.

Angie glanced over her shoulder at the boy before the door cut her view of him off then she focused on climbing the ramp. There was a thick bed of coals that had her boots steaming by the time she reached the top. She kicked a burned metal container in her haste to escape the suffocating heat inside the ring of still burning timbers that had been the barn. Once she was outside the ring she nearly ran into the smoking heap that had been the old man's truck, its bulk hidden by smoke, and the tears filling her eyes, but managed to side step it at the last instant. Then she was free of the smoke and the heat feeling the fresh summer night air on her face that was quickly covered in sweat under the heavy coat and poncho, but she continued on, the other two women catching up with her, and stepping to either side of her.

"What did he mean they'd do the rest" Heather leaned in close whispering the question her tone implying that she feared the answer.

"You know" Angie said just as softly looking around in the darkness for any sign of the guards the boy said were waiting.

The three women walked around what was left of the house, a massive pile of glowing coals with a few boards still burning brightly scattered here and there. They walked across the yard well back from the heat of the pile. Angie checking to see that her car was still parked in the drive. Stopping in front of the steps that now lead up to the empty air where the porch had once stood, the three women looked the pile over. Not even realizing they were searching for any sign that the old man had been inside when the fire was set.

"Stand where you are, and identify yourselves" a strong authoritative voice said behind them startling the women so much that they all jumped then spun around. Standing in front of them now were four men dressed in black with automatic rifles in their hands, but pointed towards the ground between the women and them.

"Identify your selves" the short man who had spoken before repeated.

"I think they are the three Servants that went missing" the man on his left said squinting against the light behind the women.

"Step for..." out of the darkness to the side four arrows streaked through the air one lodging in the short man's throat cutting off his speech. He raised a hand feeling the shaft, surprise and fear appearing in his eyes as his life blood sprayed out around the shaft. The other three were already down on the ground one with an arrow sticking out of his left eye socket, another on his knees with one stuck in the center of his chest. The man was starring at the shaft surprise on his face as he touched the feather fletching at the end. He turned his head and looked when the short man fell to his knees beside him. The man's face was pale white, and the blood no longer sprayed from his wound as most of it was spread across the ground in front of him. The last man was on his side looking at the other two, curled up around the shaft that was sticking just below his ribs preventing the man from breathing as the arrow had penetrated his diaphragm.

The three women watched with horror twisting their faces as the men were slowly dying in front of them. The short man fell forward the end of the arrow digging into the blood covered ground holding his head and shoulders up. His eyes were empty of life but Angie felt that he was still staring at her. The man with the arrow in his chest sat back on his heels looking up at the women for a moment then blood welled out

234

of his mouth, and he choked fighting for breath that would not come. He fell backwards the arrow sticking up into the air with his hand gripping the shaft. The last man was looking at them his eyes pleading for help before they closed, and his legs kicked out straight.

Heather dropped to her knees and vomited. Spewing up everything she had in her stomach, and then dry heaving as she continued to convulse. Angie felt like doing the same, but could not because all her muscles were frozen. Her eyes were locked on the short man with the arrow in his throat, and she couldn't break free from his gaze.

"That is what killing means" the boy said stepping out of the darkness, and drawing their eyes to him. His face was as hard as stone, his eyes unyielding as he looked at each of the women. "Are you still sure you can do it" his tone was demanding as walked up to them.

"You did that on purpose" Heather said from the ground looking at him with hate in her eyes for what she had seen.

"You had to know the truth of what you thought you could do" his gaze made her cringe as she forced herself to stand. "There is no shame in not being able to take another person's life" he looked at each of them again giving them a way out. "But when others are counting on you is not the time to learn the truth. Now is, can you kill" he waited for each of them to nod before looking at the next. "How about you Able, after seeing this can you and your people kill" he looked over his shoulder into the darkness where Able appeared follow by the others.

"We'll do what needs doing when the time comes" the large man said looking at the dead men on the ground. "Though a sight more merciful than this" he added seeming unaffected by the sight of the dead men.

"There is no mercy in this world" Elmo said walking past him to pull his arrow from the man's eye socket.

"Only the strong can afford to be merciful, and we are weak" Kat said as she passed on the other side, and used her foot to roll the short man over, and jerk her arrow from his throat.

"There's no mercy in killing" Jody said as he passed, and went to the man with the arrow in his middle, and rolled him over with a boot as well before pulling his arrow out.

"We can talk about mercy when this is over, and not all of your friends are still alive" Elisa said looking the group behind the large man over before walking over to pull her arrow from the chest of man on his back.

"Marshal, you care to take point" the boy asked looking past Able and his group to the young man who nodded, and started off into the darkness towards town Elmo and Kat falling in beside him. "Jamie would you set flankers, and a rear guard please" he shifted his gaze to the other man who nodded, and began pointing to individuals. "We need to move fast and unnoticed, it's only a few hours till dawn" the boy's voice was as hard as his face.

"You got a mean cruel side to you don't you, boy" Martha said stepping around Able to look at him in the light of the burning house.

"You can think that if you want woman" the boy said turning to follow after Marshal into the darkness. His head wasn't pounding anymore the little men finally giving up, and calling it quits, and he forced his leg to stiffen as he set a fast pace that he intended to keep up all the way to town.

"There ain't a mean or cruel bone in that boy's body Martha and you should ease up on him" Able said behind him, but the woman said nothing that he could hear, and he ignored them after that.

Jamie and Brenda caught up with him shedding their ponchos and coats as they walked. Then rolling them up together and tying them with a short rope that everyone carried in their pouches and slung the bundle on their backs. Jamie took his spear and bow so he could do the same then they focused on the path ahead, and the darkness around searching both for enemies that might or might not be there.

236

Sunday

A boot to his leg drew the old man from his sleep and the dream. Tizzy was making breakfast in between kissing and hugging him. They were young like before the boys were born, but in the house the Servant had burned. He could still feel her lips on his and her arms around his neck holding him close. He opened his eyes to look up at the soldier standing over him his booted foot pulled back to kick the old man again.

"I'd rather have another kiss from Tizzy" the old man mumbled sitting up.

"No talking" the soldier warned.

"Bathroom" the old man asked knowing the word, and water were the only ones the soldiers allowed them to speak.

"Go ahead" the soldier said motioning the old man up.

Climbing to his feet the old man walked across the room, and through the door into the dinning room filled with furniture. Another soldier was standing beside the bathroom door, watching the old man as he crossed the room, and went through the doorway. In the bathroom the old man turned the hot water on before relieving himself so it would be warm by the time he was done. Taking a fresh wash cloth from the shelf he washed the sleep from his eyes, and then soaked the cloth again washing his body clean. Soaking his grey hair he combed it out with his fingers, and patted it down making himself look as presentable as possible for his execution.

"Hurry up" the soldier at the door said looking in to see what was taking the old man so long.

"Just want to look my best for the hanging" the old man said grinning at him as he dried himself off with a towel from the shelf.

"No talking" the guard warned jerking his thumb to indicate the old man's time was up, and he needed to exit the bathroom.

Still grinning, the old man dropped the towel on the floor, and walked past the man. In the living room he walked over to a soldier standing against the wall, and nodded to him politely and smiled. "Water" he asked his smile spreading to a grin at the agitation that swept across the man's face. During the night the old man had made a game of asking for water until he had to go to the bathroom, and with his age it had not taken much. He had spent most of the night drinking, and walking back and forth to the bathroom until the soldiers had grown tired of the game, and warned him to stop. Of course they had not realized it was a game, but the old man had enjoyed the aggravation it had caused them just the same.

"Take your seat" the soldier said then turned, and walked into the dinning room going to fetch the old man his glass of water.

Crossing the room the old man sat back down in front of the window turning his head to look outside where darkness still held. It would not be long till daylight though, and then they would be taken to the Square. He turned his head to the other side where Marcy was sitting up her face still puffed, but not as much as it had been though. The bruises had grown making most of her face black or blue with streaks of yellow between.

She smiled at him her lips puffed and cracked making it look odd. He could see her eyes now though only a little of them as the lids were still swollen. He nodded towards the doorway leading into the dining room, and she nodded back.

"Bathroom" she croaked looking at the guard who was kicking the others awake. He turned to look at her before nodding then went back to waking the rest of the prisoners. Marcy rolled around to her knees, and used the window sill to pull herself up to her feet then crossed the room, and disappeared through the doorway.

The other soldier passed through the door crossing the room to bring the old man his glass of water. Drinking it all down the old man passed the glass back to him, and he turned with military precision, and retraced his steps. Resting his head against the wall the old man studied the others across the room from him.

Magistrate Maxwell was having the worst time of it, he was mumbling under his breath just shy of where the soldiers would punish him for talking. His face was bruised though not as bad as some of the others, but it was clear his mind was addled. He was staring into space, and had been all night his lips moving repeating the same phrase over and over. "I'm the Magistrate I can't hang." The man did not seem to want to accept the reality that soon he would hang along with the rest of them.

Councilman Becker, Susie's ex-husband was sitting up holding his head in his hands. His face had no bruises or cuts from beatings, but the fear and anguish in his eyes went clear down into his soul. The old man had always thought he was a spineless weasel, and not good enough for a woman of Susie's caliber. From the panic that would burst in his eyes now and then causing the man's head to wipe back and forth seeking a way out proved his thoughts accurate.

High Councilman Webster was sitting with his head against the wall his eyes closed, and his lips moving in soundless words. Occasionally he would reach up, and rub his neck as if already feeling the noose around it.

All of them were a bunch of worthless cowards in the old man's opinion, and not worth hanging. They should be strapped, beaten, and left to a life of toil like they had condemned so many others over the years. His stomach churned just looking at them, and he had to turn away to prevent himself from jumping up, and crossing the room to slap each of them silly.

Probably wouldn't do any good anyway the old man thought staring at the darkness beyond the street lamps. A breeze was blowing out there shifting the limbs of the oak tree in the yard, and he could almost hear the leaves rustling. Marcy's returning drew his attention from the window, and he turned his head to watch her cross the room. She looked more dignified than any of the Councilmen or Magistrates though her face was more bruised and swollen than any four of them combined. She had made peace with what was coming, the same as him, and fear was gone leaving an internal calm that no amount of physical pain could ever shake.

As she sat down mimicking him by crossing her legs, and resting her cuffed hands in her lap while holding her head back against the wall, the old man thought of another game to pass the time. Raising his hands he looked over at her, and smiled when she turned her head to look at him. Pointing to her then to him, he used two fingers to mimic a person climbing a set of stairs. Then leaned forward holding his head up high, and put a disdainful expression on his face while slowly turning his head from left to right like he was looking out over a large crowd. When his gaze settled on her, he grinned, and held his hands up next to his head making a jerking motion upwards. Cocking his head he let his tongue fall out the corner of his mouth, and slowly turned his head like a man hanging from a rope might do. His expression was so comical the young woman barked a quick laugh before she could stop herself.

One of the soldiers at the end of the room turned to look at them when he heard the sound. Seeing the old man with his hands up the soldiers eyes sharpened and he crossed the room to stand in front of the old man. As the soldier stood looking down at the old man, he in turn stared up, studying the man. He was an officer by the metal bars on his collar, his uniform neat and wrinkle free even after having spent a day and night in it. A name tag with white letters reading Walton stood out on the chest of the man's dark uniform. Captain Walton was a dark skinned man, and the way things were now could be from America or Africa or even Europe, there were no borders under the High Chancellor's reign. She owned the world, and her soldiers were chosen for their loyalty not their origin. His dark eyes were like marble that allowed no clue as to what was going through the man's mind behind them.

240

After a couple of minutes of silent study the soldier dropped to one knee, resting an elbow on the bent knee, and clasping his hands together as he looked at the old man almost eye to eye. "What ever you were doing stop it" he said in a low voice the soft tone carrying a warning. "I have allowed a certain amount of leniency because the Servant would prefer you unblemished" his eyes shifted to Marcy's face then back to the old man. "But any more games and I will have you strapped so that your face is left untouched. Do you understand" his voice was still low, but it carried an unyielding quality to it. The old man thought he might be from Africa maybe South Africa by the hint of accent in that voice though it was mostly erased. The High Chancellor preferred uniformity in her world, everyone talking the same, living the same and worshiping the same.

"I understand you perfectly Captain" the old man said deciding that angering the man was not worth a strapping this morning when he had a hanging to attend later in the day.

The man looked at him for a moment longer then rose without a word, and returned to his station starring at the front door. The Captain had been there for most of the night, and the old man wondered if he had slept any at all, or if he did his sleeping while standing with eyes wide open.

Turning his head the old man grinned at Marcy, and shrugged his shoulders saying that the man obviously had no sense of humor. The battered woman grinned back her still swollen lips managing to curve up at the corners enough to match the light shinning in her eyes through the wider slits between the puffed lids. Glancing up and out the window the old man could see that the sky to the east was starting to brighten with the coming dawn. He wondered how long it would be before they came to take them to the Square.

His answer came a little more than a quarter hour later with the sound of vehicles stopping outside that could be faintly heard through the window. His attention was fixed on playing Itsy Bitsy Spider with his fingers when he heard the sound, and knew that the time for games was up. He glanced

241

at Marcy motioning at her with a hand as he worked his way to his feet, and she followed. The Captain looked at them, but decided to ignore them as he nodded to one of the other soldiers, and the man started getting the others to their feet.

The front door opened, and a tall thick solider stepped through looking around the room at the prisoners his eyes pausing for a moment on the old man. He returned the Captains salute then turned to study the old man more thoroughly. The old man could see the golden eagles on the man's collar, and was surprised by them making him wonder how many soldiers were in the town now.

"He is the one they call Noah" the Colonel asked looking over his shoulder at Captain Walton.

"He is" the Captain confirmed nodding his head as he spoke.

"Actually Colonel I'm Albert" the old man said drawing the men's eyes to him, anger shinning clearly in both sets. He wanted to add that Noah would be along shortly, but figured he couldn't get away with so much, and besides no use spoiling the surprise they were in for.

"Get them loaded, Captain" the Colonel said sharply, and turned walking back out the door.

Captain Walton nodded then glanced at the other soldiers around the room, and they crossed the room taking the prisoners by the arm. The Captain strode across the room, and took hold of the old man personally. "You press your luck old man" he said under his breath as a warning.

"I'm going to hang, Captain, what do I have to fear" the old man replied as the Captain led him across the room, and out the door.

Outside the sun had not risen above the horizon yet, and every thing was cast in the predawn gray that gave enough light to see clearly, but muted colors. The leaves on the oak tree looked nearly black against the lighter shade of gray in the sky. The wind that had rustled them was cool and refreshing on the old man's face, he breathed it in deeply relishing the moment.

Roses were planted along the front of the house, and the old man could smell their sweet perfume in the air. He loved roses, and they would be one of the many things he'd miss when he was gone from this world.

The sun was just beginning to peak over the horizon behind the boy, and he was feeling frustrated at the way things had gone so far. He was standing on a tree covered slope behind a small housing complex that had been vacant for some time evidenced by the broken windows, and peeling faded paint. Across the street from the houses was the Servants Compound with a hundred soldiers camped in the parking lot in front of the buildings. Added with all the soldiers they had been forced to avoid during the night, plus the ones that were surely spread around the rest of the town they had not travel through. There had to be over four hundred soldiers in the town.

The soldiers were only a part of the reason for his frustration; the main cause was their lack of finding the old man. The Magistrates Hall had been nearly vacant from Jamie's report, and the man had found no evidence that suggested the old man was being held there. Their focus had turned to the Servants Compound only to find it impossible to get close enough before the Servants had assembled in the parking lot before the sun rose. He had watched closely, but had seen no sign of the old man among them as the formation had marched out of the parking lot, and along the street below towards the Moralists Square.

Leaning on his spear the boy felt his frustration grow, hours of darkness spent avoiding soldiers and Citizens alike, no sign of the old man anywhere, and no clear idea of what to do next. He glanced over his shoulder at the others spread out through the trees behind him. It had taken some considerable discussion, and the threat of sending them back to convince Able to split his people up, and assign them to the units of the boy's group. The man had argued the merits of mass fire power over sporadic cover fire.   The boy did not see either as having any bearing if they were caught because Able's people made too much noise when they were together. Stomping through the darkness unconcerned that they sounded like a bunch of cattle that could be heard at a long distance in the still night air, or even aware of the noise apparently.

"Looking like a wasted trip, boy" Able said drawing his eye from the slope to the large man standing just behind him. "Must be four or five hundred soldiers in town" the large man was starring at the encampment shaking his head at the numbers.

"You can go back anytime" the boy said turning to look at the others standing around him. Angie held the little black pup in her arms now, looking at him, with Susie and Heather holding their rifles standing behind her their attention on the soldiers down below. Martha was standing next to the young women starring at him with a sullen look on her face. Still angry that he had told her to shut up or go back when they had been discussing separating their people. Jamie and Jen were watching the surrounding trees, the soldier's camp and him all at the same time while waiting on him to decide what to do next.

"There is only one place he will be now" Angie said her tone resigned as she nodded to the rising sun.

"Boy, don't even think about it" Able said his tone incredulous as his eyes shifted from the camp to focus on the boy. "The whole town will be there not to mention the soldiers, and if we did somehow get to him we'd have to fight our way out through two or three hundred more soldiers. There's just no way, boy" his tone was pleading at the end as he saw his words having no affect on the boy.

"I came here to get the old man because you wanted me to" the boy looked at the large man, the three Servant women, and finally Martha. "Nothing has changed that I can see, but if any of you do not wish to go with me I understand" he looked

244

at Jamie and Jen at the last offering them the chance to change their minds.

"Nothing's changed, are you crazy, boy" Able exclaimed his voice tense and low to keep from shouting cutting off Jamie who had been about to speak. "Everything has changed, we're facing an army of trained soldiers, and a town full of people boy" as if repeating the facts would make the boy see them better.

"Did you really think they were just going to hand the old man over because we asked nicely" the boy said using Jen's words from earlier, and copying her sarcastic tone. He gave her a wink and a smile that she returned in kind before continuing. "He is the most wanted man in the world, and they intend to keep him till the time comes to hang him. Did you think it was going to be otherwise" the boy looked at the larger man waiting for his answer.

"I didn't expect this" the man said grudgingly nodding towards the soldier's camp.

"More the fool you then" Jen said looking at him with derision in her eyes. "You heard what the old man said they did to those countries and cities and you expected less of a reaction here" she shook her head at his apparent stupidity in her eyes.

"We'll go with you" Jamie said giving Able a look similar to Jen's. "And we'll kill them all if need be" his tone left no doubt that he felt they were capable of doing so.

"You can collect your people, and make your way out of town, and back to the door" the boy nodded in the general direction of the door, and included the men and women spread out along the slope in it. "When we get the old man, and get there I'll open the door for you. You can go back to your happy little lives then" the boy filled his voice with as much sarcasm as possible at the last.

"And if you die..." Martha left the question open speaking for the first time in hours. The sullen look gone from her face replaced with resigned fear.

"Then you'll all be stuck on this side, surrounded by enemies that will hunt you relentlessly" the boy said a glimpse of his life showing in his words and voice.

"That's not much of a choice boy, leave you to die, and be on the run forever, or die trying to help you do the impossible" her voice was filled with fear, but a trace of anger ran through it.

"It's still a choice" the boy said his voice and his eyes suddenly hard again.

"Death or death" Able said shaking his head at the choice.

"We all die" Angie said still looking at the boy. "I would rather die trying than die running, I'll go with you."

"I'll go" Susie said behind her with a tone that implied she had never considered other wise.

"I'll go too" Heather said more hesitantly.

"I guess we'll go too, boy" Able said after glancing at Martha who nodded her head in agreement.

"Then let's go, we've got a lot of ground to cover without being seen, and little time to do it in" the boy said glancing over his shoulder to where the sun stood well above the horizon now.

The sun was sitting above the Magistrates Hall shining down into the square, and heating up the already sultry air. The old man could feel it on the side of his face, shoulder, and ribs. Sweat was running down his face, and had been for most of the morning since arriving in the square. The mass of Citizens spread across the square in front of him generated an enormous amount of heat from their bodies. Behind him the equally large mass of Servants standing on the steps leading up to the entrance of the Hall of Councilors had him trapped between what felt like two ovens, and now the sun was adding its bit to broil him before he had a chance to hang.

246

Beside him Marcy was wilting under the heat her shoulders slumping, and her sweat matted hair hanging across her face as her head drooped. The other prisoners had long since given in. Their heads hanging, shoulders hunched, and tears streamed down most of their faces. The old man still held his head high though it took considerable effort in the heat, his fatigue trying to draw his chin down even just a fraction. But the old man refused to give even that much as he stared defiantly at the mass of Citizens jeering and taunting the prisoners.

He could feel their hate rolling off them like the heat that baked his body. He could see the excitement in their eyes building as the hour approached. They wanted to see blood and pain, someone else's blood and pain. Beyond the crowd a gong sounded in the High Chancellor's Temple, the vibration sweeping across the crowd like a wave lifting their blood lust higher. As the sound died away the gong rang again, and the crowd roared in anticipation. A third time the gong sounded and the crowd went silent, but in their eyes the fervor reached even greater heights. This always sent shivers down the old man's back when he witnessed it. That silent mass of people waiting with all reason swept aside by an ocean of blood lust. They should have been frothing at the mouth like a dog gone rabid, their madness was riding them at a gallop, and nothing could stop it.

The massive doors of the Temple swung open, and the crowd exhale, the old man realized he had been holding his breath as well though not in anticipation as the crowd had. Out of the open doors came a double line of priests chanting praises for the High Chancellor. Two acolytes led the procession swinging smoking braziers back and forth in front of them, and the old man had a sudden desire for a confessional. Behind them twenty priests followed carrying coiled whips held to their chest like lovers, and behind them another pair of acolytes with their braziers then another twenty priest with rods held in their hands. The procession was long each set of priest with a different implement of the Tools of Punishment held reverently in his hands.

The two lines of priest diverged around the pavilion set in the center of the square then came together once again on the other side of it heading towards the old man. The gong sounded again, and the crowd roared as the High Priest came through the open doors. He was a tall broad shouldered man who had been blessed by the High Chancellor as any could see just by looking at him. The man was beautiful as were all priests who served the High Chancellor with their unblemished skin, perfect teeth, fine angular features, and thick silky hair. There were no ugly priests in the High Chancellor's world. The old man wanted to see their faces ground in the dirt just to show the crowd that the priests got dirty like normal people did.

When the acolytes reached the line of prisoners they turned one going left the other right. The priest followed making their turns with military precision, their pristine white robes glistening in the morning sunshine, and their Tools of Punishment held out for the prisoners to see. Most did not even notice their passing, those that did shuddered at the sight of the objects that would soon be used on them. The old man simply watched the priest passing curious as to how much feeling was left in his old body, and if he would feel it when the items were put to use on him. *Probably be the first time in years this old body decides to work like it's suppose to* the thought brought a grin to the old man's sweaty face.

Those priests who passed the old man, and saw his grinning face lost a fraction of their zeal. They had never seen a Sinner with a look of anticipation on his face before, and the whispered tales that had built the old man's reputation now resurfaced. Their smooth cool features began to bead with perspiration after seeing the old man look at their Tools, and nod with a light of excitement in his eyes. It unnerved many of them, and they had to struggle to maintain the outward calm that was expected in priest of the High Chancellor.

In the Temple the gong sounded again as the High Priest reached the pavilion, and mounted the steps. The other priest stopped in place, those on the walkway between the pavilion and the Temple turned to face each other, and stepped back to the edge of the walk to leave the way clear. Those on the other side of the pavilion continued marching till they all stood in a long line in front of the prisoner. Then they stopped turning to face the condemned. The priest standing in front of the old man was a tall slender man with crystal blue eyes, and thick blonde hair that curled at the ends.

With a deep rolling voice that carried across the square the High Priest began his opening prayer. "Our High Chancellor" the way the man said it God could have replaced High Chancellor easily "has given us this day of celebration to see Her sacred Hand of Morality punish those who have Sinned against Her. Let each Citizen know Her kindness as..." the old man quit listening, and the grin on his face broadened as he thought of a new game.

"Our Father who are in Heaven, hallowed..."

"Silence Sinner" the priest hissed raising the rod in his hand in a threatening manner.

"...be thy name. Thy kingdom come thy will be done..."

"Silence" the priest raised the rod higher, but the old man saw the fear in his eyes.

"... on Earth as it is in Heaven. Give us this day our daily bread...

The priest brought the rod slashing down, and the old man stepped to the side. The blow struck air, but the man had put such force into the swing that he lost his balance, and fell to the concrete.

"... and forgive us our debts as we forgive those indebted to us. Lead us not into temptation but deliver us...

"Be silent Sinner" the priest next to the one on the ground growled, and stepped forward swinging his rod at the old man's head who ducked quickly to avoid the blow. Missing,

249

the rod continued on to strike the now rising priest in the face, smashing his nose which sprayed blood over his white robes.

"... from evil. For thine is the kingdom and the power and the glory forever Amen" the old man started cackling after reciting the ancient prayer, watching the two priests struggling to disentangle themselves both now with blood on their robes.

Angry murmurs were spreading out from those in the crowd who were watching the old man. Laughing as he stood over the two priest who could not seem to regain their feet. When one was nearly there the other would lose his balance, and reach out pulling them both back to the concrete walk. To the crowd it appeared that the old man was using some kind of magic to control the priest, and their anger was growing, threatening to disrupt the High Priest's prayer.

Raising his voice in an attempt to maintain control of the crowd the High Priest gave a quick hard look over his shoulder at one of the priest behind him. The man jumped at the burning anger in the High Priest's eyes, and rushed down the steps of the pavilion. The priest was nearly running in his haste when he reached the still tumbling priests, and misjudged his footing, or perhaps there was a bit of dirt on the concrete. Either way the man's foot went out from under him, and he stumbled into the two priest who with arms locked together were finally nearly back on their feet.

All three went down in a heap and the running priest's momentum carried him over the other two to land face first on the concrete. The rough surface scraping skin off his forehead, nose and chin. Normally such wounds would not have bled as much as his now did, red droplets falling on the grey surface then the white robes of the priest as the man tried to rise.

Throwing his head back the old man roared with laughter at the spectacle as the three priests now struggled against one another to rise. Even Marcy found the scene comical as she started laughing beside the old man. The other prisoners however like the line of priest seemed to be immobilized with shock at what was happening right in front of their eyes.

The blow came from behind the old man striking him at the base of the skull, and driving him to the walk. As if the three priests had truly been under a spell, and were now finally freed from it the priests scrambled to their feet blood still dripping from the two. The scarlet liquid staining their robes as it fell from their flesh.

Rolling onto his back the old man looked up blinking against the haze of pain to see Captain Walton holding a rifle in his dark hands. The man was breathing hard as if it had taken all his strength to deliver the blow. Sitting up the old man lifted his cuffed hands to rub one across the back of his head feeling to see if he was bleeding. To his surprise the skin was unbroken, and his head was quickly clearing of the initial pain settling into a dull throb.

"I feel sorry for you, Captain" the old man said looking up at him again. The man was still panting staring down at the old man with fear filling his eyes. "I'm afraid you are going to die today, Captain" the old man rose smoothly to his feet, his seemingly frail body full of life and energy. "God's servant has come to deliver judgment on the idolaters, and you will not see the sun set this day, Captain" the old man's voice was full of sadness for the man.

"Shut up, you old fool" the Captain's fear was thick in his words. The old man should be dead or at least dying with the force that had been in his strike yet the man stood before him warning him about his own death. It wasn't right.

"Only a fool can't learn something from a fool" the old man said grinning once again. "I give you this one chance, Captain, the Lord my God has spoken to me. If you run now, and don't look back you will live. Stay and you will die" the old man was pulling every bit of pageantry he could remember from a world that had died so long ago.

"I said shut up" the Captain raised the rifle, but the old man could see in his eyes that he was too frightened to use it again.

Turning the old man ignored the Captain, and looked to the pavilion where the High Priest was finishing his prayer. Then shifted his gaze to the crowd where many were looking at him with hate and loathing on their faces, blood lust filled their eyes, and their fists were clenched at their sides. Glancing to his right his eyes followed the three priests as they hurried along the walk away from him their eyes filled with fear as they looked back then stepping even faster when they turned away. Two new priests drew his eye as they approached from the other direction, and stopped in front of him bending down to pick up the rods that were lying on the blood splattered concrete. Their robes were brilliant white, looking fresh and pure, the old man grinned at them as they took their places filling the line of priests once more.

In the Temple the gong sounded again drawing the crowd's attention back to the pavilion though some continued glancing at the old man. The priests stepped forward one on each side of the prisoners, and took them by the arm. In the pavilion the High Priest began calling out the names of the Sinners his voice rolling across the crowd building their lust for blood once more.

"Allison Stroud" the crowd cheered. "Sinner against our High Chancellor, and condemned to pain and death on this Sunday" the crowd roared its approval.

Down at the far end of the line from the old man two priest dragged the woman... who had gone limp when the High Priest called her name... down the line of prisoners to the walkway leading to the pavilion. Then holding her there for the High Priest to inspect for a moment, and when he nodded in confirmation that indeed she was the Sinner named. They then dragged the woman across the grass to the left platform and up the stairs to the far end of the wooden frame work atop the platform. A rope hung from a pulley set in the center of the thick wooden beam of the frame, and the priest tied it to the cuffs around the woman's wrists. The rope ran through another pair of pulleys to a cleat secured to one of the posts of the frame where one of the priests untied it and pulled; raising the woman into the air. The pain in her wrist from the cuffs roused the woman from her stupor, and she kicked in vain trying to prevent the priest from binding her ankles with ropes that ran to rings set in the wooden flooring of the platform.

As the priests were binding Allison the High Priest had already called another name, and George Reid was being inspected. The man was shaking his head in denial, but the priest pulled him up the steps, and along the platform to the frame next to Allison's, and began binding him in the same manner. Beside him the priests were using razor sharp knives to cut away the hanging woman's clothes, and tossing the rags off the platform to the frenzied crowd below.

"David Mason" the High Priest called his words barely audible over the roaring crowd. "Sinner against our High Chancellor, and condemned to pain and death on this Sunday" the priest pulled the man out of the line. Tears streamed down his face as they half led half dragged him down the walkway.

"Pain and death are apart of life, Marcy, and not to be feared" the old man said leaning forward to look across the priests between them.

"Silence" the priest said gripping the old man's arm tighter in warning.

"God has set a place at his table for you, girl, and we shall dine together with him this evening" the old man grinned at her when she leaned forward to look over at him.

"I am not afraid" she smiled as best as her swollen lips would allow, and there was no fear in her voice. The High Priest called another name.

"I said silence Sinner" the priest raised his rod.

"Or what, boy, you'll beat me some before you hang me up there" the old man nodded to the wooden frames. The man had a confused look on his face for a moment then his eyes cleared, but the old man was ignoring him by then.

He watched as the other prisoners were led out of the line one by one, tied up, and hung in mid air. He watched as their clothes were cut from them, and tossed to the crowd that was screaming with excitement and anticipation for the coming pain and blood. Glancing over his shoulder once looking at the line of soldiers between him, and the Servants he searched for, but could not find the Captain. He wondered if the man had taken his advice and fled.

Then the High Priest called Marcy for his inspection. The old man smiled at her as the woman glanced over at him before walking with her head held high to stand before the High Priest. She led the two priests up the stairs and to her frame where she held her hands out for the priest to tie the rope. The old man was proud of her courage and fortitude.

"Albert Jenkins" the High Priest called. "Also known as Noah the Sinner who thought he could hide from the High Chancellor's sight" the High Priest's voice was full of contempt, and the crowd's cries were filled with rage and hate. "Sinner against our High Chancellor and condemned to pain and death on this Sunday" the priest tightened their grip, and the old man stepped forward.

"The Lord is my shepherd, and I shall not want" the old man's voice was clear and calm. The two priests looked at him, and then each other, but made no move to stop him speaking now.

"He maketh me to lie down in green pastures, he leadeth me beside the still waters" they turned to face the High Priest.

"He restoreth my soul, and leadeth me in the paths of righteousness for his name's sake" the High Priest seemed to revel in seeing the old man's lips moving as if he were finally breaking down. He nodded his acceptance of the old man.

"Yea though I walk through the valley of the shadow of death, I will fear no evil for thou art with me. Thy rod and thy staff, they comfort me" he mounted the stairs.

"Thou preparest a table before me in the presence of mine enemies. Thou anointest my head with oil, my cup runneth over" the old man reached his frame, and turned holding out his hands to the priests. The priest's eyes were nervously shifting refusing to meet the old man's as he reached for the rope, and began tying it around the short chain linking the cuffs.

"Surely goodness and mercy shall follow me all the days of my life, and I will dwell in the house of the Lord forever. Amen" the old man was looking out over the crowd as the priest raised him up into the air. He felt the cuffs bite into the thin flesh of his wrist, felt the muscles in his shoulders protest at taking all the weight of his body, and grinned at the sensations.

In the crowd he could see individuals shouting at him with fists raised high and shaking in rage. "Blasphemer", "Fornicator", "Idolater" and "Witch" were the most common words that could be heard in the crowd's shouts, but some bordered on breaking the obscenity laws. The priests tied his ankles then one of them pulled a knife from his robes, and cut the old man's pajama bottoms off. When he tossed them to the crowd the cloth was torn to shreds in seconds.

The gong in the Temple sounded again, and the crowd's cries cut off instantly leaving a silence that was more terrifying than the shouting. The prisoners now struggled in their bonds seeking to escape what was coming next while the crowd's eyes almost seemed to glow with anticipation for it. Only the old man and Marcy remanded calm in the silence. The High Priest let it stretch in hopes perhaps that it would affect the two but when the crowd began turning heads to look at the pavilion he continued the ceremony.

"Sinners you have dared to defy the High Chancellor and now you will feel Her wrath" the words carried across the

255

square were drowned out by the crowd's roar of pleasure at the end.

A double line of priest climbed the stairs and parted, one continuing across the platform while the other turned to walk behind the prisoners. Each carried a switch in their hand, the long thin flexible piece of wood looking like it had been taken from a willow tree. The priest who stopped in front of the old man had a smile of joy on his face. The old man had always figured the priests had a sadistic side to them. The gong sounded and the priest began whipping the old man's flesh.

Yeah, the body is going to work good today the old man thought at the first strike that set his skin on fire where it landed. Then the priest behind him laid his switch across the old man's back. The old man looked at the priest in front of him, and grinned while along the line the others were screaming at the first taste of what was coming. The priests would start with the switches, and then cane rods would come next, followed by all the other Tools of Punishment till their flesh was ripped, torn and bleeding. Then they would be hung. The old man glanced up at the sun sitting in the clear pale sky well above the Magistrates Hall, but still short of noon, and knew that he did not have long to endure the pain.

The boy had long since passed from frustration into anger and was now calm as he hunkered down under a low bridge across a dry gully. For the last few hours it seemed that they had been going back and forth over the same ground as if something was trying to hold them back from reaching the square. Besides the soldiers that had it surrounded. They would find a clear open path, and then half way to their destination a patrol would appear forcing them to back track the way they had come.

The soldiers in the camp had started it marching almost as soon as the boy had begun heading along the slope. The soldiers had set up a perimeter around the square, and then others had arrived joining them, or patrolling the areas outside the ring. The boy had finally split his group sending out the smaller groups to circle the square, and find a way past the patrols and guards. Which he hoped had not been as difficult for them as it was proving to be for his little group. They were constantly stopped or turned back, or forced to go far out of their way to avoid detection.

Now with the sun nearly overhead, and Angie biting her lip in worry his little group was closer to their destination than they been all morning. Martha and Angie were sweating from more than the heat as they gripped their weapons, and stared at the concrete roadbed just above their heads. Elmo and Kat were looking up as well but they were more relaxed as they listened to the even rhythmic steps of the patrol marching along the street. If they had been seen the patrol would have been racing towards them instead, and the two youngsters knew this.

When the patrol was past the boy grabbed up the little black pup, and left the cover of the bridge keeping low, well below the top of the gully's bank. The others followed keeping pace with him as they made their way down the gully just making it around a curve, and out of sight before the next patrol appeared on the street. All morning there had been a dozen soldiers on that bridge, but now they were gone, the boy wondered about this, but kept his main focus on his footing. The gully floor was uneven, and filled with large rocks that might or might not turn under foot.

On the right side of the gully were the backs of houses with a street in front where the boy could see another patrol between a pair of them. Pausing, the boy watched until he was sure they were walking away from the little group, and had not seen them. On the left was the back of red brick single and two story buildings with a narrow street running along behind the buildings. There was no one in sight on that side.

"That's the Temple" Angie said reaching a hand past his shoulder pointing to the huge white marble covered building ahead. It rose from a high foundation that was about a hundred yards from the edge of the gully. Between the two was open grass that would provide no cover for them. But a double set of doors set into the back wall of the building stood open. Inviting.

The gong went off again and Angie bit her lip looking towards the square with fear and worry in her eyes. "That's the last one; it's a whip with blades at the end of six tails. They slice the flesh when used" she had been telling them what was happening in the square since the first gong had sounded. The boy had not liked the sound of most of it, and this last was no better. "After this they will hang him" her tone was urgent as if time were running out quickly.

Looking over his shoulder at her anxious face the boy nodded then hiking the little pup up higher on his hip started off along the gully at a faster pace. It only took a few minutes for them to reach the point opposite the open doors. The boy hesitated for a second straightening enough to look around to make sure no one was in sight then set the pup on top of the gully's bank. Leaning his spear against the bank he turned to face Angie, and cupped his hands looking at her expectantly.

For a moment she looked at him with a confused expression then comprehension showed in her eyes, and she placed a foot in his hands. Lifting her quickly he looked at Martha while Angie picked up the little pup, and ran towards the open doors. Martha's bulk took more effort, but the boy got her up, and she followed behind the younger woman. Elmo and Kat both went up quickly pausing at the top to help him climb out once he retrieved his spear then all three ran for the doors. They caught the older woman before she was halfway across the open area, and Elmo and Kat each grabbed an arm dragging the woman along with them.

Slowing the boy followed behind watching to make sure they weren't discovered. He was breathing easy, but his head throbbed from the exertion. One of the little men had picked up his hammer, and was using it half heartedly against his skull.

Following the others through the door the boy saw that they were in a large open room with empty sleeping pallets spread out on the floor. In the corner to his right was a set of stairs leading up to the floor above, hefting his spear the boy led the way at a trot. The little man in his head was going to have to do a better job if he wanted to slow him down now.

Above the stairs ended in a short hallway that ran along the back wall of the building, and the boy continued trotting to the end of it. There another hallway ran down the center of the building with doors lining it, and since no one was visible the boy turned, and trotted down the hall. At the center of the building a cross hall ran the width of the building and at either end was a set of stairs leading upwards.

"This way" Angie said confidently as she stepped around the boy, and turned down the right side hall nearly running to the stairs. "The Sanctuary is above and there will be priest at the doors" she nodded to the front of the building speaking in a whisper to the boy as he joined her on the landing half way up the stairs. She was holding the little pup in the crock of her left arm, in her right she held the grip of her rifle its weight hanging from the strap across her shoulder.

Nodding at her words the boy turned handing his spear to Martha, and as he pulled his bow from across his back he looked at Elmo and Kat. They passed their spears to the woman who gave an exasperated huff at trying to hold onto the three weapons, and her rifle at the same time. The gong sounded again reverberating through the building. The boy gave Angie a questioning look as he pulled an arrow from his belted quiver, and set it in the bow when she gave an answering nod. The old man didn't have long.

Leading the other two up the stairs, while the women followed behind with their burdens, the boy reached a curtained alcove. Turning to draw the curtain back a little the boy looked into the room beyond. Directly in front of him and on the same level was a pulpit where the High Priest delivered his sermons. Aisles radiated out from the pulpit like spokes in a wheel dividing the seats into wedges. Above were steeply slanted balconies that would allow someone sitting in the seats against the wall to still see anyone standing in the pulpit.

Shifting his footing to turn his gaze towards the front of the building, the boy could see the massive bronze gong he had been hearing most of the morning. Beside it a man wearing sparkling white robes stood with a long black piece of wood in his hands, one end had a thick pad of tightly wound cloth. Evidently the instrument the man had been beating the gong with the boy surmised. The man was looking towards the front of the building, and the boy shifted his feet again till he could see the tall wide doorway. On either side of it just outside were two more men dressed in the white robes and another stood in the center. All three were looking out into the square beyond.

The boy turned holding up four fingers to Elmo and Kat then quickly signed instructions. At their nods he went through the curtain moving at a run by the time he reached the aisle leading to the doors. Bending down he laid the bow and arrow on the carpeted floor without breaking stride, and pulled his knife and hatchet smoothly as he straightened.

Reaching the man beside the gong he swung with the hatchet striking him in the back of the head before the man was even aware of the danger. Letting the handle go leaving the weapon buried in the man's head the boy shifted his knife to his right hand as Elmo and Kat raced past. They bypassed the man standing just inside the door and as his attention jerked to them Noah attacked him from behind like Elmo and Kat were those just outside the doorway. A foot to the back of the man's knee forcing him down at the same time reaching around to grasp his chin pulling the head back exposing the throat for the knife to slice across. Letting his man fall the boy stepped over helping Kat pull her man back through the doorway as he fought to keep his life blood inside even as he choked on what wasn't squirting out of him.

Looking quickly to see that no one had noticed them the boy turned to help Elmo who was struggling with the weight of the larger man. Elmo had pulled him half way back through the door when the boy reached him, and they dragged the man inside as his heels beat against the blood covered tiles of the entrance. Leaning down the boy wiped his knife clean on the man's robes as the dying man gripped his ruined throat begging for help with his eyes as he choked on his own blood. The boy ignored his pleas feeling no sympathy for the man and straightened. Sheathing his knife he walked over to pull his hatchet from the first man's skull wiping it clean before replacing it on its belt loop.

Kat handed him his bow and arrow as she passed taking Elmo his, and the two women came up the aisle looking at the dead man, and dying men with only a little paling of their faces. Shifting his bow and arrow to his left hand the boy took his spear from Martha when the women reached him.

"Now what boy" she asked handing the two youngsters theirs, but looking at the boy with eyes that wanted to flicker to the dying men on the floor. She held them firmly on him though as she waited for his answer.

"We go get the old man" the boy said turning towards the doorway.

"We go get the old man" Martha mocked behind him under her breath, but loud enough for him to hear bringing a grin to his face. "Just like that" she asked to no one special as she followed after him.

"Just… " the words died on the boy's tongue as he stepped through the door, and looked out over the square. The crowd was screaming in near ecstasy, the sound had been a muted buzz inside, but it assaulted the boy's ears now. Their attention was focused on the scaffolds setting on a raised platform where men with white robes stained red held up men and women covered in their own blood. Another man was going down the line putting nooses around the bloody people, and pulling the rope tight around their necks.

Only one man stood unaided in the line and the boy knew it was the old man though how he managed to stand the boy had no idea. Flesh was ripped and torn, chunks hanging from arms, legs, and chest. All of him covered in blood that was dried to a dirty red color or scarlet in its freshness. Across the square their eyes locked, and the boy knew the old man saw him, and recognized him even over the distance. And miracle of miracles the old man began to speak though the sound of the crowd drowned it out.

He's still alive so there's a chance the boy thought looking around the square trying to decide how he was going to get to the old man. He could see only five soldiers spread along the back of the crowd below him, and their attention was on the scaffolding the same as the crowd. On either side were twenty or so ringing the crowd, and at the far side another fifty stood between the Servants standing on the steps of the building across the square, and the platforms in front of the crowd.

The crowd numbered in the thousands though, and they stood between him and the old man. He searched for a way to get around them, or through them, but nothing came to mind. Then he realized the crowd had gone silent as if they strained to hear the old man whose words came to him clearly now.

"… unto this covenant I have kept. Now for the promises made to me I call them due. Lift not your hand…" the boy's eyes locked with the old man's across the square again and he knew the words were for him. "… till the appointed time. For you who dare call me Sinner I say to you. Fear my end for it shall unleash the whirlwind, and you shall reap the fruits of your labors. Bitter shall they be" the old man's voice held a strength and conviction that went beyond his tortured body.

"Flee this place now and you may yet find salvation and protection from the wind that will sweep this world clean" the old man's eyes swept across the crowd and those in front drew back from what they saw in them.

"Hang the old fool" someone in the middle yelled, but no one else took up the call.

"What are we waiting for" Angie asked beside the boy at almost the same time. "We have to save him" the boy had to hold his spear out to stop her from running down the stairs.

"You call to hasten the hour of your demise" the old man looked up at the doors of the Temple and the boy knew the coming words were for the woman next to him.

"Listen to him" he told her as she fought to get past.

"I tell you this now" the old man called and Angie looked across the crowd at him. "My time is nearly done and the Lord my God calls me to Him" the old man swept his gaze down from the Temple over the crowd. "When I am gone you will face His wrath given form. You will know fear like never before that shall seize limbs and freeze hearts. Death shall carry all who remain to oblivion" the old man looked at the pavilion, and the High Priest at the last.

As if the look released his tongue the High Priest screamed into the silence "Hang him."

The old man felt the trap door fall out from under him as the priest on either side released his arms. He felt the noose dig into his flesh burning as the rope pulled tight choking off his air. The priest never left enough rope for the fall to snap the neck, the crowd wanted to watch the hanged strangle to death, kicking and clawing at the rope before dying. The old man did not kick or claw though. He waited looking through pain filled eyes at the crowd who now screamed even louder as they watched the people dying at the end of the ropes.

Two minutes, he had been able to hold his breath for a full two minutes once upon a time so long ago. Now his lungs were empty before the rope began to strangle so he thought it would be less this time before he passed out. He estimated a full minute had passed, and managed to force a grin on his face as his vision began to tunnel. The crowd receding away from him as though looking through a grey tube that was growing longer with each heart beat.

Then the grey was swept away by darkness that consumed him. He floundered in it, sinking and rising then

263

tumbling over and over like he was caught in the strong current of a mighty river. He searched in the darkness for a reference point something that would tell him up from down but there was none. There was something... a distant memory... a name that he struggled to recall. His mind was sluggish; his thoughts so difficult to order, then like a ray in the darkness the name came to him. Tizzy.

With it came the image of a young woman with light brown hair in a braid that hung over her shoulder, and smiled at him with love in her eyes. He felt the darkness around him now, cold like he had never known before drawing the heat from him, and with it his essence. But he had his point now, a light that shined drawing him towards it even as the waters tumbled him.

He realized that the darkness was water now or perhaps had always been he could not remember for sure. He struggled against the enveloping depths wanting to breathe, but knowing he couldn't. A memory of a rope flashed through his thoughts, and was gone leaving no clue as to what it meant in its passing. Tizzy was all that mattered. All that there was or ever would be.

His foot kicked something unyielding in the darkness. He had a foot... *of course I have a foot* he told himself. *I have always had a foot* he thought, but a part of him remembers otherwise. His foot touched that surface again, and he fought to dig his toes into it, and then got his other foot anchored as well. With all his strength he surged upwards.

Breaking the surface of the river he drew in a deep breath filling lungs that had never known air. Shaking the water from his face that was smooth and young he waded from the river, and she was there on the shore waiting for him. Tizzy. She looked at him, and his heart leaped in his chest that was broad and thick the muscles rippling under the skin that had never felt the heat of the sun.

Memories of toil and strife fell away from his mind like the water dripping from his body. Not the ones that held her in

264

them though. They grew and expanded each breath remembered, each touch relived, and then he stepped clear of the river.

She came to him taking him in her arms, and holding him close. Her smell filled his nostrils, her warmth soaked into his flesh, and the feel of her made his heart race.

"I've been waiting on you" she said looking up at him. "What kept you" she patted his chest as if he had been overly long on purpose.

"I had things to do my love" he said taking her head in his hands, and kissing her deeply.

The boy watched the old man's body dropped, Angie turned away pressing her cheek against his back as she hid her eyes from the sight, and the little pup whined between them. The boy looked on as the crowd cried so loud he felt the vibration in the air. Then when he knew the old man was gone he looked at Kat and Elmo who had tears glistening in their eyes. The time was almost right, the boy could feel it in the air around him, in the earth below him, in the sun that shined down on him, and he knew what to do.

"Put him down Angie" the boy said softly over his shoulder in her ear. "Let him go to the old man" the little pup was whining struggling to get out of the woman's arm. As she leaned back the pup broke free on his own dropping to the stone, and racing down the steps before she could catch him.

"He'll be killed" she cried looking after the little pup.

"Not today he won't" the boy said nodding where the little pup was racing along the walk leaving silence in his wake as those in the crowd who saw him starred in wonder. "We kill them all" the boy said stepping forward and hefting his spear.

"Kill them all" Elmo and Kat said together as they stepped up one on each side of him.

"All" Angie said pulling the bolt back on her rifle, and thumbing the safety off as she stepped up beside Kat.

"You'll get **us** all killed" Martha said as she stepped up beside Elmo but she thumbed the safety off on her weapon. "The soldiers first" she asked taking aim down the sights at the far soldier on her side.

"Wait" the boy said watching the little pup circle the pavilion the priest trying to stop him but none managed, and he raced on down the walkway across the front of the crowd then up the stairs onto the platform. The boy wanted to cry as the little pup reached the old man's body, and circled the hole in the platform it was hanging in. He couldn't hear him, but the boy knew he was whining trying to reach the old man. The crowd was silent as they watched the little pup, and into this silence the boy spoke.

"I am the whirlwind, fear me" the boy cried the words sweeping across the silent crowd drawing their eyes to him as he threw his spear with such force that it lifted the nearest soldier off his feet, and into the crowd. At the same time Elmo and Kat fired their arrows striking the turning soldiers knocking them down, and the two women fired. The shots echoed across the square shattering the silence that his words had left.

"I am the wrath of God..." the boy screamed into the silence behind the shots. "... and I bring Death to you all" the boy stepped down, and fired an arrow at the nearest priest in his white robe. The square erupted with shouts, screams of fear and pain, and rifle fire on all sides, but the boy was oblivious sending arrow after arrow into the priests' ranks.

When his arrows were spent he dropped the bow then raced down the remaining steps wrenching his spear from the soldier who was trying to pull it out himself. The boy ignored the man's screams as the blade pulled free, and charged towards the pavilion. The priest in their white robes tried to stand before him, but he wielded the spear with expert precision leaving men lying behind him with their life blood pumping out of gapping wounds.

Reaching the pavilion he saw that the man who had ordered the old man's death was on the other side surrounded by his priests as if they would die to protect the High Priest. Rushing around it the boy waded into the knot of men around the man he sought, and they fell back before him. Then they were being forced towards him as those on the other side of the man were being pushed back by someone else. Finally the boy came face to face with the High Priest who stared at him with terror filled eyes asking for mercy with his lips because in his fear no sound escaped his throat. The boy drove the spear point into the man's stomach where he knew the liver was so that death would come slowly but surely. Twisting the shaft as he pulled it out to give the man some extra pain the boy drove the butt of the spear into a man's skull when he tried running past. Turning to face the next man in front of him the boy stopped his attack just short of opening the man's throat when he saw the mark of the Servants on the man's forehead.

"We're with you" the man said franticly holding up one of the soldiers rifles half in defense, as he stared wide eyed at the spear point inches from his throat, and half displaying it as evidence.

"Do you know how to use that" the boy shouted to be heard over the screaming and gunfire.

"Not really. I been using it as a club" the man shouted back, making a stabbing motion with the butt end.

Nodding absently the boy looked around, and listened assessing what was going on in the square. The crowd was split half trying to get past the Magistrates Hall on his left, and the other half trying to get out through the open streets on his right. The problem was that all the soldiers who had been positioned around the square, were now trying to get into the square the same way the people were trying to get out. From the sound of the gunfire on his left the soldiers had started firing into the crowd for some reason.

The boy looked at the people at the back of the two crowds; they looked at him with terror in their eyes, and tried to climb over those ahead of them. Those turned and seeing him pushed and shoved others in front of them all attempting to

267

flee from him. The boy knew that in that massive press many were being trampled, and he did not care.

Then Servants blocked his immediate view of the crowd as they spread along its edge attacking the people with what ever they had for weapons. Grabbing men and women by arms, hair, or throats they dragged them out of the crowd to hammer at them with fists or rifle butts. Some of the Servants had short bladed knives they stabbed with while others used short pieces of rope to strangle the Citizens with. Where they had gotten the rope from the boy had no idea. Once the person was dead or dying the Servants turned back to the crowd to pull another person from it, and begin again.

Turning from the frenzied killing the boy searched, and found Angie standing beside the pavilion reloading her rifle. Beyond her he could see Martha firing into the crowd on the open side of the square, but Angie was the one he wanted right now. She looked up and saw him and he waved her over then turned to the Servant he had almost killed.

"I would like you and ten men to help her do something" the boy shouted at him, and jerked his head at the approaching woman. The man nodded his assent then turned to the press of Servants pouring through the gap between the crowds, and started waving at them.

"I'd like you to get the old man's body, and bring him here" the boy shouted above the noise when Angie reached him and nodded to the pavilion. "Hold this place with the Servants" he pointed his spear to the sandy brown haired man with the rifle coming towards them. His blue eyes were focused on Angie intently.

"Larry" she said the name with wonder as she looked at the man. "Where are you going" she shouted turning her attention back to the boy. Fear crept into her eyes when he nodded to where the firing was the most intense. "Be careful" was all she said though then walked past him to where the Servant with the rifle was waiting for her.

Turning Noah started running for the Magistrates Hall tapping Elmo and Kat on the shoulder as he passed. The Servants had already reached them, and were dragging people from the crowd around the two teenagers. They both followed after him keeping pace as he circled the crowd running past two of Able's people. They were using their rifle butts on anyone who was trying to get to the side of the big black building. Reaching Brenda he paused long enough to ask her to do a couple of things then raced on.

Taking the steps in front of the building two at time he climbed to the open doors and raced through. When he slowed Elmo raced past, and lead the way through the maze of hallways to the back of the building, and a door that opened onto an alley way. They turned and raced along it towards the far end where the firing was coming from.

As they rounded the corner of the building they surprised a group of ten soldiers heading towards them. The leader was a big man with dark skin and gold bars on his collar. Noah caught a glimpse of the man's name tag and read the word Walton out of habit. That was all the boy had time to for before throwing his spear side armed, the blade burying in the man at the base of his throat, and toppling him back into the other men.

With out slowing the boy pulled knife and hatchet using the latter to catch the barrel of a rifle one of the soldiers was lifting. Forcing it down the boy drove the knife into the man's right eye, and as he fell dropped down with him to hook the hatchet in the back of another man's leg and sweep him off his feet. Ripping the weapon free of the leg he drove it down into the man's face feeling the bone and flesh giving way to the blade. Another man was bringing his rifle up aiming at Kat, and the boy rose swinging the hatchet upwards into the soldiers trigger arm then stabbed him under the same arm with his knife. The man's scream when the hatchet nearly severed his arm cut off, and became gasping for air as the blade pierced his lung.

The rest were down, Elmo pulling his spear from the throat of the last man standing letting him fall, and Kat wiping her blade clean on the pants leg of another who was struggling to breathe while holding his stomach. Kneeling, the boy wiped his blade clean on the shirt sleeve of the dark skinned Captain Walton while looking at the line of soldiers between the two buildings.

Sheathing the knife, and slipping the hatchet back into its loop the boy picked up the Captain's rifle checking the load before pulling his spear free. Looking at the fifty or so soldiers who had still not noticed them, his eyes lifted seeing Angie on the platform with the Servants cutting the old man's body free. Glancing at Elmo and Kat he saw that they held a rifle in their left hand, and their spear in the right ready whenever he was.

Nodding he stood and the two youngsters flanked him. *I hope you're in place Jamie* he thought briefly.

"Kill them all" he said hefting the spear.

"All of them" the two said in unison.

They started trotting forward spreading out ready to do just what they said.

Jamie was worried because it was taking them so long to get into a position that would allow them to support whatever Noah decided to do. They had been forced back from the square so many times that the man had begun to wonder if they could even reach it. Now they were making their way along a back alley between tall buildings that Susie said would bring them out on Main Street near the square. Able was still muttering about it being a wasted trip, and Elisa was giving the man a disgusted look that he was totally unaware of. Glancing at the young woman she blushed slightly, and returned to watching behind them for signs of any soldiers. Jody was ahead leading the way, and nearly to the end of the alley.

The sound of the gong going off again could be heard faintly, and Susie turned to him. "That is the last one, they'll

270

hang Albert now" she sounded hopeless as if the man were already dead.

"Noah won't let that happen" he assured her. Then seeing Jody stop at the end of the alley looking around the corners of the buildings, and turning to wave them forward he spoke to the others as well as the worried woman. "Let's move" suiting action to words he led them at a run to the end of the alley.

"Ten soldiers" Jody whispered, and nodded in the direction of the square when Jamie reached him.

Nodding he stepped past the teenager, and to the corner of the building to peek around it. The ten soldiers were standing in the middle of the street behind a pair of military vehicles parked in a V formation. Their attention was focused on the square. Beyond them he could see the crowd of shouting people, the sound nearly deafening even at this distance. Smiling Jamie turned back to the others.

"You two stay behind us" he said to Able and Susie then looked at Jody and Elisa to see that they were ready.

Hefting his spear Jamie went around the corner in a crouching run, keeping behind the line of cars parked along the side of the street. When he was nearly even with the soldiers he cut between two of the cars, and slowed letting the other two flank him. Then they were on the still unaware soldiers.

Jamie stabbed the first man at the base of his skull, and the large man dropped to the pavement. Pulling his spear free as the man went down he drove the blade into the neck of the soldier on his left as the man turned. The sharp edge of the blade opened the soldier's throat, and the man dropped his weapon grabbing at the wound. Pivoting Jamie slashed at the man on the right driving him back onto Elisa's spear. Then turning with his momentum Jamie brought the blade around driving it into, then through another soldier's arm, and between his ribs into the man's chest cavity. The man screamed at the pain for a moment before Jody's spear opened his throat. Wrenching his spear free Jamie slammed the butt of it into the

271

face of the last man then spun it sending the blade into the base of his throat. The man grasped the shaft starring down it at Jamie for a moment till his strength left him, and he fell to his knees.

Standing straight and looking around Jamie saw Susie and Able standing behind him starring at the three of them with shock on their faces. Looking at Elisa he understood why, they were all three covered in blood, he could feel it on his face, and looked down to see it on his chest and arms. "Killing gets messy sometimes" he said smiling at them.

Turning back to the soldiers he dropped to a knee, and picked up a rifle checking the load automatically then started pulling magazines from the dying men's vests, and putting them in his pouch. He noticed the crowd had gone silent once again, but he could hear someone speaking though he could not make out the words. As he rose the crowd roared again even louder than before. Glancing over the hood of the vehicles he could see a line of soldiers standing on the edge of the crowd watching what was happening.

Following their line of sight Jamie could see men dressed in blood stained robes standing beside men and women dangling from ropes. *They've hung him already* he thought feeling a twinge of guilt at not getting there in time.

Then the crowd began to grow silent again, and Jamie turned to look at the Temple entrance where he could see Noah standing. The boy was looking at the crowd, and there was anger on his face that Jamie sensed more than saw.

"I am the whirlwind fear me" Jamie heard him cry, and saw him throw his spear.

"Come on" he said to the others then raced between the vehicles towards the end of the street.

"I am the wrath of God, and I bring Death to you all" Jamie heard him cry once again as he reached the end of the street. With out a word to the others Jamie raised the rifle, and fired on the nearest soldier. As the man went down Jamie shifted his aim and fired again and again quickly. The others were firing as well at the soldiers, and the crowd both.

He paused glancing down the street to his right at movement, and saw that Jen and her group were coming out onto the street. Just ahead of them were about fifty soldiers running down the street towards Jamie. Jen and the others were firing their bows at the backs of the soldiers, and then she was among them using her spear.

Glancing down the street the other way Jamie saw Marshal, and his bunch just finishing off another group of soldiers. The man was calmly pointing to the weapons lying on the ground, and directing people to start firing on the crowd, and others to watch their backs. Smiling at the man's coolness Jamie tapped Able and Susie on the shoulder. "Watch the street" he jerked a thumb back the way they had come.

Looking back to his right he waved a hand to Jen who lifted a rifle into the air in response, and turned to the crowd opening fire with it. On the other side he waved to Marshal who gave an answering wave then went back to watching his people firing into the crowd. Jamie turned his attention to the crowd in front of him, and opened fire with the rifle, one thought going through his mind over and over. Kill them all.

Epilogue

The sun was sitting low on the horizon by the time the killing was done. The square was littered with the dead and dying, many had been trampled, but most were shot, stabbed, strangled, or beaten to death. There had been thousands in the square, and the ground was soaked in their blood now.

The boy was sitting on the pavilion steps, behind him Angie, Susie and Heather were finishing the wrappings on their dead, the old man and a Servant they called Marcy. Around the pavilion were his friends with Jamie and Jen standing close keeping an eye on him. Around them were nearly a hundred of the Servants with rifles in their hands making sure that nothing would threaten him. The boy was tired, but there was still so much to do. Martha had Able, and his bunch out with the other Servants cleaning the town of everything they could pick up, but the woman herself was staying close to him.

The little pup lying beside him on the step whined, and lifted his head looking back at the wrapped body of the old man. The boy laid a hand on his head stroking him gently knowing how the little pup was feeling because he was feeling the same way. The little pup looked up at the boy hoping that the hurt smell would leave him soon he didn't want to loose the boy too. He missed the old man terribly, but knew that he would see him again one day in that place after this one. The little pup worried about the boy, that much hurt was not good. He knew he had to take care of the boy now that the old man was gone. The One that was All had told him the boy was his responsibility now. There was so much to do. The little pup licked his hand trying to take the hurt away.

"It's ok, dog" the boy said smiling down at the little pup sadly.

"So what now boy" Martha asked from the side of the pavilion where she had been standing in the shade pulling his attention away from the little pup.

"We bury our dead" the boy said looking across the square at the bodies. Some had been children and while it had not bothered him in the heat of the fight now that fact was beginning to eat at him. The pup whined again at the stronger smell of hurt in the boy.

"Then what boy" Martha pushed.

"Then we kill the witch" the boy said rising to look at the woman with a warning in his eyes. "Come on, dog we got a lot to do" the little pup rose following the boy. So much to do the pup agreed.

The End

www.ingramcontent.com/pod-product-compliance
Lightning Source LLC
Chambersburg PA
CBHW031301170626
46807CB00001B/252